I0621130

Opaque Skye

Five Sloths Brewing book 2

Robin Andrews

Opaque Skye
Five Sloths Brewing, Book 2
Robin Andrews

Published by STE Entertainment LLC

Copyright 2020 STE Entertainment LLC
Edited by Holly Funk
Cover image and Five Sloths logo by Dee J Holmes, Bad Unicorn Design
Print Book ISBN 978-1-7345279-2-6

This is a work of fiction. Names, places, characters and incidents are the product of the author's imagination and are fictitious. Any resemblance to actual persons, living or dead, events or establishments is solely coincidental.

A Note from the Author

   If you are an author or you know and follow a few authors, this note will make total sense. If you are like me, up until writing my first book, you would have thought I was a little crazy and that's okay. As I said, I would have agreed with you prior to writing a book.

   I had always heard, "He just wouldn't cooperate with that plan," or "She was very difficult to write." In the back of my head, I always thought *Do they not know what it means to write a book?* I even talked to one author who wrote two series that I love and they intertwine because the characters know each other. I always thought the guy from series A should get together with the girl from series B. I got the chance to talk to her one time and so I asked. "Guy A and Girl B are going to get together, right?" She said, "No, they aren't. He just won't cooperate with that plan." I was very surprised that she didn't know that authors write the books the way they want them to go. But I wasn't going to call her out on that; after all, she was published and I was not.

   I am reasonably certain that was the day that the gods or powers or whatever they are that make authors successful looked down on me and thought *Oh, are we gonna show her.* I sat down a few days later to try to get started on my first book. A story that I had a basic skeleton of in my mind, and I knew my main character was a woman named Skye with light blue eyes. I started to try to fill in that skeleton and I am not kidding you; it was like virtual crickets chirping in my head. I got NOTHING. I couldn't come up with a story line beyond the bare skeleton at all. So I finally figured I would try to clear my mind and let the characters talk to me and tell me their story. Again, crickets. I got frustrated, because obviously, I was never going to write a book if I had no clue what to write. Finally, the powers that be took pity on me and my characters informed me that they weren't book one. Walt and Rayne were (insert baffled *Who the hell are Walt and Rayne?* thought) the first book, they needed their story told first. *Great!! Awesome!! So does this mean it's a duet?* I wondered. I found out (from them of course) that it was actually a five-book series; they were five frat brothers who owned a microbrewery together. So I wrote and released "Fallen Rayne."

   If you have read "Fallen Rayne," you saw lots of mentions of Jason and Sunni. So obviously, they are the next book, right? That's what authors do; they tie the next couple in to the story so that when the next book comes out, you are looking forward to seeing them get their HEA. Totally what I planned to do. I sat down and Jason and Sunni were not ready to tell their story. Apparently, they have all this angsty, conflicty stuff to go through before they are ready to tell their story.

So in the next several pages, I present to you book two (even though it was supposed to be book one and a standalone) of the Five Sloths Brewing series" "Opaque Skye." I promise you that Sunni and Jason are coming, even if I eventually have to tie them down and beat their story out of them.

Dedication

So I always wanted to be an author, partially because I was such an avid reader. My grandmother was a teacher in a one-room schoolhouse in the early 1900s in Northern Lower Michigan. She was the only person I ever watched do crossword puzzles in pen, because she never got one wrong. She gave her children a love of knowledge.

As a small child, my grandmother came to live with us for several years when she broke her hip. And I remember her getting the Reader's Digest magazine and numerous books in the mail every month. She always had a book by her chair or her bed.

Thankfully for me, she passed that respect of books on to my mom. As a small child living in a small town, our local library was housed in an old Victorian-style home. My mom used to take me there every Saturday and I was able to pick out the "limit" on books that the library allowed checked out at one time. Some of my earliest memories are walking into that library and inhaling the smell of books. The first book that I remember falling in love with was "The Tale of Jemima Puddleduck" by Beatrix Potter. I loved the way my mom read that book to me.

Lately, my mom has started to not remember things so well and has started to show signs of dementia. As a daughter, that's so very hard to see.

So I dedicate this book to my grandmother, who passed on her love of all things book related and to my mother, who encouraged me to love books and to devour them.

I also dedicate this to the authors who encouraged that love of books by giving me series to read as I grew. From Beatrix Potter, who gave me the cute garden full of bunnies and ducks to Laura Ingalls Wilder who taught me about life on the prairie, to the people who collaborate to publish The Hardy Boys and Nancy Drew. And to those that wrote the wonderful historical romance books that kept me going when I was a young mother.

I would be remiss if I didn't mention a person who is not only one of my current favorite authors, but also one of the people who has encouraged me the most in giving this whole writing thing a shot. She told me to look up any book that I love, and I will find negative reviews. Not everyone loves the same books, and that's okay because I write from my head and my heart and then I send my 'babies' out into the world and hope they are accepted and loved. Thank you, Lexi Blake, for showing me how to persevere even when I am not sure anyone will read what I write. And thank you for all the hours and hours of enjoyment I have had reading all of your worlds. Along with Lexi, I don't think my thank you would be complete without mentioning Lexi's 'gal Friday,' Chloe Vale. Chloe has had the patience of a saint when I have messaged her saying things like 'my manuscript looks all screwed up on Kindle" and she took a look at it (I uploaded the wrong file format). She gave me all the links to find all the sites I would need, she helped me find people to provide the services I needed to get my book out there (edits, formatting, etc.). So thank you both from the bottom of my heart, Lexi and Chloe. I don't think my first book would have seen the light of day if you hadn't encouraged me and given me so many pointers along the way.

Prologue

Skye looked down at the sweet little angel face that looked up at her from the pack and play in the corner. A face that looked so much like her sister, it was almost painful to see. But Cassie needed Skye to be strong, now more than ever before.

Skye had just left the cemetery where they had laid her sister to rest. She couldn't believe that Savannah was gone. It had only been a week ago that they had gone out to lunch, her, Savannah and Cassie. Savannah always had Cassie in tow. She was such a great mom, and she had doted on her little girl since she had been born a little over a year ago.

Skye leaned over and picked up the smiling little girl. Skye did her best to smile back. Just because her life had been so completely altered by that careless driver didn't mean that she shouldn't try to keep the baby's life as normal as possible. *How can life ever be normal again?* Skye wondered to herself. It never would be, but this sweet little one had to be protected from all of the chaos that life had thrown at them. Someday, when Cassie was older, Skye and David, Cassie's dad, would tell her all about how wonderful her mother had been. Even though the little girl wouldn't remember her mother at all really, they would do all that they could to make sure she knew that her mommy had loved her so much. And until she was old enough to be told all of that, they would do their best to give her the best childhood possible. Skye had agreed to move to the apartment above the garage at David's house so that she could help with the baby. David had a somewhat flexible schedule where he worked, but Skye had the added benefit of having childcare on site at the fitness center where she taught classes. So between the two of them, Cassie would never be far from one or the other. The child psychologist had said that Cassie was too young to really know that her mom was gone, but that didn't mean that there wouldn't be hurdles to jump even in the earliest stages. Children sense things even if they don't really have any idea of what is going on. Cassie might sense their pain or their sorrow. Even though it wasn't going to be easy, they had to try their best to seem like the same people they had been a week ago in Cassie's eyes. Skye had leaned over her sister's casket and wept as she promised that she would make sure Cassie knew that she was loved and she would always be taken care of.

Chapter One

Zak sat drumming his thumbs on the steering wheel and glancing around while waiting for whatever it was that had traffic at a standstill at 8:50 a.m. on this sunny Monday morning. He was going to be late for work, as usual. Not that it mattered. When you were the son of a senior managing partner at a law firm, no one really had the balls to say anything about you strolling in to the office at 9:15 or even 9:30, for that matter. Although lately his parents had both been getting on to him about being more responsible, taking some initiative, maybe even settling down a little from his playboy ways. But at 29, who wanted to settle down? Although his life had been what some would call "charmed," he still had some living he wanted to do.

Sure, he'd had all the best things in life growing up; sure, he had gotten into all the best schools because of his last name and his father's status as alumni. That didn't mean that he hadn't earned his good grades. He had studied hard to graduate at the top of his class in both high school and college. His grades at Harvard Law had proven that he did what it took to get the job done. But now that was over and he had passed the bar exam, it was time to live a little.

Zak's eyes caught on a woman getting out of an SUV parked alongside the road. Man, she was hot, with long blond hair that was not curly, but not really straight either. It framed a beautiful face: high cheekbones, gorgeous lips, and those eyes. He couldn't tell exactly what color they were from this distance, but definitely something light, like blue or maybe gray. Either way, they looked like eyes a man like him could get lost in while he sank deep into her body as it writhed in pleasure under him. A body which, from what he could see, was built for pleasure. She wasn't pencil thin like so many of the women who came on to him in the clubs, but she wasn't fat by any means either; she did have just enough curves that a man could get lost for hours exploring them.

He watched as she opened the back door and leaned in to get something out of the backseat. That was when his suspicions were confirmed: she had an ass that was meant for a firm slap now and then, maybe even a bite or two. His mouth suddenly watered at the thought of sinking his teeth into that luscious flesh. That was a woman that he could definitely invest hours and hours of his time getting to know, inside and out.

Skye felt like someone was watching her as she reached into the backseat of the SUV. She tried to glance over her shoulder to see if there was anyone there. Of course, with traffic this time of morning, it could be anyone. She didn't feel intimidated by it, just sensed it. It didn't set off alarm bells like it was someone with ill intent, just this feeling that there were eyes burning into her flesh. She shook off the feeling. If she didn't get moving, she would be late for her 9:00 yoga class and she still had to check Cassie into the daycare center the health club offered to its members and staff.

As she pulled the little girl out of her car seat, Cassie gave her the biggest smile as she grabbed a fistful of Skye's hair. Despite all that had happened in the span of her short life, she was always so happy and full of energy and life. It made Skye smile too, just to see her niece so carefree and secure. As she turned toward the road, juggling her gym bag, the diaper bag, and Cassie, she couldn't help but continue to smile at the joy this little girl could bring to her day. That was when she spotted him, the guy in the bright yellow sports car staring at her. Their eyes locked and at first she wasn't sure what to think, but then he seemed to look away like he had been caught staring, or like maybe he didn't like what he saw. She was used to that; most men didn't like women with a little "meat" on their bones. *Oh well, his loss.* She was comfortable with who she was and how she looked. Besides, she had way too much going on in her life right now to even think about a man being any part of it. Although she did have to admit for a minute there, she had felt the heat of his gaze. She felt the way their eyes locked for a brief moment, and from what she could tell from the limited view looking into his car, he was hot as hell.

Sitting behind his desk holding the file he was supposed to be reading, Zak couldn't stop the images flashing through his mind. The gorgeous blond hair, that was what he had spotted first as she had opened her car door. That wasn't a bleached blond; it was all natural. Zak preferred women who kept themselves as natural as possible. He didn't mind highlights or whatever they were called. But he had never really liked hair that looked like it came straight from a bottle of bleach. Then the face and those eyes as she'd turned to get out, the body that looked absolutely luscious as she stood up. Judging by the comparison between her and the vehicle, she couldn't have been more than maybe 5'4" or 5'5". Damn, she would fit against him so well, the perfect height to his 6'. Then when she had turned and bent over, his cock had started to harden at just the sight of that gorgeous ass in those tight yoga pants she had been wearing. All he'd wanted to do was to find a place to park and jump out and say hi. Maybe get to know her a little, get her number, ask her out for a drink. Something to get a chance at an up-close look at her. And then it had happened; she'd pulled a kid out of that car, no, actually, more like a baby. The girl couldn't have been more than maybe a year old or so. He knew little to nothing when it came to children. All he knew was that they were not in his near future AT ALL! Talk about throwing ice cold water on a flame. She had a kid, which probably also meant she was married. Not that a woman necessarily had to be married to have a kid; obviously she didn't. But there was something about the look of innocence on her face and in her smile when their eyes had met briefly that gave him the feeling that she wasn't the type to have a baby and not be with the father. Maybe not married, but at least with him, like long term, permanently with the guy. And here he had been fantasizing about another guy's woman. Thinking how gorgeous she was, how much he wanted to get inside her. Hell, when their eyes had met for that few seconds, he had felt an absolute certainty in his body that he had to have her.

He forced himself to focus on work and the rest of the day went pretty much the way most of his days went: files to read, depositions to take, clients to meet with, yadda yadda. By the time he got home, he was exhausted. It had been a tiring day and then just before he was ready to leave his father had come in and told him that he was being assigned a new case. It was a wrongful death suit that, from what his father told him, seemed pretty much a slam dunk from the facts of the case, but Zak knew that wasn't usually as much of a sure thing as it seemed. Often, judges or juries went totally the opposite way than you thought they would. He told his dad he would get started on it first thing in the morning. His father had reminded him that the workday started at precisely 9:00 a.m., not 9:15. He just nodded his agreement. On the route home, he had slowed down when he passed the fitness center. Maybe he would catch a glimpse of her again, and he would realize that she wasn't as hot as he had imagined her this morning. She was probably really not that pretty up close; after all, he had only gotten a look from a distance. But he didn't see her or the SUV she had gotten out of that morning, so his point couldn't be proven right or wrong.

He called and had dinner delivered. He lived in one of the newer apartment buildings in the city. His apartment had as much square footage as many single-family homes did. But he was a bachelor and living here alone just made things easier. There was no lawn to mow, and he had an underground garage to park his car in. If anything went bad, maintenance was on call 24/7. What could be better?

He ate his dinner and then jumped in the shower. For some stupid reason, one which he could not fathom, his mind pictured the beautiful woman from this morning. And that immediately got his cock thinking about her and what it would like to do with her. And it would not listen when he told it that she had a kid and was most likely married or in a relationship. Nope, that didn't slow his cock down even for a second. It knew he had seen a beautiful woman and it wanted him to pursue her. He wasn't going to get this off his mind unless he got it out of his system, so while he jacked off to the picture of her in his mind, he told himself that it couldn't hurt to maybe go to her gym and say hi. Maybe she wasn't married. Maybe she had a kid with some guy who had just taken off. Or maybe she had wanted a child and had just gone to a sperm bank or whatever. Some women did that, right? Like their biological clock or something. If that was the case, maybe she would be happy to get out and have a little fun, as long as he made sure she knew that he wasn't looking for a relationship. It couldn't hurt to at least try to find out what her situation was. With that decision made, his release came in long jets over his hand and onto the shower wall.

Chapter Two

For some reason, Zak was up way before his alarm. That absolutely never happened to him. But since he was up early, he might as well swing by the fitness center and see if he could find out anything about that blond-haired beauty. Was she a member, or was she staff? Was she married or single, and most importantly, what the hell was her name?

On his drive over, he decided the best plan of action was to sign up for a membership. That way, he wouldn't look so much like a stalker, even though he pretty much was a stalker. But he didn't need to look like one. They had no way of knowing that his apartment complex had a full gym and he had a treadmill and some free weights in his spare room. He was just a guy who was looking to stay in shape at the local fitness center.

When he walked in, the guy behind the counter greeted him and asked if there was anything he could do for him. Zak explained that he was thinking about getting a membership. The guy gave him a big smile and said, "Let me go grab some information out of the office." He stepped through a door and was back a minute later.

He was just beginning to explain the details of membership when the door opened. Zak glanced at the door and there she was, walking through the door, his beauty. She was carrying the same small child he had seen her with yesterday, but oddly, the child really didn't look anything like her. It had darker brown hair, and their facial features weren't very similar either. But maybe the kid just took after its dad. Who, he reminded himself, was probably the beauty's husband.

The guy behind the counter looked up and said, "Oh, hey, Skye." He pressed a button and a door opened into the fitness center. So her name was Skye; that was enough for now. He must have been staring as she went through the door because the guy cleared his throat rather loudly like he was trying to get someone's attention. *Of course he was, stupid. You were practically drooling over the girl.* He tried to sound nonchalant, but probably didn't pull it off when he asked if she was one of the members. He claimed that he might want to talk to a few people before he committed to membership.

"Nope, she's an instructor. She teaches yoga and some of the water aerobics classes." He went back to explaining the membership, but Zak wasn't paying much attention. He was too busy telling himself that guys took yoga and water aerobics too, didn't they?

When he realized that the guy had stopped talking, he said, "Great, where do I sign?"

The guy kind of chuckled like he was seeing right through Zak's smoke screen. He didn't bust Zak on it, though; he just showed him where to sign and asked for a credit card to bill the monthly fees to. When he came back out, Zak asked about Skye.

The guy said, "Look, man, I'm not supposed to talk about employees."

"Just tell me if she's single. You can do that, right?" Zak pleaded.

"You didn't hear this from me, but yeah, she's single, she has some pretty heavy stuff going on in her family, so take it easy with her." The man obviously cared about Skye and was looking out for her. Zak put his hands up in a sign of surrender and assured the guy that he got it.

He took his pamphlet of information and paperwork and headed back out to his car. He looked at the list of classes and was happy to see that the instructors' names were listed with the classes they taught. He took note of what days and times Skye would be teaching classes and decided to try to drop in to her next yoga class.

When Zak got to work it was 8:45, thank you very much, His father would be impressed. He opened the case file and realized why his father had said it would be an open and shut case. A young mother with a fourteen-month-old infant had been forced off the road when a semi driver had pulled back into the driving lane too soon. She had been forced to make the choice of hitting him or going off the road into a deep ravine. She had chosen the ravine and her car had rolled before stopping at the bottom. Even though she had a seat belt on, she had died in the crash. The baby had been fine, though. The infant seat had completely protected the little girl. He looked at the pictures of the accident scene. It was pretty gruesome. The last picture was of the young mother when she had obviously been happy and healthy. Zak stared at it for the longest time. There was something about her that seemed familiar. Like maybe he had seen her before, or maybe it was just that she looked a little like someone he knew.

Either way, this case was going to take some time. The trucker was claiming that the company had forced him to work more hours than he was supposed to by law. If that was the case, the company would be at fault in all of this too. He definitely had some digging to do. He had to talk to the driver, the first responders, the husband. He looked at the date of the accident. It couldn't have been more than a few days since the funeral. He decided to leave the husband and any other family members until last in his long list of interviews. They had barely had time to grieve; he wasn't in any hurry to bring up the pain this must have caused them.

He spent his day making a list of the people he would want to talk to and a list of bullet points he needed the answers to before he could adequately write up the case. He left the list of people he would want to talk to with his administrative assistant before he left for the day and instructed her to wait until he had finished all the other interviews before contacting the family to schedule theirs. Hopefully by the time he met with them, he would have a feel for how things were looking from the other interviews he would conduct.

When he got home, he felt like he needed to burn off some extra energy, so he ran five miles on his treadmill. When he still wasn't winding down much, he decided to take a drive over to the brewery to check out what was going on over there. If nothing was happening, maybe he would head to one of his other favorite clubs and see if he could find a woman that could hold his interest for a few hours. He wouldn't commit to more than a couple of hours with anyone because he had work in the morning, and, while he might not be the poster child for being at work on time, he held fast to the rule of spending the night in his own bed alone on work nights. Hell, any night he spent in his bed he was alone. He didn't invite women to his home. It made things too messy if the woman didn't understand his 'no strings' approach.

When he got to Five Sloths, he wasn't sure he had made the right decision to stop off there. It was Walt's night to manage, and he had brought Rayne with him. It wasn't that he didn't like Walt and his fiancée; it was more that this really wasn't a night that he needed to see one of his former party buddies settling down with a woman. Just because Walt had decided to give up the single life didn't mean Zak was going to consider that anytime soon. It seemed like Jason was sort of hung up on Rayne's friend, Sunni. They were together anytime the group had a cookout or some sort of get-together.

Oh, well, now that he was here he might as well at least have a drink or two. It was a Tuesday night; all the clubs would be rather empty. He could just have his drinks and maybe some dinner and head home. Five Sloths had his favorite microbrews and the food was pretty decent. That's what happened when you put five frat brothers together to create a menu and hire staff. They didn't settle for anything less than great food and the best selection in beer.

Zak sat at the bar rather than at the private table they tried to keep available for the owners. He might not find a woman to take his mind off of Skye, but he could at least mingle a little with other customers as they came and went. Generally, he didn't pick up women at Five Sloths anyway. It was kind of like hunting too close to home. If he met a woman and she wanted more than he did, she would know right where to look for him if he picked her up here. No, he usually did his hunting at dance clubs or places where he could just blend in and be one of the guys. Here he was part owner and most of the regulars also knew that he was an attorney. He wasn't taking any chances on finding a 'too clingy' woman in his own home waters.

"Name your poison," Walt said when he walked over to Zak at the bar.

"My usual brew," Zak began. "Is Lou back there on the grill or is it one of the other cooks?"

"Nah, Lou usually takes the busier nights," Walt stated. "Tonight we got the newer girl, Holly. She's a damn good cook though. Lou trained her on our menu."

"I'll check her skills out. Tell her I want the BBQ bacon cheeseburger and pub fries, but the burger needs to be medium rare," Zak said.

"Got it." Walt walked back toward the open window that led to the kitchen. He placed Zak's order and came back with the microbrew that Zak preferred. "It's pretty quiet here. What are you up to?"

"Just burning off some excess energy tonight, I guess," Zak stated.

"You usually do that between the sheets with a hot blonde, if I'm not mistaken," Walt chided.

"Ha, ha, funny man." Zak rolled his eyes. "Okay, yeah, most of the time that is my M.O. Tonight's just different, I guess. I got a new case handed to me today and while I am pretty sure it's going to be easily winnable, it's not easy to have to tear open this one in court."

"What's the case?" Walt asked with all seriousness. They all knew there was a time for joking and being the playboys they typically were, but as attorneys, they all knew that there were some cases that just ripped your heart out.

"Young mother pushed off the highway by a semi driver. The car rolled, killing the mom while her infant daughter lay sleeping in a car seat in the back," Zak stated somberly.

"Most likely drunk or tired," Walt offered. Zak nodded his head in agreement and Walt continued. "Like you said, probably winnable, but not something you want to drag out in court. At least the kid was probably too young to actually understand what was happening."

"Yeah, there is that, although now the kid has no mom. Seems like the parents were in a good solid relationship, so at least the kid has a dad," Zak offered. Not that that would make up for not having a mom. Dads were good and all, but it always seemed like moms were the ones that were generally closer to the kids. It was that way for him growing up. Walt walked away to tend to another customer and Zak couldn't help but think about Skye. Was she a single mom? If she was, did he have any right to try to take any of her time away from her child? He had told himself that a single mom might like to get out and have fun. But what about the kid? If she was hesitant at all about leaving her child, he would have no right to try to persuade her otherwise. Kids needed their moms. Zak wasn't sure where that would leave him when it came to dating Skye, but there would only be one way to find out. Until he met her and talked to her, it was all just speculation on his behalf.

Zak finished his meal and a couple of glasses of brew and then headed out. He stopped to say goodnight to Walt and Rayne on his way out the door. The regular servers were tending to the dwindling crowd, so Walt had taken a place next to Rayne at the bar. He would still tend the cash register, though. It wasn't that they needed to be the ones to cash out customers, but it gave them a chance to see how the customer had enjoyed their meal or if they had any comments or complaints. They were all certain that things like that were what had made them as popular as they had become in the short time they had been open. People liked to associate a face with the owners or operators of a business.

Chapter Three

When Zak got up Wednesday morning, he flipped through the pamphlets from the gym while he ate his breakfast and had his morning coffee. There was a list of classes offered which conveniently also listed the instructor for each class. Perfect, he thought to himself, now to pick a class or two that Skye taught. Maybe, just maybe he could find out more about her and see if she was up for a little 'no strings attached' fun. Couldn't hurt to ask, anyway. If she was a single mom, she might enjoy getting out for a nice dinner, some drinks and then a little adult fun. There just happened to be a beginner's yoga class this afternoon. Men did yoga, right?

The gym wasn't very far from his apartment, which also meant it wasn't very far from where he worked either. He had time, so he decided to go home and get out of his mandatory work uniform, which actually was a tailor-made suit. He threw on some sweats and also packed a gym bag with shorts and his toiletries. He arrived at the gym about fifteen minutes before the class was supposed to start, so he put his bag in a locker and went to have a look around the place. He found the room where Skye was just finishing up her current class. Damn that woman was hot when she did some of those yoga positions. He didn't know the names of any of them yet, but he would label them hot, hotter and even hotter. Those yoga pants and her skintight tank top had him thinking all sorts of dirty thoughts. He realized that he needed to keep his hormones in check; it wouldn't be cool if he was sitting in the class with a hard-on for the sexy instructor.

The class let out and several people went and talked to Skye for a moment or two, but eventually the room emptied out and the new class started to head into the room. He figured that since it was his first time it would be proper to introduce himself to the teacher. He walked up to her and when she looked up at him, he lost every single syllable in the English language. Those eyes that he had thought were something light like blue or gray turned out to be the most beautiful shade of blue he had ever seen. It looked just like the sky on a bright, sunny, almost cloudless day. She was looking at him with a puzzled look on her face. *Oh yeah, right, say something, dummy*, he chided himself. He pulled his thoughts back to the reason he had walked up to her in the first place and introduced himself. He told her that this was his first time, he had just joined the gym the day before. He asked her if she thought he would be able to catch up with whatever the class had learned in previous sessions. She assured him that if he followed her instructions he should be fine. She also suggested that he choose a mat in the front of the class so that his view was unobstructed. Zak thought that was the best and worst suggestion ever. Up close, he could watch her body bend into all sorts of delicious positions, and he would probably have to take a cold shower after the class was over.

After 45 minutes of trying to bend his body into a pretzel, Skye told everyone they'd done a good job and she would see them next class. Zak wasn't sure if he should approach her again after class or if that seemed too overzealous. But as he was walking toward the door, she called out his name, so he walked over to see what she wanted. She asked him if he had enjoyed his first class. She also asked if he thought he would be able to catch on to the positions and if he planned to come back next time. He told her he would be there as often as he could, unless he had a work commitment that he couldn't get out of. She smiled at him and told him it was nice meeting him. He agreed—it had been way more than nice meeting her, but he had to play this cool. He couldn't come on too strong at the start or he would scare her away. It was going to kill him, and he would probably be taking a lot of cold showers for a while, but it would be worth it in the end if he could get her to at least go out with him.

Skye watched the new guy—Zak, he had said his name was Zak—walk out of the room and turned to make sure there wasn't anyone left in the class. She didn't want anyone to see her drooling over the hot new guy. That man was sin on a stick. He had to be 6'2" or more, wavy brownish-blond hair and deep blue eyes. He had muscles everywhere she had been able to see in his shorts and tank top. She would bet he had an amazing six-pack hidden under that shirt too. She wondered why a guy like that was just joining a gym. It was pretty obvious that he already had a workout routine. Maybe he'd just moved to this area and he was looking for a gym. Whatever the reason, she was going to just be thankful for the eye candy that apparently would be in her beginning yoga class. She knew that right now, trying to start a relationship wasn't a good idea, but having eye candy wouldn't cause any harm.

Chapter Four

Zak had figured if he didn't want to start with the family, the best person to talk to was the trucker. He was likely to be a hostile witness as far as talking to Zak went, but he had to try. The driver had maintained that the accident was the fault of the company rather than the driver himself. Zak wasn't sure how that could be possible, but if he approached it right, maybe the driver would open up as to why he felt that way. The driver was most likely on paid leave of absence from his job until this could all be settled. He had received a ticket for the accident, but as of yet there were no charges against him, and as far as Zak could tell, there might not be charges at all. It made no sense to him. The man had been negligent; he had pulled back into the driving lane too soon and had forced the woman off the road. That was what the accident report said. Zak was surprised that the prosecutor hadn't filed any charges yet. He would have to call one of the assistant DAs and see if he could find out where that was going at on their end. Zak picked up the phone and dialed the prosecutor's office. When the ADA came on the phone, Zak asked, "What can you tell me about the case where the trucker ran a woman off the road? I'm representing the family in the civil suit and I was just curious what's going on on the criminal end. From what I've heard, no charges have been filed yet."

He confirmed that there had not been any criminal charges filed at this point. ADAs usually were a pretty closed-mouth group, but Zak still wanted to try to figure out where they stood on this. So he asked why that was. The ADA said, "Look, I can't go into it yet because it's still an open investigation, but let's just say that from what we know so far, there may be bigger fish to fry."

Zak thought about that for a moment before asking, "Do you mean the trucking company? I've heard the driver is trying to pin this on them."

"Let's just say there are rumors of some less than ethical practices going on there, possibly even some law breaking, and until we finish sorting that out, we are better off letting the trucker be our informant rather than our enemy. I am sure he will get charged with something, but at this point, I can't say much. We have to look at the big picture and what might be worth a plea deal if we get the info on something bigger." The ADA was talking somewhat quietly; probably he was in the office and didn't want too many people to hear that he was leaking information to the "enemy."

"Gotcha," Zak replied. "But, like I said, I'm representing the family in the civil suit. I won't even begin to try to figure out where your case is going, but if you know or hear anything that might help out my case without compromising yours, I would appreciate a heads-up."

"Understood." With that, the ADA hung up.

So that was interesting. If the prosecutor had some potential information against the trucking company, it might be more prudent on his behalf to wait to see just what they came up with before he decided what way to proceed with the civil suit. He called his client, the husband of the woman and father to the baby, and explained without giving any more information than he had to just what was going on with the case. He told the husband that he felt it best to wait to see what the criminal investigation turned up before they proceeded with their case. He also told the man that if that wasn't okay with him, they could proceed with the case as it stood now. His client assured him that he wasn't in a hurry as much as he was committed to make sure someone was held responsible for his wife's death. No amount of money would bring her back, but someone needed to pay in some way. Zak promised him that he would do his best to make sure someone was held responsible for this accident and told him that he would be in touch with the client in the next week or so, as soon as he heard anything more.

Chapter Five

Zak was determined to at least talk to Skye at the next class, and hopefully get a chance to ask her out for a drink sometime. He was sincerely hoping the guy at the desk had been right and she was really single. The last thing he needed was some jealous boyfriend coming after him. He walked into class the next day and there were already several people standing around talking. An older woman was talking to Skye, so it looked like he might not get a chance to talk to her until after class.

Just like the last time, watching Skye in some of those positions did something for his libido. This woman was hot as hell. Honestly, he couldn't put his finger on one specific characteristic that made her hot. It was more like it was just the whole package. Everything was proportionate, she had some great curves on her, but she didn't look fat. She was obviously in good shape if she taught these classes. Her eyes, though—Zak had heard that the eyes were the window to the soul. But her eyes just looked like a wide open blue sky on the most beautiful clear day you could ever imagine. It undoubtedly was the reason her parents had given her the name.

After the class was over, he waited until the room had cleared out for the most part before he approached Skye. When she looked up and saw him there, he thought he saw a brief flash of something there. Dare he hope that she had some desire for him too? He knew he desired her probably more than he had ever wanted anyone before. There was just something about her that did it for him.

"Hi, Zak," she said with a smile. "Is there something I can do for you? You seem like you are starting to get some of the positions, and I am sure you will catch on to the rest if you keep working on it."

"Oh, yeah. I am getting the hang of it." He wanted to talk about positions all right, but not yoga ones. "Actually, I was wondering if I could take you out for a drink sometime. Nothing super spectacular, but maybe we could go to a local brewery and have a few beers."

Skye thought about that for a moment. She really hadn't done anything fun in quite a while; she had spent every waking moment since she'd received that phone call with a deep sadness that she couldn't get past. She obviously put on a good face, since Cassie didn't seem to sense how blue Skye really was. She had to keep it together for that little girl. But she didn't have to spend twenty-four hours a day seven days a week with her. She could do something fun in the evening or on a weekend when David was with Cassie. She obviously was taking too long to make her decision because Zak interrupted her thoughts.

"Look, if you don't want to or if you can't because I'm a member here or whatever, I understand. I just think you are really pretty and I would like to take you out for an evening of fun," Zak explained. If it was the whole membership thing, it looked like Zak was going to be canceling almost as soon as he had joined. Because if that was what it took to get her to go out with him, he was perfectly fine with that.

"No, that's not it," Skye assured him. "I just have to figure out the logistics is all. I can work it out; it just may take some planning."

Ah, yeah, she probably needed to line up a babysitter for her daughter. "Sure, I totally understand. You tell me what times work best for you and I will work around that."

"Um, I should be able to do Friday or Saturday evening," she said.

"Great, let's make it Saturday. Fridays can be a bear with my job and I wouldn't want to have to cancel if something comes up at work. Would you like me to pick you up, or do you want to meet me there?" He didn't want to put her in an awkward position. If she felt safer having her own car for their first meeting, he totally understood; a lot of women did that. And maybe she just wasn't ready to tell him about the kid yet, so if he showed up at her house, she would have to explain that. Either way, he was fine.

"I think I'd like to meet you there," she said.

"That's totally cool with me. Do you know where Five Sloths Brewing company is?" he asked.

"I do. I've always thought that was an odd name though." She was sort of laughing about that one.

"Yeah, it is an odd name, and there's a story behind it," he agreed. He didn't want to lay all his cards on the table and tell her he was part owner of the place. "Maybe one of the owners will tell you about the name when we are there. So I asked you for drinks, but that place has some fairly decent pub-type food too, if you want to make it dinner and drinks. But if not, that's fine."

"Dinner and drinks sounds good. I've had a lot going on lately and it will be nice to just get out and be waited on and have some fun for an evening," Skye said.

"Great. Want to meet me there about 5:30?" he asked. He knew that on Saturday nights the place didn't really get busy until after six. So that would give them some time to settle in before the place got crowded and therefore loud because of all the people.

"Sure, that sounds great," she agreed.

"See you then," Zak said and turned and walked out of the room.

Skye was excited and yet nervous about going out with Zak. He was one seriously hot man, but she knew absolutely nothing about him really. She had seen him the day he joined the gym and he had been in a suit, most likely on his way to work. But that didn't help any. Downtown Grand Rapids had tons of businesses, lawyers, accountants, banking companies, lots of places where the employees wore business attire. And she knew that now was not the time to start anything like a relationship. Her life had to be the last priority right now. She would have to explain to Zak that she was great with going out and having fun, but she couldn't even think about long term or anything serious right now. Most likely, he wasn't either, since they were both young, but she didn't want to mislead him either. But she really could use some fun dates and maybe even a little "friends with benefits" action to get her through this period of mourning silently so that she didn't upset Cassie. She had to be the rock for Cassie and for David right now. Besides, she wasn't really allowed to talk to anyone about the accident because the police and the lawyers had told them all that they couldn't tell anyone about it until the criminal and civil cases were both settled. Supposedly if they talked too openly it could jeopardize either aspect of the legal system.

Chapter Six

Friday had been one hell of a day, just like Zak had predicted when he had talked to Skye on Thursday. It always seemed that way in the legal system. Criminal cases all had their sentencing hearings on Friday. Everyone was trying to get paperwork filed or cases on the docket and that all had to be done early in the day, because by Friday afternoon, many judges left early and so did the senior partners in law firms. So, while it usually ended up being a short day for the higher ups, it left the "worker bees" with a bunch of stuff to try to get filed or settled before they could go home.

But now it was Saturday. Zak usually tried to get up at the same time every day just to set a pattern, but this Saturday he had decided he would let himself wake up whenever his body decided it was ready to. He knew if he got up early, he was just going to spend the whole day wishing it was 5:30 already.

He got to the brewery about 5:00. He wanted to give his friends a heads-up on what he was doing and also make sure that he got their private table. The table was still a part of the main dining area, but it was sort of set off in almost like a little alcove of its own. When the guys were designing the place, they had realized that this area was a perfect spot to put a table that they themselves could use for a date or a private business conversation and they could also give it to regulars who requested it for similar situations. They always kept a "Reserved" sign on it so that people who might be waiting for a table didn't get upset because there was an empty table right there. He walked over to the bar and spotted Jason. He was sitting there like he seemed to be several nights lately, flirting with a blonde named Sunni. She was a friend of Walt's fiancée. Tonight was Pete's night to manage the restaurant/bar, but often on weekends more than one of them was there if they didn't have other commitments. The weekends tended to be busier than weekdays and it never hurt to have a couple of managers on hand to handle the bigger crowds. He told Jason that he was planning to use the table tonight if no one had already requested it. Jason immediately asked if he was using it for business or pleasure. He shook his head and told Jason he should mind his own business but finally admitted that it was for pleasure; he had a date. That kind of surprised Jason because of all of them, Zak was the one who didn't "date." Oh, yeah, he spent time with women, but he didn't date. Most of his time with a woman was spent in a hotel room having no strings attached sex.

"Whoa, man, this woman must be special if you are going to date her and not just bang her," Jason chided.

Zak looked Jason in the eye and said, "Lay off. This isn't anything serious either, I'm not looking for more than a nice evening that will hopefully end up in a bed somewhere. This woman has a kid and I don't know her whole story, but I don't think it's a great one. She has these beautiful blue eyes, and she smiles, but it always seems like it doesn't go all the way to her eyes. Like maybe she's been hurt, probably by whoever got her pregnant and apparently didn't stick around." Jason started to object but before he could say anything, Zak assured him that he would make it clear to her that he was just in it for the fun. And if she wasn't okay with that, they would have one fun evening in the brewery and go their separate ways. Jason just shrugged and went back to talking to Sunni. Zak also told Pete they would be using the table so that he knew to keep it clear.

****

At 5:20, Skye found herself sitting in the parking lot of Five Sloths Brewing Company. That really was an odd name, and she hoped to meet one of the owners and ask for the story. The sign out front even had a silly looking sloth lying at the top of a pyramid of keg barrels. She was debating with herself on whether she would seem too eager if she walked in now, but then if she didn't walk in and Zak pulled in, he would see her sitting in her car and he might think that she had lost her courage. She actually had lost her courage several times that day. At one point, she had convinced herself that she heard Cassie sniffling and told David that maybe she should stay because Cassie might be getting sick. He had assured her that he hadn't heard any sniffles but if it did become a cold, he was pretty sure he could handle it. And he had her cell phone number if something happened and he needed her. He also told her that she should go out and have fun. She deserved it after all the help and support she had been giving him and his little girl the last few weeks. He said if she didn't start going out and having a life, it was just going to make him feel like he was being too much of a burden. She assured him that they weren't a burden at all. She was happy to help and she told him she would go out tonight. She didn't tell him that it just might not be the date she had planned. If she lost her nerve to see Zak, she could always go out somewhere, see a movie or something. She could even go back to her apartment and pack. She was moving out in the next two weeks so she could be closer to David and Cassie. When David and Savannah had bought the house, they had fallen in love with it immediately. It had a small apartment above the garage, but they had never rented it out. They didn't want some stranger living that close.   But now that the circumstances had changed, it turned out to be the perfect solution for Skye. She could live there and still have her own privacy, but she would be right there if something came up unexpectedly and she was needed.

Sitting in the parking lot of the brewery, she called her best friend, Autumn. "Hi, can you talk me down from a freak-out?" Skye said in a rapid spew.

"Okay, first, what's the freak-out about?" her friend asked.

Skye quickly explained where she was, why she was there and that she thought this might be a huge mistake. She wasn't ready for a relationship, she couldn't promise to be available all the time, and her first priority was Cassie. That was where her friend finally got a word in edgewise and got her to stop her rambling.

"Okay, first of all sweetie, breathe," Autumn said. "Is this your first date with this guy?" When Skye responded in the positive, she continued. "Then just be honest with him. You don't have to tell him your life story; in fact, it's probably best that you don't. Just tell him that you have a lot going on in life now. You can say it's family stuff or you don't have to give any details. Simply say that you are open to a little fun and going out, but you aren't looking for anything steady or long term at this point." She hesitated, and then asked, "Are you open to a sexual relationship if it doesn't have strings attached to it?"

"Definitely. He is hot as hell," Skye responded. "But I'm not sure that's a good idea either."

"Listen to me, girlfriend. This is the twenty-first century, and it's almost the start of a new decade. Men don't think poorly of women who are looking for something sexual. In fact, most likely that will take a lot of pressure off him. He's probably open to sex too, but the relationship stuff takes time for men. If he knows right up front that you're okay with that, he will probably be very happy to oblige," Autumn assured her. "Now, go in there and knock that man off his feet."

"Okay, I will," she said quietly, then with more feeling, she added, "Thanks for always being there for me. This hasn't been an easy month, but you've always been there when I needed you."

"You're welcome, my friend, any time. Have fun tonight." Autumn disconnected the call.

Skye looked heavenward and hoped that her sister was up there somewhere watching over them all and that she would be happy with the way they were trying to make a life for Cassie even when they themselves had huge holes in their hearts from losing her. And with that, she got out of the car and walked toward the door.

When she got inside, the place wasn't super busy. It was probably a little early for most of the weekend crowd. She spotted Zak sitting at the bar and started to approach him, but he turned around and met her in the middle and then escorted her to a table with a reserved sign on it. "You made reservations?" she asked.

"Well, let's just say that I know the owners." Zak smiled and pulled out a chair for her at the table.

"Oh, good. Maybe you can ask one of them to tell me the sloth story. I'm dying to know," she said.

"Okay, look, Skye, full disclosure here," Zak said, and his look gave her a weird feeling. "I'm one of the owners. I don't tell women that right off because some of them get weird about it."

"What do you mean weird?" she asked.

"Well, usually, I try not to tell a woman too much until I know her better. Some women can really get nasty if things don't go the way they want them to in a relationship. I once ended up with a woman stalking me. She would show up here night after night hoping I would be on duty. She showed up and called my day job repeatedly. It was a real mess. So I just keep my personal business quiet at first."

"Then why did you tell me?" she asked.

"I can't really explain that, except that you don't seem like the stalker type to me." He shrugged and went on. "I may regret that, but I don't think I will."

"No, trust me, you don't have anything to worry about with me. I was actually wanting to clear up a few things and now is as good a time as any." She probably looked like she was a little terrified to say what was coming next. She just wasn't sure how to say it or how he would take it. "I just...really have a lot going on in my real life right now...family things, things I really don't want to talk about. I'm not really looking for anything more than some fun times to get away from real life when I can."

"I can live with that," Zak agreed. "I'm actually just looking for some fun times too. My parents are pushing me to settle down and I'm just not at that place yet. I mean, it hasn't been that long since I finished school, you know?" He looked at Skye and she nodded. "So we agree, go out and have fun when we can, but don't stress about commitment or even feeling like we have to get super involved in each other's life. We just get together and have some fun. And after the date is over, we go our separate ways and maybe see each other again when it works into our schedule."

"I like that," Skye agreed. Zak nodded and then told her to look over the menu. He would gladly give her suggestions if she wanted them, but she could have whatever she wanted.

They placed their orders. Zak got his favorite beer, but Skye decided to try a flight, small glasses of several different beers so that she could try to see what she liked. When the server walked away, Skye asked for the story of the brewery name.

"Okay, well, it's pretty stupid really," Zak said. "But here goes. Four of my frat brothers and I decided we wanted to go into business after we graduated. We all went to the same college, and even to the same grad school. Four of us were law school, one was business administration. So here we are, still basically stupid frat brothers, trying to decide on what type of business we want to own. Of course the obvious answer was a microbrewery. All the free beer you can imagine, right?" He chuckled and looked at Skye. She appeared to be listening intently but he could tell she was trying not to giggle. So he went on, "I'm pretty sure it was the night that we were interviewing brew masters, trying to figure out who we wanted to hire when we realized that we didn't have a name for the place either. We had probably had way too much beer, but we got to thinking that the one thing that none of us had ever been called or compared to was a sloth. See, we were always at the top of our class. We often competed with each other for awards for academics and all that, and we had worked our asses off for most of our lives. We just wanted to be sloths for a while and not have to be super motivated or super driven. I'm not sure if we were motivated or if we were driven by our parents, but either way, we just wanted to be able to decide to be sloths for a while. So that was the birth of Five Sloths Brewing Company."

He looked at Skye and she was laughing a little.

"I see the irony now," she said. She looked around and realized that the place was really starting to fill up. "It doesn't look like being sloths has hurt your business any," she chided.

"No, and honestly, a big part of that goes to my friend Jason. He was the business major. When we opened this place, he was named the managing owner. The rest of us come in to be managers for a night or two a week, but Jason is the one that does all the actual managing of the business end of it all. We would have tanked a long time ago if he hadn't known what he was doing."

"I can tell you have a great relationship with your friends," she said.

"Yeah, I really do," he agreed. "But what about you? Any stories about you that I should know?"

Skye was a little panicked for a minute. She really didn't want to get into her current life; it would drag anybody down, and she was trying to have fun for one night. She started to stammer a bit, trying to say something that would suffice. "Well, uh, there's really not a lot to tell. I'm an instructor at a fitness center, but you already knew that. I'm originally from a small town in Indiana but moved up here for school and just ended up staying because my sister was here. Pretty simple really."

Zak could tell that she really didn't want to talk about her story right now. Maybe she had been hurt or maybe she was embarrassed about something. Either way, he didn't want to put her on the spot. He reached across the table and put his hand on hers and told her, "Listen, Skye, you don't have to tell me anything more than you want to say. Like I told you, I want to keep this light and easy for both of us. We go as far as we both want to. You don't owe me any story you aren't wanting to tell. Okay?"

She looked at their hands and then up into his eyes. A definite zing of something happened when he was touching her and looking into her eyes like that. She didn't pull away; she just continued to stare into his eyes. When they both heard the server clear her throat, they pulled apart, realizing that she couldn't set the plates on the table the way they were sitting.

They had pleasant conversation for the rest of the meal, just typical mundane stuff. *What kind of movies do you like? Are you into any specific sports?* Just easy things that weren't threatening or feeling like it was getting too personal. They did a fair amount of flirting back and forth too. When they had finished eating, Zak asked her if she would see him again sometime. And she agreed to another date the next day. He didn't have to work, she didn't have to work and David would be with Cassie. It was the perfect set-up.

Zak was excited that Skye agreed to go out with him again the next day. He told her he would like to take her out on his boat for a picnic on Lake Macatawa. It was a little over a half hour drive, so they agreed to meet at the brewery at ten o'clock the next morning. Zak helped Skye out of her chair and then walked toward the exit. On his way out, he grabbed one of the stuffed sloths that they had for sale at the brewery. It might be kind of silly, but he sensed that Skye had some pretty heavy stuff going on in her life right now and it seemed to be making her sad. So he handed her the sloth and told her that since she knew the whole story, he wanted her to have something to make her think about the evening and hopefully it would give her a smile.

Then he walked Skye out to her car and started to give her a kiss good night. He figured he would lean in and give it a shot. If she didn't respond or seemed to be hesitant, he would make it a quick peck. But when their lips touched, she responded beautifully. She rose up on her tiptoes so that their mouths reached easier and put her arms around his neck, so he placed his arms around her waist. He pressed his tongue against her lips and she eagerly opened so that he could explore her mouth fully, and she did some exploring of her own. They were in a fairly dark corner of the parking lot, so Zak took a shot and ran his hand up from her waist to cup her breast. She didn't object to that either; in fact, she seemed to really like it. After they had been making out and doing some fondling, Zak's head finally registered just what they were doing. As much as he would like to, he was not going to strip her down and fuck her right here in the parking lot of his bar. He pulled away, and he could hear the protest in Skye's moan. But he assured her there would be a lot more tomorrow when they had more privacy. He opened her car door and made sure she was buckled in tight, then leaned in to give her a more chaste kiss before closing her door and watching her drive away.

He went back into the brewery to let Jason and Pete know that he was going home. He found Pete at the bar and asked him if there was anything they needed before he headed out. He made a detour to the kitchen to ask the chef what some good ideas for a picnic on a boat would be. The chef gave him a few pointers and then he went to the office to talk to Jason. He was kind of worried that Jason might be stringing Sunni along or giving her false hope for a relationship.

Zak had watched Jason with the woman he had been flirting with all night. Zak headed into the office to talk to him. Jason looked up when he walked through the door.

"What's up, man? Is that the yoga instructor/single mom I've heard you are wanting to hook up with?" Jason asked with a devilish smile.

"Yeah, whatever," Zak replied. "Look, I saw you out there with Sunni and you two are hitting it pretty hot and heavy lately, but considering your circumstances, I thought you had realized it was best to just step back for a while, with what happened last time and all."

Jason just shook his head and then looked Zak in the eye and said, "Really, man, pot meet kettle."

Zak put his hands up in surrender. "Look, dude, I'm not trying to get in your face, and yes, I know I sound like a hypocrite, having a no strings attached thing going with a single mom, but this is different."

"Yeah?" Jason scoffed. "Exactly how is it different? We both have a sexual relationship going with women we don't see as a long-term thing."

"I'm just saying, if things go bad with Skye and me, it's no skin off anyone's nose. But you are playing with fire, man. That girl is Rayne's best friend. You hurt her, and I guarantee you that both Rayne and Walt will not be happy with you." Zak just shook his head and added, "You do you, man. Just be careful. We don't need a woman coming between any of us."

Jason said he would make sure that it never got to that point and they did the fist bump thing that they had been doing for years. Then Zak headed out the door, and Jason returned to the blonde at the bar.

****

As soon as she got into her car, Skye called Autumn. "I did it; I went in and I had an amazing time. He was so great about me not wanting to talk about some things. He told me there was no pressure," she said excitedly.

"That's awesome, girl," Autumn said. "But what are you doing alone so soon? Wait, please tell me you didn't head to the bathroom so you could call me."

"No, I'm driving home."

"Well, that's no fun," Autumn complained.

"We did have a pretty hot makeout session in the parking lot and tomorrow he is taking me out on his boat for a picnic." Skye was so excited she thought she should probably be pinching herself. She was so looking forward to just getting away and having a day where she didn't have to think about Savannah or Cassie or all of the crap that had happened in the last few weeks.

"That's so great, Skye," her friend said. "You deserve a little fun in your life right now."

They talked the rest of Skye's drive to her apartment. When Skye got home, she grabbed a glass of wine and took a long bath to try to relax. She was pretty sure she wasn't going to fall asleep easily tonight. She would bet she was going to be too excited to fall asleep at any decent hour.

Chapter Seven

Zak got up before his alarm, which was an odd occurrence for him, especially on a weekend. He wasn't sure why it had happened. It couldn't be that he was anxious or excited for today. He had been with his share of women over the years. He wasn't sure why this seemed like something different than his past dates. He showered and then went to his wine fridge to try to figure out what wines he wanted to take with him. He didn't know if she liked red or white, so he decided to pack a few of each. Then he headed to the local deli to pick up all the things he wanted to take for their picnic. He also needed to buy a picnic basket; he had honestly never gone on a picnic before. He wasn't sure exactly why that idea had come to mind last night, but he liked the idea of being alone with her out on the open water.

Skye woke after what had been a night filled with dreams. Actual dreams, not nightmares like she had been having so often lately. These were sweet dreams; some had even been sexy dreams. She didn't dream about the white picket fence and all that; that wasn't in her future anytime soon. But she did dream of doing fun things with Zak. She dreamed of being out on the water under the clear blue skies. She had happy dreams for the first time since Savannah's accident. Maybe there was life after the death of someone who had been a part of your life since before your first breath.

When Skye got to the brewery, Zak was already there waiting for her. He was standing by a little yellow sports car. She thought it looked familiar. Then she remembered the hot guy that had been staring at her in traffic a few days ago. She walked over to him and said she hoped she wasn't late. He assured her that she was early, and then he went to open her car door for her.

Zak was wearing board shorts and a tank top. Skye felt like she had dressed appropriately because she also had shorts and a tank top. She also had her bathing suit on underneath in case she wanted to try to tan.

When they were driving down the highway, Skye decided to ask her question. "Were you the one that was looking at me the other day when I was getting out of my car at the gym?"

Zak said, "Yeah, you caught me. I thought you were so beautiful that I was kind of staring at you."

"But you looked away when I looked up. I thought you had decided I wasn't someone you wanted to know," Skye admitted.

How did he explain this without coming off as a jerk? The reason he had looked away was that he had seen her with her kid. But since they were keeping this light and not deeply personal, she hadn't told him she had a kid yet. And he didn't want to make her feel self-conscious about him knowing it before she told him. So he just said, "I don't know. It was like you caught me and I didn't want to seem like I was being a creeper or whatever. I just panicked I guess and got my eyes back on the road."

"Oh, but then you joined the gym."

"Yeah, I wanted to try to meet you or at least find out about you, so I joined the gym," he stated. "I wasn't sure if you were a member or on staff, but I wanted a chance to meet you. Hopefully that doesn't sound too stalkerish."

"No, it's kind of nice actually. I kind of thought you didn't like what you saw," she said shyly.

"Nothing could be further from the truth," he assured her. "I liked what I saw a lot but I didn't have any way of knowing if you were single or if you would want to go out with me, so I had to try to seem like a normal guy."

"That's very flattering, that you would go to all that trouble from just seeing me on the street," Skye remarked.

"When I see something I want, I go for it," Zak admitted.

They spent the rest of the drive talking about Zak's boat and whether Skye had ever been out on Lake Makatawa. She told him that she had only been on small ones, like row boats when she was a kid. Her dad used to take her out fishing.

"Does he still like to fish?" Zak asked.

"No, he's gone, my mom too," Skye said sadly.

So her parents were an okay topic even though it seemed to make her sad, but she wasn't open to telling him too much about herself. At least not her current situation. But that was okay; he figured it had to have been painful for her, whatever it was. And if it was that she had gotten taken advantage of by a guy, she would be even more likely to not want to talk about things. It wasn't exactly first date or even second date material to say *Oh, hey. By the way, I have a kid from a total jerk face that left me high and dry*. He had promised her a day of fun and that was exactly what he was going to try to give her. A day away from whatever it was in life that had her guard up right now.

When they got to the marina, Zak swiped a card that allowed them into the parking lot closest to his boat. He opened Skye's door and helped her out of the car, then he got out the picnic basket and the insulated wine bag. Skye offered to help but he told her he had it, and then said, "Come on, I want to show you my boat."

"Is boat a euphemism for something else?" Skye asked, giggling.

"Well, no, I actually do want to show you my boat, but I would also be happy to show you lots of other things too," Zak flirted.

"Is this one of those I'll show you mine if you show me yours type of deals?" she asked, trying to keep her face serious like she was offended over the thought, but she couldn't keep from laughing.

"Well, I promise you, that if you show me yours, I will definitely show you mine." Zak sort of growled that a little bit.

As they walked down the docks that lead to Zak's boat, Skye spotted the last one on the end. It was not what she would call a 'boat.' A boat was something you rowed, or maybe something that had pontoons on it and floated along in the water. This seriously looked like a small house. "Is that yours?" she asked, pointing to the one at the end.

"Yep, that's my baby," Zak confirmed.

"When you said boat, I was thinking like maybe a small speed boat or maybe even a pontoon boat. I was not expecting something that is bigger than most of my apartment combined," Skye stated.

Zak just chuckled and said, "Well as they say, go big or go home, so I went big." He set the basket and the cooler down on the dock and helped Skye onto the boat before going back down the ladder to get the picnic stuff.

While he was getting the paraphernalia into the boat, Skye looked around a little. It appeared that the boat had a downstairs compartment that probably held a bedroom or maybe even two if they weren't huge. There was a galley with a small stove, refrigerator and sink. A person could honestly live on a boat this size for a while before having to go back to shore to restock supplies.

When Zak had put the food in the galley, he untethered the boat from the dock and then motioned for Skye to follow him to the wheel of the boat. He started up the motor and started to steer them away from the shore. When he got away from the other boats, he said, "Come here, I'll show you how to steer."

Skye walked over to him and he placed her hands on the wheel and put his hands by hers. She was essentially trapped between his hard body and the wheel. Not that she was complaining. She could feel the heat of his body. He wasn't pressing her tight to the wheel, but he was right there behind her. She wouldn't be able to step back at all without bumping up against him. He helped her steer toward the middle of the lake and then he told her he was going to put down anchor here so that they could have their picnic or sunbathe or whatever.

They decided to eat on the back deck of the boat where they could also soak up some sun. It was a beautiful day. Zak couldn't have planned it any more perfectly. He asked if she preferred red wine or white wine. She admitted that she didn't know a lot about wine, but of what she had tried before white seemed to be her preference. Zak brought out the picnic basket and a chilled bottle of white wine.

Skye was impressed with the amazing goodies he had packed in the picnic basket. There was an assortment of cheeses and crackers. There was also a plate of cold meats and some spinach artichoke spread and a fruit mixture with berries and melons. He had also included a dessert that looked amazing, but Skye said she would have to wait on that; she was too full from all of the food she had already consumed.

They decided to stretch out in the sun and let the food settle. Skye stood up and took off her shorts and tank top, revealing the bathing suit underneath. Zak had known she was hot, but this was almost too much to bear. It was a one-piece, but for a one-piece, it revealed a lot and was sexy as hell. It was a little low cut in the front and the sides where a higher cut at the thigh than most one pieces. Basically, all her parts were covered, but it was kind of showing them off in a very tantalizing way. Zak pulled his gaze away from her long enough to pull off his own tank top.

Zak offered to help Skye with her tanning lotion; he definitely didn't want her getting a sunburn. It might derail his plans for later if she was hurting from too much sun. She agreed and stretched out on her lounge chair so Zak could lotion her back. Applying lotion to her back was safe enough, although her skin was so soft and warm he was definitely looking forward to touching more of her. When he got to her legs, it became a little more challenging. Her legs weren't long, but they were well defined with all the yoga and other athletics she participated in. He could feel the muscles in her calves and thighs and began to picture those legs wrapped tightly around him. He was starting to get aroused at that thought. He tried to tell his body that there would be plenty of time for that later. He was going to be doomed if she wanted him to do her front. Thankfully, when her back was done, she rolled over and reached out her hand for the lotion.

It might be a good idea to lie on his stomach for a while so that she didn't notice the hard-on that was rapidly tenting his shorts. When she was done with the lotion, Skye stretched out on her stomach too. They turned so that their heads were facing each other and shared some light conversation in between just relaxing and soaking up the sun.

****

When Zak had pulled off his tank top, Skye had to remind herself that she saw buff guys at the gym all the time; this wasn't anything special. But her suspicions were confirmed: Zak had a six-pack—actually it was almost more like eight. He wasn't super muscular, like he was some sort of meathead obsessed with being super buff, but he was very well defined. He also had a little bit of hair on his chest, which had always been a bit of a weakness for Skye, and that led to a trail of hair that led to the waistband of his shorts. The more she saw of him, the more she liked.

After the small talk had kind of died out, Zak rolled to his side so that he could look her more fully in the face. He reached out a hand and brushed the hair back from her face. He caressed her cheek with his thumb. She smiled up at him, so he decided to go for it and ask if she wanted to go below deck to the bedroom. "Skye, I am perfectly content to just lay here with you and talk, but I would really like to take you below deck so we can pick up where we left off last night. There is absolutely no pressure if you aren't ready for that."

Skye turned her head so that she could kiss the thumb that had been on her cheek. She smiled playfully before she took his thumb into her mouth and swirled her tongue around it. Then she pulled away and said, "I would really like to go below deck and see where things go." Skye knew that she was kind of playing with fire. She didn't really know much about Zak; she knew he was obviously smart and somewhat wealthy, but she didn't even know what he did for a living. He said he'd graduated from law school, but that didn't mean he was an actual attorney. There were other things like politics and some businesses that used law degrees. She didn't even know his last name. But she also knew that she hadn't told him much about herself either, and she wanted to keep it that way. She was just hoping for some hot, steamy fun that might take her mind off real life every now and then. They were both consenting adults, so there was nothing wrong with some no strings attached hook ups. She knew that right now was not the time to try to start a relationship that was more than just light and easy. Cassie was the only person that she was completely committed to at this point. Besides, she could use a little stress relief right now.

Zak stood up and then reached out a hand to help Skye to her feet. Not that she needed help; she taught yoga after all. She was probably more limber than he was. The idea of her being limber like that did something for him when he thought about it. No, taking her hand wasn't really about helping her up as much as it was about touching her, feeling some connection. He had never been one to get into deep relationships, but he did have to have some sort of connection; he had to feel a little electricity going between them when they touched. And this electricity could light the whole city block that he lived on. He had never felt this much of a connection with someone before.

When Skye got to her feet, he didn't let go of her hand; he pulled her in the direction of the steps that would take them to the bedroom below. He wasn't really pulling, more like directing. She wasn't hesitant at all to follow him. When they got into the stateroom, he couldn't hold back any longer. He wrapped her in his arms and began devouring her lips. She seemed to be as hungry for him as he was for her. When he broke away to try to get his breathing and his libido under control, he told her, "Skye I want you so badly that I may be a little overzealous. If I do anything that hurts you or that you don't like, just say so and I will slow down."

Skye didn't want him to slow down; she wanted to be out of her head for a little while and she had no doubt that really great sex would give her that brief respite from the sorrow and the strain. She would never consider Cassie a burden, but she had not been prepared to become a surrogate mother to an infant. She thought she had time before she would have to settle into a routine of daycare and diapers, formula and spit up. If Zak could give her a few hours on a boat and take her mind off real life for a while, she was all in. She wasn't exactly sure how to convey that in words, so she just dove back at his mouth to begin kissing him passionately again.

Zak reached behind her neck and untied the strap of her bathing suit. With a slight tug, it fell around her waist and he got his first feel of her amazing breasts. She was more than a handful and that was perfectly fine with him. He cupped one breast and brushed his thumb across the nipple. It was already peaked and hard; she was obviously as into this as he was. He rolled her nipples between his thumb and fingers, and she responded with a low moan. He put a little more pressure into it and she tried to get even closer to him. It seemed like she was trying to climb inside him through the connection of their mouths. He knew that sooner or later, he was going to have to stop kissing her and taste those hard buds, but for now, he was just enjoying the feeling of their tongues swirling around each other.

Skye wasn't going to be able to take much more of the attention he was giving her nipples without going off like a rocket. She had always had very responsive breasts. She could come just from that stimulation. She pulled her mouth away to say, "Zak, please, if you keep that up, I'll come."

Zak didn't think that sounded like a problem. He had known a few women who could come from just nipple stimulation and that had always been a huge turn-on for him. He ignored her protest and went back to her mouth to keep that connection going. She tried to pull away a little again and he just kept pursuing her until he had her up against the wall. She was still trying to protest so Zak pulled away and looked in her eyes and asked, "Am I doing anything that is hurting you or is too much in a bad way?" She responded that he wasn't and he said, "Good, now, as for you not wanting to come, that's really too bad, because I want you to come and come hard over and over from every type of attention I give you. Understood?"

She sort of whimpered a little but nodded her agreement. He continued to alternate between caressing and pinching her nipples and fondling her breasts. His actions were making it so that she would get really close to orgasm from the mild pain but then he would slow down to caresses. This man was going to drive her insane. Finally, after what had seemed like an hour, he pinched her nipples really hard and didn't let up until she came with a scream. She heard Zak say, "Good girl." For some reason, those words felt really good to hear. She had never had a man say that to her before. She was just barely starting to come down from the high that the orgasm had given her before Zak was pulling the rest of her bathing suit off and laying her at the foot the bed so her legs dangled off from the knee down. He spread her legs and immediately put his mouth on her pussy. He was not giving her a chance to think; he was just going forward. He had told her he would stop if she asked him to, and she really did believe that he would, but unless she voiced an objection, he was obviously planning to go full speed ahead.

Zak couldn't wait to taste her. Her mouth had been so sweet, but he was dying to taste her juices after her orgasm. He would lap up every drop that he could get and then he would go to work at trying to get another orgasm out of her before he finally took his turn. No one had ever complained that he was a selfish lover. He wasn't a gentle lover by any means, and he was rather dominant when it came to sex, but he always made sure that the woman was well taken care of before he got his orgasm.

Skye couldn't believe how amazing Zak's mouth felt on her. She'd had guys do oral on her before, but none of them had been this determined. His licking had felt amazing, but when he started sucking, it became beyond intense. She was going to be going over the edge again in no time if he kept up these actions. She felt him insert two fingers and begin pumping them in and out. She was getting so close to going over again, but when he crooked his fingers to touch that tender spot inside her while also sucking hard on her clit, she couldn't hold back another second. She came harder than she had ever come in her life.

Zak really liked hearing her scream out his name when she had her orgasms. It let him know that they were connected at least for this time and place. Even though she was drifting a bit, she was still grounded enough to know who she was with. It might be a little bit about his ego, knowing that he had put a woman in that place, but really, it was more about just feeling that connection. He kind of felt like when a woman screamed his name during orgasm, it was a little like a 'thank you' and a little like a 'more please.' And he would definitely oblige the more part. He was more than ready to sink himself deep inside her.

While she was still a little spaced out from that last orgasm, Zak took off his shorts and rolled on a condom. He got on the bed and helped her readjust so that her head was on the pillow beside him. He looked into her eyes and asked, "Everything good? Do you still want to do this?" She smiled—it looked a little loopy, but it was a smile nonetheless—and nodded her head. He got on his knees between her legs and slowly started to inch his way in. She was so wet, he slid in easily, but he still went slow. He didn't know how much she could take. He was rather large, at least compared to most of the guys he had seen in locker rooms over his school years. When he was fully inside her, he paused for a second, partially to let her acclimate to his size and partly to rein himself in. She felt so amazing that he wanted to pound into her, but he wasn't sure that she would be okay with that. Maybe he should work up to the rougher stuff. He started rocking slowly back and forth into her body. She was meeting him with every thrust. When he had a pretty good rhythm going, she wrapped her legs around his waist and he heard her say "harder." He could do that; he could definitely go harder and faster. He went from a steady rocking motion to a hard pounding motion and she just kept right up meeting him on every thrust. Where had this woman been all his life? He assured himself that he wasn't thinking that in a romantic way—he definitely didn't see it as a happily ever after type of thing—but he would definitely like to become regular fuck buddies with her, if she was up for that. He felt his release starting and he needed to make sure that she came again too. If he could make her orgasm with him, or right before him, it would make him come so much harder. He worked his hand between their two bodies and began circling her clit in hard fast motions. When he knew he didn't have any more time to waste or he was going to be going before her, he used his thumb and forefinger and pinched her clit hard, holding on as she rode out her orgasm, which of course triggered his. He came longer and harder than he had in a long, long time; actually, he didn't remember ever coming that hard or long. This woman definitely met his every dream sexually.

He went to dispose of the condom and wash himself off a little. He also left the cabinet open a little so that Skye could find a washcloth if she needed one later.

Chapter Eight

They both dozed a little after their vigorous sex. When Zak woke up he realized that they should probably head back to shore. They still had to drive back to the brewery and then both had to drive home. He wasn't sure what Skye's schedule was like tomorrow and if she had a babysitter watching her kid, but she would probably rather be home before too late. As he got out of bed, Skye stirred and looked up at him. He explained, "I'm going to go up and pull anchor and head back to shore. You can take your time."

Skye was sort of disappointed, but she realized that it was probably for the best. Real life was always going to intrude on the fun times. The day was getting away from them; it was already late afternoon. She got up and looked for a bathroom. She found it and went in and freshened up a little with one of the washcloths she found in the cabinet. She would make a point of telling him that she had dirtied one because she wasn't sure how he handled laundry for things on the boat. She got dressed, this time without her swimsuit. She had brought undergarments in case her suit had gotten wet or something. She hadn't been sure when he said a picnic on his boat if they would be swimming or what. She got back up on the top deck just as Zak was nearing the marina.

When his stomach growled, Zak realized that it had been several hours since they had eaten, and they hadn't eaten the dessert at all. He asked Skye if she would like to have dinner at one of the restaurants near the marina or if she needed to get home. She told him that she thought dinner sounded nice. Zak was happy to hear that she wanted to have dinner with him, but that just puzzled him more on what her situation was at home. Obviously, the baby was being taken care of by someone. Maybe she had a friend or family member that she lived with that helped with the child. Or maybe the father was involved and he had the child on the weekends. That would be ideal for Zak. He could see Skye on the weekends when her kid was with the dad and then during the week they could both focus on work and other obligations. Whatever the situation, he was happy to have as much time with her as he was able. His buddies all thought that he was a playboy. And, for the most part, he was. But that didn't mean that he wanted to bed a woman and then be done with her. At least not every time. There had been women over the years that had served one purpose and one purpose only. But for the most part, in the last few years, it had involved more than just taking a woman to bed. No, he hadn't had any real long-term relationships, but he did take the woman on a date and spend time with them outside of bed. It was never a deep and lasting connection, but the connection had to be there just the same.

They stopped at a little diner that Zak assured her was amazing and he was right. Again, they had pleasant conversation about everything and about nothing. They didn't get into personal topics like family but they did talk about things like sports and movies, light stuff that didn't really put a person out there if they weren't ready for someone to know their personal business.

When they got back on the road, Zak reached over and took Skye's hand. He pulled it to his lips and kissed it and then let their joined hands fall back onto the console between the seats. They were fairly quiet on the drive home; it just felt nice to hold hands and just "be." Zak parked near where her car was in the parking lot and went around to open her door. He walked her to her car and when she unlocked the door he opened it. Before she got in the car, though, he pulled her in for another deep and lingering kiss. He told her that he had really enjoyed their day together and he was hoping they could do it again soon. Skye wanted to get together with him soon too, but she wasn't sure what his motive was. She needed to make her position clear.

"I'd love to do more of what we did today, but I will be honest. Right now, Zak, I'm really only looking for a friend with benefits, or maybe just more of a fuck buddy. I don't want to mislead you, so I wanted to put that right out there."

"That's all I'm looking for right now too," he assured her and then added, "I have to admit the sex was great, and I would definitely like to have more of it." He gave her a devilish smile.

"Then I'd like to see you again," Skye agreed.

"We never did get to the dessert, so I thought maybe you would like to take it home with you," Zak said. He handed the box from the bakery to Skye.

They exchanged phone numbers and then Skye got in her car and headed home.

Zak decided to head into the brewery for a beer or two and see how the day had gone. Jeremy was on duty tonight. So Zak went behind the bar and got a tall glass of his favorite brew and then sat on one of the stools. The place was somewhat busy, but not overly hectic. There were a few couples on the dance floor and when he looked at them, he wondered to himself if Skye liked to dance. He thought about how little he knew about her really, but that had been the way they both wanted it. Still wanted it, he reminded himself.

"You look a million miles away, my friend," Jeremy said from the other side of the bar.

"Nah, not really. Just got back from a day out on the lake with a woman I met recently."

"Ah, she didn't turn you down, did she?" Jeremy joked. "I know how badly that would hurt your ego."

"Nope, definitely did not turn me down. In fact, I think I had the most amazing sex I have ever had." He paused then said, "Who am I trying to kid? I know it was the best sex I've ever had."

"Then why do you seem like that's a bad thing?"

"You know me. I'm not ready to be a one-woman man. I've still got too many seeds to sow as they say. But if this was the best I've ever had, how do I move forward? Will other women leave me wishing that I was back with Skye? I just don't know what to think really."

"And it would be bad if you had a monogamous relationship with her?" Jeremy asked.

"Well, it wouldn't be, if it were just sex and dating, but I am definitely not ready to settle down, and she has a kid," Zak lamented. "You know I'm not ready for that in my life."

"I get where you are coming from," Jeremy consoled him. "What does she think? Is she looking for a marriage proposal? Is she looking for a new daddy for her kid?"

"She hasn't even told me she has a kid. I just know because I saw her carrying the kid into daycare a couple of times," Zak said. "Really, we haven't talked about much of anything personal. We both agreed to keeping it light."

"Then what's the problem? Have fun while it lasts. If she gets to be too clingy, I know you know how to let her down. You've been breaking up with women for years when they started wanting too much. How hard can that be?"

"You're right, I should just enjoy the sex and not worry about the rest," Zak agreed. The problem was, there was a part of him that maybe, kind of, wanted to get to know more about her. If she didn't have a kid, he was sure he would want to make it more of a relationship than just 'fuck buddies.'

On his drive home, Zak kept thinking over his day with Skye. She had been exactly what he liked in a sex partner. She had met all of his desires. If he was looking for something more permanent, she would be the perfect woman for him—if she didn't have a kid. There was just no way he was ready for a kid. But still the sex had been incredible, and even when they were just chatting while they had lunch and laid on the deck, conversation had been easy. They seemed to like a lot of similar things. He could go with her to a chick flick, if she would go to an action movie with him. They had pretty much the same outlook on sports, they liked to watch football, but weren't really obsessed with it. They preferred to participate in most sports than to just watch. They were what most people would say was a great match.

When Zak got home, before he got out of his car, he decided to text Skye, just to make sure she had gotten home safely.

Hey, just wanted to make sure you got home okay.

I did, thanks for such a fun day.

No problem, I enjoyed it too. We'll definitely have to do it again sometime.

For sure. Well, I'll see you at the gym.

Right, yeah, you will. Sweet dreams Skye.

Thanks, you too. Good night.

Good night.

What the hell? He had never said anything like that to a woman before. 'Sweet dreams'? Who the heck was he turning into? Maybe Walt was rubbing off on him. Walt was engaged to be married. His wedding was coming up in a few weeks actually. Maybe that was it, he was just getting a little mushy because he saw his friend be really mushy with his fiancée. Zak shook his head and got out of the car. He decided to go into his workout room and run a few miles on the treadmill. He really had been lazy all day and he didn't feel ready to go to bed just yet. A good run should help wear him out enough that he could sleep. He ran his usual five miles, but he still felt too charged, so he ran two more. When he was physically exhausted, he drank a big glass of water to re-hydrate. He was physically tired, but his mind wouldn't shut off. He just kept thinking about how much he had enjoyed the day. He decided to have a few fingers of scotch to help him relax even more. Then he took a quick shower and went to bed. He knew if he let himself think too much, he was going to be jacking off to the memories of the day with Skye. So he rushed through the shower. When he crawled into bed, he still had images of Skye in his head. How beautifully she had responded, the look on her face when she had an orgasm. He tossed and turned for a while but finally, he was able to fall asleep.

His dreams were just more of the same thoughts that had been running through his head, but there were also other images there. Not just the sexual ones. There were images of them going to concerts, and movies, even just sitting in the park. He didn't do those things, at least he never had. Never anything that seemed like simple dating. The image that bothered him the most was the image of him and Skye sitting on a park bench while a little boy ran around in front of them. He was absolutely certain it was a little boy too. It looked something like the little girl he always saw Skye with but not exactly. When he woke up, he was giving his best attorney argument to all the reasons that that dream was absolutely not going to happen. There was no way that his brain was suggesting that he have a kid with Skye. He wasn't even ready for one kid, let alone two. Yes, he wanted kids, in a few years, not right now. It would change his whole life. He would have to move because this apartment wasn't really built for a family. There were a lot of singles in the building and even some couples, but it wasn't super kid friendly. Besides, kids needed a yard to run around in, they needed a place to ride their bike, and downtown Grand Rapids was NOT that place. He would have to give up going out to bars and clubs just to have fun and unwind and maybe find a woman to hook up with for the night. His brain reminded him that in the whole time he had been hooking up with women, he had never found one that did it for him like Skye did. He told that part of his brain to be quiet.

Skye was lying in bed after showering from her day on the boat. She was looking at the text Zak had sent her. It wasn't like it was romantic or anything; it was just a nice sentiment, probably how he had signed many texts to women over the years. But still, it was nice for someone to wish her sweet dreams. Other than last night, when she'd had dreams of Zak, it had been close to a month since she had had sweet dreams. She read the text again, hoping that her mind would take his suggestion and give her sweet dreams. She was so tired of the nightmares she had been having. She so desperately wanted life to go back to how it had been a month ago. She would give anything to have her sister back.

She had gotten a voicemail while she was out on Zak's boat from David. He said that the attorney's office that he had hired had let him know that they were holding off on filing the lawsuit until they found out if there were going to be any criminal charges. In one sense, she was glad to have it put off because having to go through a trial would be like scraping an open wound. But in another sense, she just wanted to be done with the trial so that they could start trying to get to some sense of normal. Not the normal they'd had before, but they would adjust to a new normal. It wasn't like any lawsuit or any settlement could bring her sister back. It might be nice if there was some money to set aside to help Cassie with college expenses when she got to that age, but Skye didn't want any money. She knew that David wasn't in it for the money either. He just wanted someone to be held responsible for Savannah's death. Unfortunately, in today's society, if there weren't any laws broken, the only way to hold someone responsible was to sue them. The truck driver had been ticketed and fined, but that hardly seemed like a just punishment for what he had done. But if David was right, there might be actual criminal charges that would at least hold the driver responsible for running the car off the road.

She looked back at the text from Zak, hoping that somehow it would clear these maudlin thoughts from her brain. She tried to focus on how much fun the day had been. She really had enjoyed herself with Zak. It was easy just to be with him. They'd had long periods of silence, but it didn't feel awkward like it did with some people. They were just enjoying each other's companionship. And the sex had been mind-blowing. She had never had that many orgasms in one encounter. If she were in a different place, and not having to focus on Cassie so much, and if Zak was in a different place and wanting to keep it light, she could really see herself falling for this guy. She wouldn't, well, she kind of had fallen, a little bit, but she couldn't entertain those thoughts. Now was not the time for falling for a guy.

Her mind would not shut off easily, but she remembered the dessert that Zak had sent home with her. Maybe she could enjoy a bite or two before she fell asleep. She got back up and went to see what the dessert was. She hadn't allowed herself the indulgence to even look earlier; she'd been afraid that she would eat the whole thing. She opened the box and O.M.G. could the man be any more perfect? He had gotten strawberry cheesecake drizzled with chocolate. It was probably one of her favorite desserts, and it went so well with her favorite wine. So maybe a few nibbles and a few sips of wine would help her brain to shut off for the night.

She took a small slice and placed the rest back in the refrigerator, poured a half glass of wine, and went and sat by the window looking out on the street below. She didn't live in a bad neighborhood. It wasn't great, but the crime rate was reasonably low, and the rent wasn't outrageous. Although now she would be moving and David had already told her that there was no way she was paying him rent. She had decided that she would still put the amount of rent aside each month so that when it was time for her to move again, she would have plenty of money for deposit and all that. It would be nice to be able to set some aside for what her mother had always called a "rainy day." Her father had always told her, "You never know when a tire might need replacing, or a battery go bad." Her dad was always so handy with cars. Her parents had been older when they had first had children, and neither of them had been really healthy people for the last several years of their lives. Skye was sad that they were gone, but also relieved that they hadn't had to go though one of their children dying before they did. They had both died of natural causes, after having lived the lives they had wanted to live.

Finally, after the wine and the cheesecake and letting her mind remember the good times of her childhood, Skye decided to try going to bed again. She cuddled that silly sloth that Zak had given her to her chest and finally drifted off to sleep, and her dreams were sweet. She dreamed about doing things with Zak. She actually had some sweet dreams with Savannah in them. Memories of the good times they had had over the years growing up. When she woke up, she still felt the sorrow of knowing that her sister was gone forever, but she would keep trying to focus on the good memories and try to keep the nightmares at bay.

Chapter Nine

When Zak got to work the next morning, he was still trying to shake the images of Skye that had plagued his dreams—oh, not the erotic ones; those he had thoroughly enjoyed, and they could stay in his brain forever. But the ones from his dreams that he really wasn't sure how to deal with so he tried to just shove out of his brain. It didn't really work, but he kept trying.

It was a tiring day, but tonight he and the guys were meeting at the brewery to go over how things were running. They did it every month. The brewery was closed on Mondays, so it was the perfect time to doublecheck inventory, brainstorm ideas, and look at the financial reports, all the things that came with being a part owner in a business.

When Zak got to Five Sloths, the others were all there already. He went over to the bar and grabbed a beer and went to sit with his friends. They always started out with just some time to shoot the breeze. They were always having fun harassing someone. Tonight, it started out with razing Walt about being surprised that his 'ball and chain' had let him out of the house. But soon, the teasing turned to him since he was the latest guy to show up at the brewery with a woman. They wanted all the details of who she was and what she did and was she any good in bed.

Zak told them that she was a yoga instructor at a local gym and that her name was Skye. The rest he pleaded the Fifth Amendment on. They all just laughed and made comments about how she must be good if she knew all those yoga poses, either that or Zak was pleading the Fifth because she was so horrible in bed that he didn't want to relive it by sharing it with them. He just told them all to fuck off. And with that, the actual meeting began.

Jason passed out copies of the financial report for the month. He pointed out that line items 18 and 37 were both debits in the amount of $15.85. That was because two of their stuffed sloths had been stolen with no money received. Zak knew he was one of them but before he could speculate on who the other was, Walt looked at Jason and said, "Yeah, yeah, take my sloth out of my share of the profit if you need to. It helped Rayne come out of her shell, so it's well worth it." After Walt had agreed to pay for his, Jason turned and gave Zak 'the evil eye' as they would say. He just flipped Jason off and said, "Do what ya gotta do, man."

Other than that, things seemed to really be going great with the brewery. The profits were always rising. They discussed if they wanted to change any of the brews they were featuring now because fall was not too far off. They decided to wait another month before rotating to any different beers. The ones they had now seemed to be selling well. And then they set themselves to the task of doing inventory. Each took a different aspect and went to their part of the bar. Zak always checked the dry stock, paper products, cleaning supplies, that sort of thing, making a note of what things they needed.

When they were all done with the inventory, they always sat around and had a couple of beers and just caught up on each other's lives. Walt asked them all to stand up for him at his wedding that was coming up in October. They all agreed, of course; no way was any of them getting married without the full support of his brothers. They might not be brothers by blood, but the things they had gone though over the years made them brothers just the same. They had always had each other's backs.

It was late when Zak got home. It always was after the meetings because they had too much fun just hanging out. Being busy professionals, they didn't get to do that as often as they would have liked. He pulled his phone out of his pocket and realized that he had missed a text when he'd had his phone on silent during the meeting. It was a text from Skye.

Thank you for the wish of sweet dreams last night, that and Sigma helped me to get a peaceful night's sleep.

Should he text her back? It was pretty late, and he would be seeing her tomorrow at the yoga class. He had put it in his schedule so that his administrative assistant wouldn't schedule him for anything else. Of course court would overrule it—he had no choice if a judge put him on the docket for a certain day. He hadn't been sure he wanted to put down yoga, though, so he had put it down as a class at the gym. That worked. He decided to text Skye even though it was late. Hopefully if she was sleeping she had her phone silenced so it wouldn't wake her up.

I'm glad it worked; I hope tonight is just as pleasant. I'll see you in class tomorrow.

He was just starting to undress when he heard his phone ping with another text. He grabbed it to see what she had written. *Really, Zak,* he thought to himself, *you jump to read a text from a woman now? Not like you at all.* But that didn't stop him from reading it.

See you tomorrow. Good night.

Good night. Sweet dreams.

He finished undressing and went to bed. He would shower in the morning. As he lay there, his mind kept trying to figure out what it was about this woman that seemed to have him acting differently than he usually did with women. He thought about all the aspects of their interactions. Actually, maybe what she had said in her text was part of it. She had implied that maybe she hadn't been getting peaceful sleep lately. He knew there was something going on with her; he just wasn't sure what since she seemed to steer away from any personal topics. It could be that she was hesitant to tell men about the child. Some would judge her, others would embrace it and others, like himself, would really not be affected by it much. If he had been looking for long-term, the child would definitely be a red flag for him, but he wasn't, and he had made sure she was okay with that. But she still might feel awkward sharing that with someone. After thinking that all through, Zak realized that most likely the reason things felt different with her was the mystery behind it all. With most women he dated, he knew pretty much all about them. But Skye seemed reserved and secretive, so she was somewhat of a mystery to him. That had to be it. With that thought, he rolled over and soon fell asleep. He had those same dreams again, though. That was getting to be annoying.

Chapter Ten

By Friday of that week, Zak had decided to not wait any longer to hear from the DA before at least talking to the family. He didn't want them to feel abandoned by their attorney at this time of such a great loss. It wouldn't hurt to have their statements anyway, because no matter what happened with the criminal case, the civil case would move ahead at some point, so Zak told his assistant to call the family and set up meetings for the next week. He knew there was a husband and a sister. The child would be too young to give any testimony as to what happened, but he planned on telling David Miner that if at all possible, he wanted the child in the courtroom during the actual trial, It was amazing what seeing a child whose mother had been taken away at such a young age did to both judges and juries. For sure, it was a sympathy vote, but anything that helped with their case was a good thing.

He planned to call Skye and see if she was available to go out anytime this weekend. He had seen her at yoga class, and that had been even worse torture than it had been the week before. Now he knew what she looked like naked, he knew how her body moved, he knew what it felt like to be deep inside her. He thought about dropping the class because she was a huge distraction, but then he reminded himself that he couldn't care less if he learned anything about yoga, but he did enjoy watching her do the poses. He would just have to wear baggy workout pants to try to hide his arousal.

Skye had seen Zak at yoga class on both Tuesday and Thursday. They had smiled and been pleasant, but hadn't really talked or anything else. Skye knew that the fitness center didn't have a strict policy against instructors dating clients, but she had asked Zak to keep it professional anyway. She didn't need coworkers asking all sorts of questions. And Zak had honored that request. She would admit that when he looked at her there was a heat that hadn't been there before the past weekend, but he didn't say or do anything to cause any suspicions to arise.

On Friday, she had a message on her voicemail when she finished her classes. It asked her to call some law firm. Most likely it would be about the lawsuit against the truck driver. As much as she did not want to make that phone call, she knew she needed to. She would much rather be able to not have to go through all the questions the attorney was sure to ask. But David deserved to have some compensation. Not that money would ever be an adequate trade for the loss of your wife. It was more symbolic, showing that he was having to take some responsibility for his careless actions. Cassie definitely deserved for the man to pay. David was planning on putting whatever he got into a college fund for Cassie. He wanted only the best for his little girl. She called the law office and was scheduled to have a meeting with Mr. Owens on the following Wednesday.

She had barely hung up from that call when her phone rang again. It was Zak. She tried to sound happy and upbeat when she said hello. She must not have pulled it off, though, because Zak's first question was if everything was all right. She told him that she was okay; she was just tired and had a lot on her mind. When he asked her if she was up for a date on Saturday, she told him she had to move some things to her new apartment during the day, but she should be done by dinner time. They agreed to meet at the brewery again and then she told Zak she was really looking forward to just getting away from it all for a few hours.

Skye's move on Saturday had ended up not really being very strenuous. David had hired a moving company, pretty much all she had to do was pack the few dishes and clothes that she had kept out until the last minute. Her lease would be up at the end of the month, but she wasn't going to wait till the last minute. Living above David's garage would make the logistics of helping with Cassie so much easier. By 4:00 she was completely moved. She was going to be living out of boxes until she had some time to put things away, but at least they were all in her new place. She quickly showered, put on the clothes that she had kept out of the boxes so she would have them for tonight, threw on some make-up and headed out the door.

When Zak saw Skye walk in, he walked to the door to meet her. He took her to the table and asked her if she knew what she wanted. She did because the last time she was here, there were a few things that she'd wanted to try but she'd only had one of them. So she picked another off her list of "sounded amazing."

After their order was placed, Zak looked at her, noticing that she looked tired, or maybe it was sad. He just wasn't sure which it was. She definitely wasn't her usual cheery self. "You sounded off on the phone yesterday, and now you seem a little subdued. Is there anything wrong?" Zak asked.

"Not really wrong, just some things that are sort of stressful right now. But I'll be fine," she assured him.

"Is it anything I can help with?" Zak asked.

Skye knew something he could do to help; she just wasn't sure how to go about asking for it. What the heck, it couldn't hurt. She was sure that nothing she could say would really surprise Zak. It might be unexpected coming from her, but definitely not shocking in general. If Zak was the playboy she thought he was, it would take a lot to shock him. So she laid it right out there. "The best way you could help me is take me away from all the stuff going on in my head for a few hours."

When she said that, Zak paused for a moment. He could do that, he knew how, but would she be up for his way of doing things? And it would mean taking her to his apartment; all of his toys were there. He hadn't packed it like he usually did when he knew he was going to pursue a little BDSM type of play with a woman. He didn't consider himself a Dom in the traditional lifestyle sense, but he was dominant, and he did enjoy some of the forms of play that lifestyle was known for. He must have been sorting things out in his mind too long, because he became aware of her starting to apologize for being too forward and telling him to just disregard what she'd said.

Oh, that was so not going to happen. He was not going to let her feel like she needed to apologize for asking for something she needed. She needed to know that he couldn't be effective if he didn't know what she was thinking or what she felt she needed. He put a finger over her lips and said, "First of all, hush. You have every right to ask for things that you need from me." He removed his finger but placed his hand over hers on the table. "Secondly, I was thinking about the request. I wasn't hesitating for any other reason, okay?" When she nodded, Zak continued. "Have you ever done any sort of BDSM play, like light bondage, spankings, even just as a fun thing?"

"No, I've heard of it but never done anything beyond one guy wanting to blindfold me. He wasn't that great in bed anyway, so it really was just bad sex with a blindfold instead of bad sex without a blindfold," she admitted.

"Okay, so hear me out for a minute." He looked to her for a nod or some form of agreement. When she nodded, he continued. "I have found that being tied up and blindfolded can help a woman get out of her head space at least for a little while. I have also found that some women respond to a small bite of pain and can go even further out of their heads for a longer period of time. Now, I am by no means a sadist. I don't want to spank a person because I enjoy causing them pain. However, I do enjoy when things like spanking or flogging with a light hand really does it for some women. I think you might be a woman that does enjoy it to a point. From some of the things that happened on the boat, I get the feeling that you might like a little roughness with your sex. If you want to try this, there are two things that are paramount to it working. The first is that you have to have a safeword that will tell me to stop. Some people use the traffic light system. If you say yellow, we slow down and talk about what is getting overwhelming. If you say red, I will stop immediately, untie you and step back so that you know you are completely safe. Understood?" She nodded, so he added, "The second thing is that you need to trust me, trust me enough to believe that I have no ill intent, and that I will stop if you use a safeword."

She knew she trusted him to not have ill intent. Hell, if he had wanted to off her for some reason, he could have done that on the boat and she would currently be resting at the bottom of Lake Makatawa. She also believed him when he said he would stop at any time if she needed him to. What she didn't understand was why she just couldn't say 'stop' or 'no.' She asked him and he was very happy to explain it to her.

"Well, we can try that route if it's what you feel more comfortable with. But just think about this first. It's a proven fact that women often say no or stop, because their brain is telling them that they shouldn't be enjoying this. It's dirty or it's wrong so your brain is saying stop not because your body wants it to stop but because your brain tells you that it should stop. The other part of that is if your brain is floating nicely in a fog from a couple of orgasms, in your brain, you may be thinking *Please don't stop*. But when your brain is not fully in control, any one of those three words may come out of your mouth independently or in any combination. Any combination without the whole phrase leaves a lot of possible misunderstandings. Now, some people do use a random word like"—he looked down and noticed her plate of eggplant Parmesan— "eggplant for example. That's not a word most people would be thinking or saying during sex. So if you say eggplant, I will know that there was something that was bothering you." He looked into her eyes. Damn, those eyes were so beautiful. "Do you get what I mean?"

She nodded. She got it now. "The traffic light is fine," she said.

"Great. Let's finish our food and then we can head out."–*to his place*. He didn't say that, but that would be where he would be taking her. He had never had a woman there before. Usually it was just easier to go to her place or to a hotel. That way he could make the quick exit when he wanted to. But he couldn't see a good reason to have to go home and pack his 'toys' and then meet her somewhere. Most likely she wouldn't have volunteered her apartment anyway, since she had told him she was in the process of moving.

Skye was sort of excited and sort of nervous, but she made herself finish her meal. One, it was absolutely delicious and two, she might need the energy later if it was going to be the way he said it was.

As they walked hand in hand out the door, Zak suggested that they ride together in his car. That way she wouldn't have to worry about trying to find parking near his building. Again, what the hell....he was basically inviting her to spend the night if she wanted to. She wouldn't have a car to leave in unless he called her a cab, and that sounded like a really dickish thing to do. If she wanted to call a cab, he would definitely pay for it, but he couldn't be the one to call and basically kick her out in the middle of the night. If she wanted him to, he would bring her back here to her car.

Chapter Eleven

When they got to Zak's apartment building, they parked in the underground garage and Zak helped her out of the car. He put his hand at the small of her back and directed her toward the elevator. He swiped a card over the card reader and the elevator doors opened for them. Skye's old apartment didn't have all the fancy hi-tech security stuff this building did. Hell, they were lucky if the elevator worked. She had walked up more than her fair share of steps since moving in there. Oh well, her new place was just one floor up and David would be right there most of the time if she needed help. When the elevator opened, there was a small hallway with only two doors on it, one to the left and one to the right. Zak headed for the one on the left. He swiped his card again and the lock disengaged. He held the door open and guided her in with his hand still at the small of her back. He reached for the switch and turned on a few lights. Not a lot of lights, it wasn't really bright, it was dim, but adequate to see your way around. It was pretty typical of a guy's apartment: big screen TV, black leather couches and chairs. A mini bar in one corner. An iPod dock with some pretty good sized speakers. Basic male bachelor pad.

Zak asked Skye if she wanted anything to drink.

"Just water, please," she requested. The last thing she wanted was to get overly tipsy from alcohol. She wanted to be out of her head for a bit, but Zak's way sounded so much better than getting drunk.

Zak filled a glass with ice water and then reached in the refrigerator and grabbed a slice of lemon and a slice of lime and put them on the rim of her glass before he handed it to her. His libido wanted him to take her to the bedroom and get down to business. But he didn't want to make her feel uncomfortable. He motioned for her to take a seat on the couch. He went and got himself a flavored seltzer out of the mini-fridge. No more alcohol for him tonight; he needed to be in full control of all of his faculties for the evening.

"This is a nice place," Skye said, looking around.

"Thanks. It's got four bedrooms which is probably more space than I need, but I have one room as a study and one has a treadmill and weights in it. So I have a guest room and my room." He thought about maybe taking her into the guest room; that would feel less intimate than being in his room. He could easily move his kit down the hall a few feet. But something inside him told him that there was no reason he couldn't have her in his bedroom. He had never actually slept with a woman before—oh, he had napped a bit after some great sex, but never actually spent the night. He would probably be able to get to sleep if she was still in there. Maybe. Hopefully. If not he could always get up and read, or catch up on some work or something. There were always ways to pass time.

Zak sat beside Skye on the couch and they talked a little more about the apartment and the view. His apartment overlooked the river. It was kind of obvious that they were both a little nervous. Well, Zak wasn't nervous; at least that was what he kept telling himself. He was just trying to put her at ease. She had drunk most of her water and was kind of just rolling the glass around in her hands, so Zak took the glass from her and set it on the end table.

"Don't be nervous, Skye. We go at your pace, remember," he reminded her. He took her hands in each of his and she turned to look up at him. He leaned down to give her a kiss. It started out as something that would hopefully feel kind and gentle to her, but as usual when they started kissing, it turned much more passionate very quickly. There was definitely something about this woman that got him amped up. It wasn't very long before they were trying to tear each other's clothes off again. Instead, Zak pulled away and reached under her legs with one arm and put the other around her back. He picked her up and carried her to the bedroom.

He set her on the bed and sat beside her. "Like I said earlier, I'm not a true lifestyle Dom, but in the bedroom, I do like to be in control of how things go. So if I tell you to do something like take off your shirt for example, I expect you to do that, unless you need to use your traffic light to slow things down. Understood?" Skye nodded. "That's another thing that needs to happen. I need to hear your voice. I can tell a lot by your voice. I can usually get an idea if you are nervous or aroused or a number of other things just by your voice." He corrected, "So let's try this again." He repeated his earlier statement.

This time, Skye said, "Yes, I understand."

He told her that he was pleased to hear that. "Another thing. This is your first time, so please feel free to ask questions or tell me thoughts. If you are particularly enjoying something, I want to know it. If something feels odd, but not so bad that you want me to stop or slow down, you can tell me that or ask me what I am doing. It's all about open communication when we are doing this. I also ask that if something feels like you don't like it, give it a few moments to settle in your brain. If it's overly painful or distressing, of course, say red and we'll stop immediately. But sometimes with new sensations, your brain automatically says, *That feels weird, I don't like it,* and it may actually be something you'd really enjoy if you give your brain and body time to adjust to the new sensation." She agreed and so he told her that he would like to watch her undress, not just tear her clothes off, but to go slow and tantalize him a little. Not that he needed to be tantalized; he was full-blown ready to get going on this, but it would give her a start on getting her mind in the right place. He wanted her to feel sexy and not be embarrassed to show herself to him.

Skye stood up and tried to do what he'd said he wanted. She was nervous, but she closed her eyes and tried to think of this sort of like a strip tease. She had never done one, but she had seen them in movies. She didn't put any dance moves into it or anything, she didn't really know how to do that, but she tried to undress like a stripper might.

"Very good," Zak praised her. He stood up and took off his tie. He wasn't wearing a full suit, but he had on a dress shirt and a tie. He walked around Skye, not touching her at all, but getting very close to her body. He noticed a slight shiver. She wasn't cold; that was a different kind of shiver. When he got behind her, he put his tie across her eyes and tied it in the back. It was a makeshift blindfold of sorts. He had regular blindfolds, but this just seemed like the way to go on this one. When he had it tied around her so she couldn't see, he walked around her again, and this time he did touch her. Light caresses of his thumb here, a light scrape with his fingernail there. Skye sometimes jumped at the shock of the touch when she couldn't see what was going on, but she never flinched. There was a difference between being startled and being scared. She was definitely not scared. He didn't want to do anything to scare her; startle her, yes, surprise her, yes. But not anything that should scare her. He helped her to sit back on the bed and told her to stay there while he got some things out of his closet.

Skye sat on the bed and tried to regain her composure. Zak had definitely gotten her aroused already. If his touches and caresses hadn't been enough, the tie he had put over her eyes totally smelled like him and that just added to the sensations she was feeling. She sensed Zak come back into the room more than heard him. He must have taken his shoes off; he moved almost silently across the plush carpet. When he was standing in front of her, he cupped her chin and caressed her cheek with his thumb. She took a deep breath. With her eyes completely unable to see, the sensations were definitely more intense.

"I'm going to help you reposition on the bed. Basically, I want to have you lying in the middle." He picked her up just enough to be able to pivot her body lengthwise on the bed. He told her to lay down and stretch her arms high above her head. She did as he said, and she felt a soft rope being tied around her wrists, and then he placed an end of the rope in her hands. He wrapped her fingers around it and told her, "This end will pull everything and the rope will let you free. It's a safety precaution that should always be followed in this type of play. If you panic, pull this, no matter what. I don't think it will come to that, but there have been weird accidents where the Dominant got hurt or had a heart attack or something and you can't leave a person tied up too long. So pull this if you feel like anything is wrong."

Skye knew he had tied her hands together, but what she hadn't realized was that he had also tied them to the headboard somehow. She couldn't move much at all. She had a little wiggle room in the part around her wrists, but not enough that she would be able to pull herself free. She wrapped her hand around the end of the rope that would set her free. She didn't think she would need it either, but she didn't want to be trying to find it if something went wrong.

Zak started running something all over her body. She thought it was a feather because it tickled. He ran it all over her torso at first. He ran it up and down her legs. It was almost too much when he ran it over that area that was at the top of her legs, bordering on her pussy. That area had always been a sensitive spot for her. After that, he ran something else all over her body. She wasn't sure what it was, but it was hard and rough and felt kind of scratchy, like maybe sandpaper. When he ran it over her nipples, she felt them get harder. Next, he ran something that felt like fur all over her body. It was soft and kind of silky. It was odd when he ran it over her peaked nipples, and she felt them peak even more. After he had caressed her whole body, he told her that he was going to help her roll over so that he had access to her back. He flipped her over, gently but with absolutely no problem at all. The rope had obviously been tied so that she could pivot around somehow. He ran the feather over her skin again, and she realized that the different textures were making every nerve on her skin become more aware. Every sensation was heightened.

Zak had observed every flinch, every low giggle, every deep sigh. He was memorizing her body and which areas were more sensitive. He knew her nipples would be sensitive, but it seemed like every woman he had known had other places that were also more sensitive. They could vary from stomach to upper thigh, to ass, but every woman had them somewhere.

Zak stepped away for a moment to collect the next toy from his bag. It was a fairly lightweight deerskin flogger. He began by brushing it over her skin just to keep those nerve endings on alert, then he raised it off of her and started doing a figure eight swing. It was hitting her, but not any harder than a massage would be. After he had covered her entire back with those light swings, he put one knee on the bed so that he could put his face down near hers. "Everything still okay, Skye?"

She sounded a little groggy when she answered, "Yes. It felt like an amazing massage."

Ah, that was what he was hoping for. Then he asked, "And this?" He swung the flogger harder this time so it hit with a distinctive thud. He heard the intake of her breath. It was probably a little pain, although not really much. The inhale had most likely been out of surprise rather than actual pain. Just to make sure, he placed his hand over the pink spot that he had just hit, giving it warmth. He leaned down again and asked, "Still with me?"

"Mmm-hmm" was all Skye said.

Hmm, so his girl liked a small bite of pain. Wait, she wasn't his girl, at least not like that, like in the girlfriend/boyfriend way. Maybe he had thought that because right now, at this moment, she was definitely his plaything and they were both having fun. He continued with the harder hits, alternating them so that no swing hit in the same spot as the one before it. He listened closely for any words to come out of her mouth. Mostly, she just looked like she was drifting off to sleep, although he knew that wasn't where she was drifting. He decided to try an even harder hit on each of her butt cheeks. He heard the sharp intake of breath again, but she immediately went right back to her drifting, not saying anything.

He told her he was going to roll her back over again. Whether that registered in her brain he wasn't sure, but she didn't protest when he rolled her back to her original position. He tied her feet to the bedposts at the foot of his bed. He could tell that she was getting very wet from all of his attention. He began with the flogger on her front, but he kept the hits on the softer side on her upper body and went a little harder on her legs. She was beginning to squirm, at least as much as she could when tied the way he had her.

He was curious what she would do if he gave a small swat to her pussy area. She just rose up after the hit, almost like she was following it to try to feel it again. He tried another swat, slightly harder than the last. Again, she seemed to be arching to try to get more. So he placed one final hit right on the spot where her clit was peeking out and she let out a scream. At first he thought it was pain, but then he looked at her and realized she had just had a massive orgasm. Zak had never known a woman who could orgasm just from moderate pain stimulation.

Zak realized that Skye was saying something so quietly that it was barely audible. He leaned closer to her mouth to try to make it out. She was just repeating the word 'please' over and over. He had to be certain of what she was asking for. "Please what, Skye? Please stop? Please what, sweetheart?"

He still wasn't getting an answer; she was really flying in subspace. He asked her, "Do you need yellow or red? Skye, you have to try to tell me what you want me to do. Please what, Skye?"

Skye heard what he was saying, and she was pretty sure she had answered him, but he kept asking, so maybe she hadn't actually said anything. She was definitely feeling floaty, kind of like that one time she had been in a car with a few people that were smoking pot. She felt a little high. When she heard Zak trying again to get her to tell him what she was saying please about, she mustered up enough clarity to ask. "Please, fuck me."

It wasn't said with much real clarity, but the words were understandable at least. They kind of ran together into something that was more like *plsfkme*. But she had done her best to speak with some amount of clarity even though her brain was mush.

Zak had never heard better words. He grabbed a condom and got it on as quickly as he could. He untied her feet but left her hands tied and the blindfold on. He crawled between her legs and started to enter her. She was soaking wet, so she had obviously enjoyed his attention. He had never met a woman like this. If he were in the market for a long-term relationship, this woman would be it. Well, if she didn't have a kid she would be perfect—if he was looking, but he wasn't, so it wasn't worth thinking about. He plunged into her and began thrusting hard, and again, she met him thrust for thrust. Her pussy felt so good and tight, it almost felt like it was trying to suck him back in when he pulled out. It didn't take long until both of them were screaming out with their orgasm.

Zak reached up and pulled the piece of rope that would loosen Skye's arms, and then pulled the rope off of her before he got up and went to dispose of the condom in the bathroom. When he got back to the bed, Skye was lying there with a very contented look on her sleeping face. This would be the time when he should do something, like go and brush up on some legal procedure or go watch a movie. Anything but crawl into bed with Skye. He didn't cuddle. Sex was a separate thing. He had great sex, but when the sex was over, it was time to part ways. Actually, what he should probably do was wake Skye up and give her a ride back to her car. That would be the best way to keep this where he wanted it. Sex, but no romance, no cuddling, no commitment. But, to be honest, the sex had been pretty exhausting for him too. Did he really want to have to get dressed just to drive her back to the brewery? It wouldn't be a big deal just to sleep beside her. When they woke up, he could run her to her car and then get back to his regular routine. Although tomorrow was Sunday, so it would be another day that Zak would have most likely called Skye to see if she wanted to do something. Last Sunday they had been on his boat and that had been a fun day. Maybe they could do something fun tomorrow too. He wouldn't worry about it now. He would get a little sleep and see how things felt in the morning.

Chapter Twelve

Zak woke up and realized the sun was coming up and he had a very warm body draped across his. Skye had her head on his chest and his arm was cuddling her tight. She also had one leg hooked over his, with a knee very close to a part of him that was starting to get aroused by the fact that he had a beautiful naked woman draped over him. He tried to move her over a bit without waking her, but he wasn't successful. She began to stir.

Skye woke up to feeling someone move in the bed next to her, actually more like under her. She was obviously lying on someone else. As the fog of sleep cleared a little more, it registered. She had fallen asleep after Zak had given her the best sexual experience of her life. He had also made her get out of her own head for a while, and for that she was extremely grateful. She had fallen so dead asleep that she either hadn't dreamed at all, or she was so wiped out that she didn't remember them. Either way, another night with no nightmares was a plus in her book. She probably shouldn't have spent the night. How would she have explained waking up in a cold sweat screaming her sister's name? She realized he was trying to move her off of him or get out from under her somehow. She pulled herself away and apologized for having fallen so deeply asleep. She began to get up and said, "I'll get dressed and get out of your way."

Zak grabbed her arm to halt her progress. "Skye, you don't need to apologize. I fell asleep too. It's not a big deal," he assured her. When she sat up, the sheet had dropped to her waist and Zak couldn't help but notice her breasts. She really did have great breasts. His cock was definitely noticing her great breasts. He was starting to get even more aroused than he had been when he had woken up with a naked woman lying against his chest. No one had ever accused him of not being fast on his feet. He took her hand and said, "I have a great idea. Why don't we take a shower? We both need one, right? Let's conserve water and shower together." He tugged on her hand as he started to get up off the bed.

Skye agreed with him that it did make more sense to conserve water. "Can I use the restroom first?" she asked.

"Oh yeah, sure, of course." Zak stepped aside and allowed her to pass him and go in the bathroom. He grabbed out some clean clothes to put on after the shower, but he realized that her clothes were still lying in a pile on the floor where she had stripped for him the night before. If they did decide to go anywhere, he might have to run by her place to let her get clean clothes. Skye opened the bathroom door to let him enter. He turned on the shower and checked for water temperature.

"I think your shower is bigger than my entire bathroom in my old apartment," Skye commented.

"Yeah, I've thought about the fact that I could practically host a party in here," Zak joked. He let her step in before him and then he joined her. He adjusted the spray so that it wasn't hitting her in the face. He was several inches taller than her, so what hit his chest was going right for her face. He reached for his washcloth and his body wash. It was a little masculine smelling, because there was never a reason to have anything feminine in his bathroom. He asked her if she was okay with that body wash. If she wasn't, he probably had a bar of soap from a hotel or something lying around somewhere. She said it was fine, but she took it from him and asked if she could wash him. He had absolutely no objection to that.

As Skye washed Zak's body, she got more and more aroused, but then again, so did he. She got her hands very soapy and started to rub lather all around his dick and balls. He was getting harder by the minute. She stroked him with her soapy hands, and he leaned back against the shower wall to give her full access. Just because he was the more dominant one, it didn't mean that she couldn't pleasure him a little in the shower. If he told her to stop, she would, but if he didn't, she was going full speed ahead. After she had him very aroused, she stepped back so that the spray from the shower head would help her rinse the soap off of his body. He started to try to take the soap and washcloth from her, but she held it back. She then sank to her knees and guided him into her mouth. She had wanted to taste him since she had first seen him naked. Actually, probably more like since she had seen him in her yoga class. There were definitely some positions that gave her a great view of his body even though it had been fully clothed.

Zak let her explore on her own for a while, but it was getting too intense, so he placed a hand on either side of her head and guided her motions. She was really good at this and if he didn't control the rhythm he was going to go off in her mouth and that was not where he wanted to come. When he couldn't take it anymore, he gently pulled her head away. He saw the objection in her eyes, but he silenced it by saying it was his turn to have fun. He helped her stand up and he took the washcloth and the body wash and began washing her body. He wanted to be sure that he touched every inch of her. He had hoped that getting her mouth off of him would help slow his libido down a little bit, but it didn't help as much as he had hoped. He gave her an orgasm with his hand and then he lifted her so her face was even with his and gave her a deep lingering kiss. She started to wrap her legs around him, but he pulled his head away to stop her. "I need to go grab a condom," he stated.

"I'm on birth control, and I'm clean, but if you still want a condom, I totally understand," Skye said. "I know neither of us is looking for a commitment, but all I ask for is monogamy or we go back to using condoms."

Hell, he had never had sex without a condom, so he knew he was clean. Besides, he had just had his yearly physical last month and everything was good. He looked into her eyes to be sure he saw honesty there, and he did, so he lifted her up and grabbed on to her ass when she put her legs around him. He had his hands full of her ass, so she reached between them to position his cock at the entrance to her pussy. When he was fully inside her, he paused for a moment while two thoughts ran through his head. First was, *What the hell are you thinking? You don't know for sure she is on birth control, just because she claimed she was. Look what happened to Jason. That could happen to you too.* The other thought, though, was the one that was louder in his head. And that was that he had never felt anything so amazing in his life. It was like his dick was wrapped in warm soft satin. He was not going to last long with how good this felt. He turned so that her back was against the shower wall, she was between his body and the wall, so it was easier to only hold her with one arm. He needed to use the other to make sure that she went over that edge with him. He adjusted their positions so that he could play with her clit while he rocked in and out.

Skye was absolutely losing her mind with this man. She had never been okay having sex without a condom, even though she was on birth control. You never knew what you could possibly end up with if you had unprotected sex. The only way she could explain it was that he had her under some sort of spell, Not that she actually believed he had hypnotized her or anything like that, but there was definitely something about him that made her lose all her good sense. She felt the orgasm coming hard and fast after he started playing with her while thrusting hard. What she didn't expect was that when he came, feeling his hot semen rush into her would make her orgasm all over again.

Chapter Thirteen

When they were done with actually getting cleaned up in the shower, Zak broached the topic of what to do today and if she wanted to go to her apartment to get other clothes.

Skye thought about that for a few minutes, not really sure she wanted him to take her to her new apartment. It wasn't that she didn't trust him as much as she didn't want her two worlds to collide in a bad way. Zak was her 'have fun on the weekend fling' while David and Cassie were her real everyday life. She made up the excuse of having everything at her apartment still in boxes so it would take her a while to find the right box and go through it. She asked him if he could take her to the gym instead. She always kept an outfit or two there in case she decided to go somewhere after work. Although for the last few weeks, the only place she went was to take Cassie home.

Zak parked in front of the gym and Skye ran in to change clothes. He had told her that whatever she wore was fine; he had on jeans and a polo shirt. He figured she would probably dress similarly. Just after Skye walked through the doors to the gym, his phone rang. It was Walt. He picked it up and said, "Hey, Walt, what's up?"

"What's up is that everyone else is here for brunch and you aren't. You didn't forget that Rayne wanted all the groomsmen to come to brunch today to have input on what the guys are wearing, did you?" Walt explained.

Well, shit! He had totally forgotten. He was in a predicament. He didn't want to leave Walt hanging, but he had asked Skye to spend some time with him today and he didn't want to be the jerk who canceled before they got started. "Shit, Walt, yeah, I forgot that was today," he said sheepishly.

"Well then get your ass over here. We're waiting for you, man," Walt said.

"The thing is, I promised a friend that I would hang out with them today, and I don't want to be a jerk and back out at this point."

"Bring your friend along. If you see the amount of food Mrs. Steele prepared, and then what Rayne added to it, we can feed an army platoon," Walt insisted.

"Okay, I'll try," Zak conceded.

"No! Try not! Do or do not, there is no try," Walt joked in his best Yoda voice, which by the way was pretty crappy.

Zak just laughed and said goodbye. What was Skye going to think? Would she even want to go? She might just want him to take her back to her car and call it a day. He hoped she didn't because this brunch thing wouldn't last all day. They could still spend the afternoon and evening doing something fun together. But it would be a bunch of people that she didn't know. She might not want to be subjected to that.

When Skye got back in the car, Zak seemed a little weird. She wasn't sure why until he broke the silence.

"So here's the thing. I really want to spend time with you doing something fun. But I totally forgot that my friend Walt, one of the other owners, is having a brunch today for all of his friends to get together and get some of their wedding plans figured out." He was rambling, he knew he was. But he wanted to get it out there.

"Oh, sure, no problem," Skye said, trying really hard not to sound bummed. "You can just drop me off at my car if you have time. If you don't, I can take a cab or the bus."

"Well, actually," Zak said with a little wince, "I was hoping maybe you would want to go with me to brunch. Walt said there's enough food to feed an army platoon and that you would be welcome to come. But if it's weird for you or if you're going to be uncomfortable, I totally understand if you don't want to go."

"Oh." Skye thought about that for a minute. Was he asking because he actually wanted her to go, or was he just trying to not let her down? It might be kind of fun to meet the other Five Sloths guys, and Zak had told her that one of them was engaged and one was dating someone, so it might give her a chance to make a few friends from Zak's circle. Not that they would be together long term, but since Savannah's death, Skye really hadn't had any friends to talk to. It might be fun to spend a day with people that she didn't have to explain anything to, or try to seem okay when they offered her their condolences.

Zak interrupted her thoughts. "Look, I was really hoping to do something fun with you and I am sure we still can. This brunch thing shouldn't take too long and we can be on our way. I'll tell you what. If you go, you get to pick what we do for the rest of the day. Anywhere you want to eat dinner, or anything else that sounds fun to you, it's your pick." Why the hell was he trying so hard to convince her to go? He didn't even know this guy that was practically begging a woman to go to a brunch with him. It was like some lovesick schoolboy had taken over his mind.

"Well, if you really want me to, then yes, I'll go," Skye agreed.

"Great, let's get going then." That was all he could say. He was still baffled over his actions, but it wasn't like he could backpedal now and say, *Oh on second thought, maybe you shouldn't come with me.* All he could do was hope that everyone was on their best behavior and no one got too much into Skye's business. Maybe he could give them a heads-up somehow.

Skye wasn't really surprised when they pulled up in front of a rather large home in East Grand Rapids. Once they hit the general neighborhood, she knew it would be a nice house. It seemed like Zak was rather wealthy and so was his friend. Zak got out of the car and came around to help her out. "This is a beautiful home," she commented.

"Yeah, most of us guys wanted something with less maintenance and in the city, but Walt always wanted a house. He figured he could keep it until he had a family, or he could sell it when the markets were up and make a nice profit," Zak said. He crooked his arm so she could take it. "Ready?"

"As I'll ever be," Skye said.

Zak thought about just turning around and taking Skye somewhere else. She didn't seem to be too sure about being here. But before he could make that move, Rayne opened the front door and motioned them to come inside. Zak put his other hand on Skye's hand that was resting at his elbow. He hoped she wasn't going to hate this too much. They would go inside, have a couple of mimosas, he would give his input on the tuxedos, and they could be on their way.

When they got to the porch, he made the introductions with Skye, Walt and Rayne. The rest were waiting patiently inside. Zak asked if he could speak to Rayne for a moment, so Walt offered to take Skye in and introduce her to the rest of their friends. In a quiet voice, he explained to Rayne that he didn't know exactly why, but Skye did not like to talk about her personal life much. He knew that there had to have been a tragedy, or something that had gone south for her, but he didn't know what it was. He asked Rayne to try to help him steer people away from asking her too many questions.

"No problem," Rayne agreed. "We'll make her feel welcome without feeling interrogated."

When they stepped into the house, Walt was still making the introductions. Sunni was there along with all the guys. Today would be Jeremy's day to manage at the brewery, but that didn't open for a few hours yet, so he was here to give his input. And of course to eat food. That man could outeat pretty much anyone Zak knew.

When they got to the table, he pulled out Skye's chair then took the one right next to hers. It appeared that in the time it had taken them to drive over, Walt and Rayne had set another place at the table just like Skye had been planned on all along. Rayne sat next to Skye and Sunni across the table. The women began small talk with Skye to help her feel comfortable. They didn't ask questions that were very probing; they kept it light. Mostly things like did she like this food or that food as things were passed around. And of course, Rayne could talk all day about her wedding coming up, so she also engaged Skye in questions about what she thought about this color combination or what she thought about the cake flavor choices. Mundane things that let Skye feel welcome but didn't cause her to be uncomfortable.

When brunch was over and everyone had their fill of the food, Walt's housekeeper came to clear the table. Before she had a chance to do much clearing, Rayne grabbed the pitcher of mimosas and motioned for Sunni and Skye to grab their glasses and follow her out onto the back deck. Zak headed into the other room with Walt, but before he got completely out of sight, he turned and looked at Skye. He tried to do his best *Are you okay with this?* look. Skye smiled and gave him a little nod. Apparently, she liked Rayne and Sunni and felt comfortable enough with them to at least stay for a little while. Zak would check on her often to make sure things were still okay. He might not be looking for anything serious with her, but he would never treat any woman poorly. His friends would understand if he needed to get Skye home.

Zak took a lot of ribbing from his buddies about bringing a girlfriend to the brunch. He tried to explain that she wasn't really a girlfriend, but she had spent the night and he had promised her a fun outing today, because he had forgotten about the brunch. He didn't want to be rude and back out on the promise, so he brought her here for brunch so they could continue their plans after.

"That's your story, you stick to it, man," Walt said.

"No, really, we have both agreed to a friends with benefits sort of thing," Zak assured him. "She has some stuff going on in her life right now. I don't know exactly what it is, but she just wants to get away from real life once in a while and I am happy to oblige her in that capacity. Besides, she has a kid and you guys all know that I am not ready to settle down like that."

"Don't knock it till you try it," Jason chimed in.

Zak knew that Jason was perfectly happy with having his son, but, on the other hand, he wasn't willing to open up to Sunni, so they really were kind of in a similar situation.

"Okay, okay, we'll let you off the hook for now," Walt said. "We have a few decisions to make before Jeremy has to leave. So let's get down to business." He brought out some big notebook that had a label that said 'My Wedding Planner' on it. They started through the process of looking at tuxes and shirt colors and all the other fun stuff that must go into planning a wedding. Zak was totally overwhelmed; he had no clue what colors looked good with what. Or which style of tux he liked best. His input was, "Whatever Rayne and the other guys like is fine with me."

****

Skye was a little nervous about going out on the back deck with the two other women—not because they hadn't seemed nice; they really had made her feel welcome in a room full of strangers. But she was afraid they were going to ask her questions she wasn't prepared to answer. The backyard was beautiful though. She commented on how pretty it was out there.

"Well, the pool and hot tub have been here for a long time. But when I moved in a few months ago, I started slowly adding flowers and the decorations," Rayne said.

"It's lovely," Skye said.

"So first of all, if we get too nosy, just tell us. We are fine with you not answering," Rayne assured her, and Sunni nodded in agreement. *Oh, here goes*, Skye thought. "How long have you known Zak?" Rayne asked.

That one was simple enough. "A couple of weeks, I guess," Skye answered.

"Cool. I don't know any of Jason's friends super well, but Zak has always seemed like a nice guy," Sunni commented.

"He is," Skye agreed.

"How about this? I don't want to get all up in your business," Rayne said. "So why don't you give us the condensed Wiki on Skye? Only what you want to share."

"Oh, well, I'm a yoga instructor and I teach a few water aerobics classes at a gym downtown. I'm from a small town in Indiana but moved up here to be closer to family," Skye stated.

"Oh, I would love to try some water aerobics classes," Rayne replied. "See, I used to be a dancer…"

"You still are a dancer," Sunni interrupted.

"Okay, yes, I still dance. I was a professional dancer but had a bad accident and was in rehab for a long time. I think water aerobics would be a great way to stay limber and tone up."

"I'm sorry to hear about your accident," Skye consoled her.

"It's okay. Walt and Sunni really helped me get past it. I was pretty depressed for a while, but when an awesome man like Walt comes along and pushes you to get better, you try," Rayne said.

Skye figured that the best way to not have them ask her questions she didn't want to answer was to try to get them to talk about themselves, so she started asking leading questions about Rayne's wedding, and with that Rayne was off, talking about colors and dresses and caterers and everything wedding. Skye was pretty sure she wouldn't be asked anything for a while. If you want a distraction, ask a future bride about her wedding plans!

One of the things that became clear to Skye was that she and Rayne had the loss of parents in common. Rayne had said that her parents weren't here to be able to give her away or go to her wedding, but she was going to do her best to make it a special day that they would have been proud to have been at. Skye told her that she had lost her parents too. She didn't go into a lot of detail; just that they had been older when they had her and they had both not been in good health in their last few years of life. She was glad that they had died reasonably close to each other because she never could have imagined either of them being happy for long without the other. They had married young but put off having kids until they were more settled in life. Sunni said that her parents were still living, although they were what most people called snowbirds. Really, they were more like wanderers. They didn't have a specific home; they had a large RV and they traveled a lot. Most of the year they stayed in warmer climates, but in the summer they did come to Michigan to spend time with her.

About an hour later, Jeremy came out to thank Rayne for inviting him and apologized for having to leave, but it was his day to manage the bar. Rayne thanked him for coming, and Sunni asked him if he knew whether or not Jason planned to head over to the brewery too. He said that Jason had offered, but he told him it was no rush. Sunday nights weren't usually too busy, and the crowd tended to leave earlier because most had to get up and go to work the next day.

Chapter Fourteen

Zak always enjoyed hanging out with the guys, but he was a little worried that Skye might not be enjoying herself. So he left the guys to go check on her. He found her out on the back deck sipping mimosas with Rayne and Sunni. She was talking and laughing as he walked up. It looked like she wasn't totally bored with being here. As he walked up, all three women glanced up at him.

"Don't tell me you've come to take Skye away," Rayne protested. "We are having fun out here."

Zak glanced at Skye and said, "Well, I promised the lady that if she would accompany me to brunch, she got to decide what we do for the rest of the day. So that decision is up to her."

"Oh, please stay," Rayne pleaded. "We rarely get a chance to have girl talk around all these testosterone-filled men. It's nice to have someone new to talk to."

Skye thought about that for a minute. She really did feel comfortable here. They hadn't asked her a ton of questions that would have been painful to answer. Mostly they had talked about Rayne's upcoming wedding. And they had giggled over Rayne's stories of how totally Walt glazed over when she tried to talk about some of the wedding details. Apparently, he didn't care what flavor of cake they had or if they had a buffet or a seated dinner. He just wanted to be married by the end of that day. The rest was up to Rayne. Skye didn't really have many girlfriends. Her sister had been her best friend and she had a friend named Autumn that she had known since high school. She had co-workers from the fitness center that she went out to lunch with sometimes and they had gone to see a few movies, but she could really use more women in her life. She looked at Zak and said, "I'm fine staying here for a while longer if you want to hang out with your friends."

"If you're really sure," Zak asked. "But we are definitely going to head out in time to get dinner, any place you want to go." Zak gave her a wink and headed back to the study.

"Zak seems really into you," Rayne said.

"I don't know. We both have things going on right now, so we agreed to something light and easy. I'm not really ready for a steady relationship. It's nice to have someone that likes to have fun but isn't looking for anything too deep," Skye said.

"Okay, he just seems like he really wants to make you happy, or at least comfortable," Sunni remarked. Skye did have to admit that even though they weren't boyfriend and girlfriend or in some huge relationship that you had to put a label on, Zak was a gentleman and was always concerned with her being okay with whatever went on with them.

She found out that Rayne had taken some of the money from her settlement in her accident case to open a dance school. Because she had the money, she made classes available to anyone regardless of ability to pay. Sunni was a massage therapist, so her schedule was somewhat flexible.

About an hour later, Zak came outside again and asked Skye if she was ready to go. She got up to leave and Rayne and Sunni both told her they hoped they would see her again sometime and that it had been nice meeting her. Rayne also made a point of reminding her that she was invited to their wedding. Sky wasn't sure if she would be going to it or not; she had no way of knowing if she and Zak would still be seeing each other then. And, if they weren't, she definitely didn't want to go to one of his best friends' wedding.

When they got into Zak's car, he asked her if she had a place she would like to go for dinner. She said that she had always wanted to go to the Melting Pot, but it had never worked out for her to get there.

"The Melting Pot it is then," Zak said, starting up the car. "I hope Rayne and Sunni were okay. I mean they didn't talk your arm off, or make you feel left out. "

"No, they were both really nice," she assured him. "It's always nice to meet new friends."

Zak refused to let his mind go down the path of trying to figure out why he had been okay with letting his latest fling meet all his closest friends. He still knew very little about her. But then again, he hadn't been exactly forthcoming on the details of his life either. Hell, they didn't even know each other's last names. And that was the way he liked these types of things. The only really personal thing he knew about her was that she had a kid and that wasn't because she had told him; that was because he had seen it. Speaking of the kid, he wondered how it worked out that she could spend the whole weekend with him and not have to check in with a babysitter or whatever. He was pretty sure that the 'baby daddy' must get the kid on weekends, who knew? It wasn't his problem and he kind of liked her not having to leave to get home to the kid. This way, they could have fun on the weekends and life went back to normal during the week. Although this would be a new normal. His friends wouldn't let this go, he knew that. He had never brought a date to a 'family get-together.' He had taken women to large company parties with the firm, but never to an event that was more like getting together with family than actually getting together with his family. The guys had become closer to him over the years than any real relatives. Well, as they say, you made your bed, now go lie in it. He had made the decision to take her and he would have to live with all the ribbing he would be taking for it. He had no doubt in his mind that when he got his fill of Skye, like he did with all of his hookups, they would lay off of him again. They were just having fun with it now because he had never been one to do much more than a few casual dates with any woman, and he had definitely had his share of one-night stands. Skye was just so in tune with what he liked in bed that it might take him a little longer to get her out of his system.

When they got to the Melting Pot, Skye enjoyed her meal more than she ever had any meal in her life. The place made several different kinds of fondue and you could pick fruits or meats to dip in them. Zak often flirted with her and fed her a bite of this or that. When a drip of cheese had fallen on her chin, he leaned over and licked it off. He never did anything inappropriate for being in public, but he definitely made Skye very aroused by the way he was flirting. She almost wished that they could go back to his place, but she knew that wasn't wise because she had to be up to take care of Cassie first thing in the morning so David could get to work.

After a wonderful dinner, and even more wonderful flirting, Zak drove Skye back to the brewery to drop her off at her car. He thought about asking her into the brewery. He was sure they could find someplace to finish out the evening right. He could tell the guys he needed the office for a bit and lock them out. Then he could bury himself in Skye for a while. But that wasn't so appealing, because for one it would just give the guys more ammunition to harass him with, and two, he didn't think that was the way he wanted to treat Skye.

Fortunately, she had parked in the far corner of the parking lot so she didn't take the good spaces that patrons would be using. It was dark enough that they had an epic make-out session before they said goodnight. It left both of them wanting more.

On his drive back to his apartment, Zak was wondering if there was any way he could convince Skye to see him during the week. He didn't want to have to wait until next weekend to have more of her. That would probably depend on whether or not she had a babysitter. He wouldn't expect her to spend the night or anything. When he parked his car, he pulled out his phone and texted her.

I had a great time this weekend. I'd love to see you again soon. Let me know when you are available.

He didn't get a response right away; most likely she was still driving. He went up to his apartment and decided on a glass of scotch to help him unwind for the night. He had just sat down with his scotch when an incoming text from Skye hit his phone.

I work during the day, but I could probably get away for a few hours in the evening.

Great. Can you see if you can work something out for tomorrow night? After our goodnight kiss, I'm hoping to see you sooner rather than later.

I'll let you know tomorrow. Thanks for a great weekend.

It was my pleasure. Good night and sweet dreams.

She had said a few hours. So obviously during the week, she had more constraints with babysitters and such. He started to think about the best way to utilize a few hours with her. If they went out to dinner, that could take up the whole evening and he wouldn't get any alone time with her. If they just got right to the sex, it might seem like he didn't care if she had eaten; his libido was more important. Again, not something he had ever worried about with any other woman. He had to admit to himself that Skye wasn't like any other woman he had dated. He had different feelings about her. Not feelings like falling in love or anything close to that, but he did feel differently about her. Maybe it was because she had a kid. He wasn't interested in being around the kid or of having kids, but she was a mother; maybe that made him more respectful of her. He wasn't sure why he was feeling this way, or really what he was feeling. He couldn't define it or explain it. It just felt different. He realized it wasn't something he would be able to figure out easily and there was a part of him that wasn't sure he really wanted that answer. He finished his scotch and went to shower and get ready for bed.

Chapter Fifteen

Zak was trying to trudge through another Monday at work. The life of an attorney wasn't what they made it look like on TV. They always showed the glamorous parts, like court proceedings and such. What no one ever saw was the hours of research, depositions, and filing court documents that were the bulk of the job.

When his phone vibrated with a text around 12:30, his day began to look up. Skye said she would be available at 6:30 this evening, but she also reminded him she needed to be home at a decent hour because she had to work the next day. He could live with that.

Now, what to plan to make the most of their time together. He decided to call one of his favorite restaurants and get a to-go order that he could pick up on his way home. He texted her back with his address and told her to text him when she was pulling into the parking garage. He had shown her the guest parking area when he had taken her there on Saturday night.

Skye was excited but also nervous about going to Zak's apartment again. With this being a weeknight, she definitely needed to leave at a reasonable hour so that she could get home to sleep. She would have to be able to take over for David at 7:00 a.m. so he could get ready for work. She would just have to be very careful not to fall asleep at Zak's house. Although, after the great sex they always had, it was so easy to want to doze off.

When she got to Zak's apartment building, she parked, then texted him. A minute later, he was walking out of the elevator to come greet her. He took her upstairs and showed her to the kitchen. He told her he had ordered from one of his favorite restaurants, but he wasn't sure what she liked, so he had ordered several things. He offered her five choices that all sounded delicious, and she picked the Icelandic lobster. He picked a steak for himself. He said the other three would be great for him to warm up for the rest of the nights this week. He took the two meals out of the warming oven and took them out of their tin foil containers and put them onto plates. Skye offered to help, but he told her he already had everything set. They walked into his dining room, and he did indeed have everything set. There was silverware and cloth napkins, even a couple of bottles of wine, one red and one white. He asked her which she wanted, and she said white. He helped her into her chair and then he poured the wine and sat down himself.

The food was absolutely amazing, and they made pleasant small talk while they ate. Simple things like *How was your day* and they talked a little about how much Skye had enjoyed her time with Rayne and Sunni. She teased him a little about having met all of the sloths now. He chuckled at that. But again that flash went through his brain about what had made him invite her in the first place. He was just going to enjoy her company while this lasted. He knew from his track record that eventually he would get to where he didn't have this same drive to be with her. Once the sex cooled down a bit, he had no doubt that he would walk away as he always had before.

When they were done with the food, they worked together to clear the table and then took their wine into the living room. They sat on the couch and began with a few touches, which turned into a few kisses, which turned into something way hotter. He took her wine glass and set it on the table, then stood up and reached down to carry her to the bedroom. He knew that they wouldn't have time for all of the things that he wanted to do with her, so he had to start with what he wanted most. He had never had her ride him and the idea of seeing her breasts bounce as she did sounded like a really great idea to him. She must have been as anxious as he was to get the night going, because she was already undressing. When they were both naked, he took her hand and led her to the bed. He lay down and pulled her toward him. They kissed and caressed for a while before he started sucking on her nipples and giving them gentle bites. When she started to try to pull him onto her, he reversed her motions and rolled to his back, pulling her on top of him. "I want you to ride me, Skye. I want to see your body as you take pleasure from mine. Whatever pace or angle you need. You take your pleasure from my body tonight. Do you want me to put on a condom?" he asked. "I have them in my dresser."

Skye thought about that for all of two seconds. She thought it was odd that he didn't keep them in the nightstand; that would be much more convenient for anything happening on the bed. They had already done this once with no condom, and she was on birth control. She wanted to be on him too badly to take that extra time. She just shook her head and began to straddle him. She used her hand to line his cock up and then slowly sank down on it. That first feeling was unreal, and she paused for a moment before she began to move.

"Oh, hell, yes," Zak said. "That feels amazing." At first he closed his eyes, just to feel her warmth and wetness all around him. But he opened his eyes when she started to move. He wanted to see her face and her body as she moved above him.

She started out somewhat slowly. He wanted to encourage her to move faster, but he had told her to take her pleasure from him. So he remained quiet. She began moving faster and when Zak saw her breasts bouncing up and down, he couldn't help himself; he reached up with both hands and began pinching and pulling on her nipples. That made her move all the more. It was kind of like an 'up, down, pivot her hips' kind of thing and she was practically grinding on him on the downstrokes. He had to admit it was amazing. It was like she had a natural rhythm for riding a man. She didn't seem to be thinking about it or trying to figure it out; she just moved like it was a dance she was very used to doing. Zak didn't think she had been with a lot of men before, though. Other than the fact that she was absolutely amazing in bed, she didn't come across as a strong, confident woman to him. He was sure she had dated, but he didn't think she had a bunch of sex in her past either.

Skye realized that if she angled just right, her clit could touch his lower abdomen on the down strokes. So she pivoted when she was down so that she was about ready to go off in no time at all. Zak's attention to her nipples was definitely making this ramp up really fast. She stopped on the downward movement and just rotated her hips because she was about ready to come, and the feeling of her clit rubbing on his muscular abdomen was too good to stop. She came, moaning out his name, and a few seconds later, he held her hips and made a couple of deep thrusts and followed her over that ledge. Skye collapsed onto his chest, too out of breath to do anything else for a bit. He wrapped his arms around her and held her while they both tried to catch their breath. It felt really good to be in his arms. The real world couldn't intrude when they were like this. Skye realized that she was starting to like being with him way more than she should. It wasn't just the sex, although that was amazing. But she liked to sit with him and share a meal, and flirt across the table. She liked just being held by him. She knew that he wasn't looking for anything that came close to romantic entanglements. So she kept those thoughts quiet, but they were there all the same.

Zak was really starting to love this feeling. He loved just holding her, listening to her breathe, feeling her soft skin up against his. He realized that he could really get used to just being able to roll over and fall asleep with her beside him. But he knew that could not happen. She needed to get home because she had a kid at home and thinking about that was like throwing a wet blanket on the whole idea of having her be more than just a great sex partner.

Skye was still trying to catch her breath. That had been some amazing sex. She wished that real life didn't have to intrude on her time with Zak, but it always does. When she was able to breathe again, she asked him if he minded if she took a shower. She asked him if he wanted to join her and so he did. They had what most would call a 'quickie,' but it was still some of the best sex Skye had ever had. Zak walked her down to her car and kissed her good-bye.

Skye looked at the clock on the dashboard. It wasn't super late, so she decided to call Autumn.

"Hey girl, what's up? Still seeing Mr. Hot Mystery Man?" Autumn asked.

"I just left there," Skye said.

"Why does it not sound like you are happy about that?" Autumn asked. "Are you not happy about having been there, or are you not happy because you had to leave?"

"Just not happy because life sucks sometimes, I guess," Skye answered. "He is such a great guy, and I love spending time with him. And I feel like maybe there could be something there, but I'm afraid to open up to him. He has always said that he isn't looking for anything more than fun, and I agreed to that, but sometimes I feel like I wish there could be more." Skye paused for a moment before continuing, "And I know that right now, I can't really commit to anything anyway because Cassie has to be my main focus."

"I am sorry, I am going to preface this statement with that apology right up front. But this has to be said," Autumn stated. "I get that you lost your sister, and that was a terrible tragedy. I get that you want to try to make Cassie's life as normal as humanly possible right now. But I can guarantee you that Savannah would not want you to keep your entire life on hold. If something can grow between you and this guy, go for it. There are two points to be made here. First off, I know David would understand if you wanted a little less time taking care of Cassie. Single parents work it out all the time. If that means that Cassie has to go to daycare or have another babysitter besides you once in a while for you to be free to work on your own life, then so be it. And, two, if this guy is worth having around long term, he would understand you needing to help with Cassie sometimes. If he can't handle that, then he isn't the guy for you. Simple as."

"I know, I do, I know, but I just don't want to be another person that Cassie loses because I went all into a guy who turns out to not be worth it," Skye admitted.

"I hear you. But you have to have your life. Stick with the status quo for now and see if you think this guy might be the real thing. If he is, then David will understand you backing off a little to work on your relationship. If it ends, or he never wants to get serious, then you aren't out anything if you just let yourself go with the flow. It's not like David would keep you out of going back to spending more time with Cassie if things don't work out with this guy."

"You're right. I know you are," Skye agreed. "And it is true that I have no idea where Zak stands on the whole idea. I may be the only one that wants to try for more. Neither of us has been overly forthcoming with personal information. I don't even know his last name or what he does for a living. And really all he knows about me is that I teach classes at the fitness center and that's only because he saw me there. Maybe I am better off just keeping things as is for now. I'll see if he seems to open up more."

"You do what feels right for you. All I'm saying is that I know that David and Savannah wouldn't want you backing out of something that might end up good for you," Autumn assured her.

"I'm pulling into my driveway now, so I will let you go. Thanks for always being a sounding board for all of my issues."

"Anytime. That's what besties do," Autumn said. "You take care of you, boo."

"Thanks, we really need to find a time to do a girls' night or something. I miss seeing you," Skye lamented. "Talk to you soon. Good night."

When she got inside, Skye wanted nothing more than to have a glass of wine and go soak in the bathtub. But first, she needed to text Zak and let him know that she had made it home safely. He had asked her to do so when he kissed her goodnight.

I made it home safely. I hope you have a goodnight.

A few moments later a reply came.

Glad to hear it. Goodnight, Skye and sweet dreams.

Why was the man always wishing her sweet dreams? Part of it felt nice because since he had started doing that, she had less and less of the bad dreams about Savannah that had plagued her since her sister's death. The problem was that most of the time, the dreams either turned out too sweet, like a happily ever after sweet, or they went from sweet to totally hot in seconds. Oh, well, it wasn't like she could change her dreams. So a relaxing bath with a glass of wine and then off to bed. She had an early day tomorrow.

Chapter Sixteen

Zak sent Skye a text on Tuesday morning letting her know that he wouldn't be at class. He had gotten forced into a meeting that he just couldn't miss. His father had insisted that he be there, and as much as he loved ignoring his father's overbearing ways, he knew that none of the partners would be happy if he missed it. He didn't concentrate very well in the meeting because his mind kept going back to Skye. Would she feel as disappointed as he felt that he wasn't going to be able to be in class today? Tonight was his night to manage the brewery, so he couldn't take her out. Maybe he could see if she wanted to stop by and have dinner or something.

A little voice inside him warned that he was getting way too invested in this relationship. He had never felt the need or desire to see a woman as often as he wished he could see Skye. That was probably the heart of the problem, it was desire. He honestly had never been with a woman so in tune with him sexually. He convinced himself that it really wasn't that he wanted to see her as much as it was that he wanted to bang her, and he wouldn't do that at the brewery, so asking her to stop by seemed pointless. That was another thing that the little voice kept reminding him of. Before Skye, he wouldn't have minded taking a woman wherever they were. He had not taken women to the brewery because after the one stalking incident, he hadn't wanted to give away personal information, but if he had, he would not have an issue taking them to the office or even the back storage room for a quick hard fuck. But he couldn't see himself doing that with Skye. He was pretty convinced that it had something to do with her being a mother. There was nothing else that was different about her than any other women that he had dated. He was telling himself that it was sort of like a Madonna complex. His mind wouldn't let him reduce a mother to a woman to hook up with in the back room. That was his story and he was sticking to it.

The meeting was boring as usual, but finally, the workday was done and he could head to Five Sloths. He really liked being there and chatting with the customers. It was always a nice change of pace from the rather stuffy legal profession.

When he got there, Jason was there, and so was his little boy. Ryan was a very energetic four-year-old. But he was also a very well behaved little boy. He knew that he wasn't allowed to run around in the customer section of the restaurant. He sat patiently in the office while his dad finished up the supply order. Zak wasn't big on children, but he had to admit Ryan was a good kid. Jason never brought him if he was planning to stay for the evening, but sometimes, if he just had an hour or so of work, he brought the little boy with him.

As soon as Zak walked into the office, Ryan greeted him with a big smile. "Hi, Uncle Zak!" he said enthusiastically.

"Hi, Ryan. Are you helping your dad work tonight?" Zak asked.

"Nope, we had to come here for some um...um....what did you call it, Daddy?" he asked Jason.

Jason looked up and smiled at his son. "We had to order inventory."

"Right, inbentory." Ryan said. "Then he is taking me for pizza!" Jason smiled at the mispronunciation—the kid was only four—and then he ruffled his hair.

Jason looked at Zak and asked if that was going to be a problem, or if he thought he would need anything. Jason assured him that if he wanted him back, he would take Ryan out for pizza and then drop him off with his grandparents for a few hours. Zak told him that he had it under control; he should enjoy the evening with his son. Tuesdays weren't an overly busy day. They had a decent-sized dinner crowd, but usually the place got pretty dead by 9 p.m. They had great staff, and for the most part, there really didn't need to be one of the owners there and the shift would still run smoothly. They just liked to have one of them around in case there were any issues or complaints. And it was always great to have one of the "sloths" there for customer rapport.

Zak started to leave the office but turned back and asked, "Hey, Jason, what's it like having a kid?"

Jason raised his eyebrow and asked, "Why, are you having one? No, wait. You are thinking of getting more serious with someone who does."

"Maybe," Zak admitted. "I'm really not sure yet."

"Well, I can tell you that it's the most rewarding hard work you'll ever do. Especially as a single parent. I don't know what I would have done if my mom hadn't been willing to help me at first. I had no idea how to change a diaper, let alone make formula and what to do when he was fussy or sick. But I also wouldn't change it for the world. If I could go back and not get her pregnant, I might do that, just because of all the legal hassles and all the crap she flung at me. But I wouldn't go back and not have Ryan for anything. He's my world," Jason explained.

"Okay, one other question," Zak continued. "Why haven't you told Sunni about him?"

"Well, that has a two-part answer," Jason said. "I'm enjoying time with Sunni, but it's light and easy. No heavy entanglements, because one, I'm not sure she would even be interested in kids. And, two, until I know that I am ready to be serious with someone, I'm not putting Ryan in the mix. He is too young to expose him to someone that he might feel connected to and possibly have that person walk away. I won't have a revolving door of women who he thinks might become his mommy until I am sure that I am ready to have that person be fully in my life. I know there are no guarantees; she could still say no. But I'm going to give it my best to wait until I think there is a real potential with someone."

Zak thought about that for a minute. It made a lot of sense. No parent who cared about their kid would want to have them get attached only to get hurt. Maybe that was why Skye was so careful to not talk about her little girl. "Thanks, man, that helps a lot."

Zak started to walk out of the office but Jason stopped him. "You need to do the same thing. You have to decide if you care enough about Skye to accept her kid. If you don't and she is okay with it just being no strings, then go for it. But if you even start to think of wanting more, you have to figure out where you stand in regard to kids."

"Yeah, I hear what you are saying," Zak admitted. The problem was, he wasn't sure what he thought about kids. He had never really been around any kids except Ryan. And he really hadn't been around Ryan all that much when he was truly a baby. It had only been in the last year or so that Jason had been bringing him to the brewery and to get-togethers with the guys. He tried to not think about it and get back to work.

Zak had to admit, though, that not thinking about it was pretty much impossible. He pushed it to the back of his mind when he needed to focus on a customer or had to run the cash register. But other than that, it kept popping right back up, front and center. What would he think about a relationship with Skye if that had to include a kid? And did he even think he was ready to give that a shot? He was pretty sure that Skye would see things the way Jason did. She wouldn't expose her kid to someone she wasn't sure was at least thinking long term.

At around nine o'clock, there was a bit of a lull that started over the brewery. It happened this way most nights before a workday. Zak found himself picking up his phone to dial Skye. He would normally text, but there was a part of him that just wanted to hear her voice to see if he could pick up any signals from her. When she picked up her phone, she sounded a little stressed. "Hey, Skye, I just wanted to call and see how your night was going," he began.

"It's going okay," she sort of mumbled.

Zak thought he heard a male voice in the background and he definitely heard her child in the background somewhere. The child he totally understood; she had a kid. But he didn't understand the male voice at all. Was the baby-daddy more a part of the picture than she wanted him to know? His mind started racing with all of the possibilities that could be happening right now. Maybe she lived with the guy but they were only together for the baby. She had told him she wanted to be monogamous while they were together and Skye just didn't seem like a woman who would say that knowing that she was getting a piece on the side. Even if it was her old flame. He had to set those thoughts aside because she was kind of hanging there waiting for him to say something. "Sounds like you're a little busy there. I don't want to keep you," he stated.

"No, it's all right," Skye assured him. It sounded like maybe she was moving to a different part of the house, but then he was sure he heard a car pass by in the background so she must have stepped outside to take the call. "I was just finishing something up, but I can talk now."

"Great," Zak began. He wasn't going to try to pry any further. Either she was or she wasn't being monogamous, but he would bet she wasn't sleeping with baby-daddy. She might be living with him to share expenses and child duties, but there was no way his Skye had asked for monogamy if she knew she couldn't promise it herself. "Anyway, I'm at the brewery. It's my night to manage, so I thought I would give you a call."

"That's really sweet of you," Skye said.

It sounded like maybe she was walking somewhere, but Zak continued, "Right, we had a lull and I just wanted to call and apologize again for missing class today."

"It's no problem, really, everyone has life to deal with at times," Skye assured him.

"Well, I won't get out of here until pretty late, so I wanted to call before you went to bed to tell you that and to wish you sweet dreams," Zak continued. "I wasn't sure what time you go to bed, but I wanted to try and catch you before I have to get busy with closing the place." Why was he explaining why he had called her, and better yet, why had he called her? It wasn't like he actually owed her an apology for missing yoga. It wasn't like he owed her an explanation of what he was doing every night. It wasn't like she was his girlfriend. His thoughts were interrupted when he realized she was talking.

"That's really sweet of you. I'm probably going to take a shower and maybe read for a while, but I will be going to bed soon," she explained. "Thanks for calling. Have a great rest of your night," she said before adding a good night and then hanging up the phone.

That phone call had been wrong on so many levels, Zak didn't even know where to start. She wasn't his girlfriend; he didn't owe her a call every night explaining his whereabouts. He didn't have to tell her good night and sweet dreams every night. But he had to admit, he did wonder what she was reading. Did she enjoy the steamy romance novels that a lot of women loved?

By the time he got home, his brain was exhausted. All of the back and forth in his mind as well as the struggle to keep it out of his mind had made for a very tiring night mentally. He took a shower and then decided to pour himself a double of scotch. The guys had made it a policy that when it was their night to manage, they never had more than one beer an hour and never any of the 'hard' stuff while on duty. He wasn't planning to get drunk, but maybe a little more than usual would help shut his mind off and let him sleep.

He ended up pouring himself another double and then headed to his bedroom. He got into bed and leaned up against the headboard and just let his mind wander wherever it might want to go. And of course, it went to thoughts of Skye. He thought about her a lot of the time lately. When it came right down to it, he was pretty sure that if there wasn't a kid to take into account, he would want to try for a more committed relationship with Skye. She was definitely all he could dream of in a sex partner and although they hadn't discussed a lot of personal details, what he did know about her seemed to mesh really well with his thoughts and ideals.

He wouldn't admit it to anyone else, but Skye had definitely gotten under his skin way more than any other woman ever had, especially in the short time they had known each other. Usually after one or at the most two times with a woman, he was ready to move on. They held no more appeal for him at that point. But he just kept wanting more and more of Skye. He didn't necessarily understand it, but he knew it was true. He sipped his scotch and let the thoughts flow through his mind. Admittedly, they sometimes tried to turn sexual, but he set that aspect of it aside. He had no doubt at all that he wanted her sexually, and that they were definitely compatible in that area. It was the rest of life he had to try to figure out. And that wasn't going to be easy. He would just have to give it time. He wasn't going to make a decision like that after only knowing her for a short time. He would just have to try to spend more time getting to know her and see how things progressed. He looked at his clock and saw that it was really late. He would have liked to text Skye one more time to let her know he was heading home, but by the time the brewery closed and he took care of the register and all of that it was always late. He was glad he had thought to call her earlier and chat with her a bit.

After he finished his scotch, he turned off the bedside lamp and tried to go to sleep. Sleep didn't come easy. He tossed and turned, and when it finally did come, he had dreams about Skye and some little brown-haired boy running in a park. He wasn't going to ask himself who that little boy was.

Chapter Seventeen

Skye was not looking forward to Wednesday afternoon. She didn't have classes to teach, so normally, she would take Cassie and go home. But she had to go and give her statement to the attorney that David had hired. The ladies in the daycare at the fitness center were more than happy to keep Cassie past her normal time. She really was a very easy baby to take care of.

She headed downtown to the building that housed the Owens, Jensen, Hallowell and Stein law offices. She made her way up to the floor that the security guard at the front door had told her to and got off the elevator. The receptionist pointed her down the proper hallway to Mr. Owens' office. She introduced herself to the assistant at the desk and the assistant picked up the phone and asked someone if they were ready for their next client. He must have answered in the affirmative because the assistant told her to go right in.

When Skye walked into the big office, the man had his back to her looking at something in a law book over near his bookshelf. He was younger than she had thought he would be. When she thought of attorneys, she usually pictured someone like Ben Matlock or Perry Mason. When he turned around, Skye couldn't believe her eyes.

It was Zak. How could it be Zak? The surprise registered on his face as soon as it did hers. She said questioningly, "Zak, what are you doing here?" at the same time that he said, "Skye, what are you doing here?"

Zak answered first, "I work here."

Then Skye said, "I'm supposed to be giving my statement to my brother-in-law's attorney."

"You're Ms. Pierson?" Zak asked, slightly stunned.

"I am," Skye affirmed.

"Then that makes you the little girl's aunt." Zak sounded like he was still sorting this all out in his head.

"Yes, Cassie, her name is Cassie. I'm her aunt." Shouldn't an attorney know the name of the little girl who was the whole reason for this case? Skye wondered to herself.

"This is so awesome," Zak said. "This changes everything."

Skye was confused. What did this change, and how did it change it? "What do you mean?" she asked.

"I have been going nuts trying to figure this out. I want to get to know you more and see where a relationship might go, but I've been under the impression that that little girl I saw you with a couple of times at the gym was yours. I wasn't ready to commit to a mom with a kid."

"Cassie, her name is Cassie," Skye said more adamantly.

"Right, Cassie," Zak agreed as if that point wasn't important in the least. "I had seen you with her going into the fitness center, so I assumed that you were her mother. Now that I know you aren't, it makes all the difference in the world."

"Wait, are you saying that you wanted to keep this as a friends with benefits sort of thing because you thought I was a mother, but now that you know that I'm Cassie's aunt, you are ready to consider something more?" Skye asked.

She didn't make it sound like the same wonderful thing that Zak considered it to be, and he wasn't sure why. "Yes, I didn't think I was ready to pursue a single mom, but you're not a single mom," Zak exclaimed.

Skye was shaking her head and backing out the door. "I can't do this right now," she said. She turned and started to walk out the same way she had come in. The woman at the desk tried to stop her, but she just told her, "I need to reschedule; I'm not feeling well." She picked up her pace heading back to the elevator. She heard Zak closing the distance between them.

Zak grabbed her arm to halt her progress, and said, "Skye, wait. We can figure this out."

Skye just looked at him with tears in her eyes and said, "I can't do this right now" as she tried to pull out of his hold.

He let her go. He had no idea what he had said wrong, but the hallway in the law firm wasn't the place to try to sort that out. It would be just like his father to hear about it and think that Zak was harassing a client. "We will figure this out," he said as the elevator door began to close between him and Skye.

Skye made it to her car and got in and closed and locked the door. She wasn't about to let Zak walk up and open the door if he had decided to follow her out. She couldn't talk to him right now. She called Autumn, and when she answered, Skye said, "I can't believe he would say that."

"Hold up, you can't believe that who would say what?" Autumn asked, puzzled.

"Zak," Skye remarked, trying to tone down the crying so her friend could understand her.

"What did he say?"

"He said that it made all the difference in the world that Cassie is my niece and not my daughter," Skye lamented.

"And that's a bad thing why? She is your niece." Autumn was getting really confused.

"No, he said that he was against having a relationship with me when he thought she was my daughter, but now that he knows she's my niece, it changes everything according to him."

"And you don't think it's okay for him to feel that way?" Autumn guessed.

"No, because even though she is my niece, I spend a lot of time with her. If he can't handle being around kids, then we have no business being together. I will always have Cassie as a huge part of my life," Skye explained.

"Okay, I get where you are coming from, sort of. I do see your point, but I think I am missing something here," Autumn consoled her. "How about I come over after David is home and you and I can sit down with a glass of wine and figure it out?"

"Okay," Skye sniffled. "You're the best."

"Dry your tears, and you can tell me all about it tonight. It may not be as horrible as it first seemed to you," Autumn assured her.

When Skye got home, she took Cassie into David's house and waited until he got home. She hoped that Zak hadn't called him to try to figure out what had happened with Skye. She did need to give her statement, to help David's case, but she wasn't sure she could give it to Zak. Maybe there was some other attorney or paralegal or something that could take it.

When David got home, he didn't say anything about the case, so Skye didn't either. She told him that Autumn was coming over tonight and if David didn't need anything more, she was going to her place. David assured her they would be fine, and she headed out to the stairs alongside the garage. She wasn't hungry, but she knew she should eat something. She looked in the fridge and found some cheese dip. That was protein, right? Chips and cheese were about all she could handle for food right now. She couldn't focus on cooking.

What the hell had he thought that would mean when he told her it changed everything? Well, it did change everything. She knew now that she couldn't keep seeing him if he wasn't okay with her having a child in her life. She wasn't Cassie's mom, but she still had a huge commitment to that little girl. Way more of a commitment than any man would ever have from her unless he was her husband. She didn't need a man in her life if they weren't going to be okay with her having such a huge role with Cassie.

Her phone started ringing and she knew that it would be Zak. She glanced at the phone and saw that she was right. She put the phone on silent and stuffed it under the pillow on the couch. She didn't want to see it or hear it. She wanted him to stop calling her. It was hard enough to keep up her resolve of ending things with him; she didn't need to have his face on her call screen all the time.

When Autumn arrived, Skye asked her to text Zak and request that he not call Skye anymore right now. She had a lot to think about. She pulled out her phone long enough for Autumn to copy the number and then turned it off, not before noticing that there were four voicemails and about a dozen texts, all from Zak. She couldn't deal with them right now.

She explained to Autumn exactly why she felt what Zak had said was wrong. She was a part of Cassie's life whether he liked it or not.

Autumn honored her friend's request and texted Zak, although she added her own spin on it.

Hi, my name is Autumn. I am a friend of Skye's. She asked me to text you and ask you to give her some space. She just doesn't feel that she is ready to talk to you at this point. But I will say that she definitely has some feelings for you. Just don't give up on her.

She put her phone on silent in case he responded. She didn't want it to upset Skye.

They spent the evening talking and catching up. Skye got teary-eyed whenever she talked about Zak. She was also worried about what to do about the statement. She knew she had to give one. David and Cassie deserved to have full representation, and her input would be important, but she wasn't sure that she could talk to Zak at this point. She told Autumn that she would call and see if maybe one of the other attorneys could do it, or even Zak's assistant.

By the time Autumn left, Skye was feeling a little better. Talking about or thinking about Zak was still too painful, but they had talked about all sorts of things while drinking the bottle of wine Autumn had brought. Skye had definitely needed some time with her bestie. She hadn't really had much time to catch up with her since Savannah's accident.

When Autumn got ready to leave, she checked her phone and there was a response from Zak. He said some things that she wasn't going to repeat to Skye right now, but he also wanted her to make sure that Skye knew that he would drop out of the yoga class until they had a chance to try to work things out.

Autumn gave Skye a huge bear hug and told her to hang in there; she was sure it would work out for the best.

When Autumn got home, she texted Zak to let him know that she had passed on his message about the yoga class. He texted her back asking how Skye was and saying that he really didn't understand what he had said or done wrong, but whatever it was, he was sorry if he had hurt Skye.

She asked him to give it a few days. Skye might see things differently once she had some more time to think it over. And, if not, Autumn would at least keep him posted on how Skye was.

Chapter Eighteen

Zak walked into work at 8:50 a.m. Thursday morning. His assistant was surprised to see him because he had put his gym schedule in the main calendar so she knew that he was supposed to be coming in late on Tuesdays and Thursdays. He thought about taking it out of the calendar, but he wasn't fully ready to admit defeat yet. His assistant told him that Ms. Pierson had called to see if she could possibly reschedule her statement and asked if she could just do it with the assistant. Zak knew why she was asking that; she didn't want to see him right now. But there was no way he was going to handle this any less than professionally. "Can you call and see if Walt Jensen is in yet this morning and ask his admin if he has a few moments for me to come down and talk with him?" He walked into his office to take off his suit coat. They weren't required to wear them around the building, but everyone had to have them in case they were needed in court or if they had a client come in. His admin buzzed the intercom to let him know that Walt was in and he did have a few minutes free.

Zak walked down the hallway to Walt's office. The firm was divided up by type of law practiced. Walt wasn't far from him because they both handled personal injury and similar lawsuits. Their friend Pete was in a different area altogether because he practiced criminal defense. Zak asked Walt's admin if he could go in and she nodded in the affirmative and told him that Mr. Jensen was expecting him. Having the law firm belong to three of the fathers of the guys, the whole Mr. part got confusing at times.

Still, he knocked and then opened the door slowly in case Walt was on the phone or something.

"You look like you either didn't sleep or you went on a bender last night," Walt commented.

"Actually, a little of both," Zak admitted. When Walt raised his eyebrow in question, Zak continued, "Look, I screwed up and I only understand about half of what I did wrong, maybe even less." When Walt sat back and settled in to hear this story, Zak continued, "You know the case that I told you about, the truck driver who ran a young mother off the road and killed her?"

Walt nodded and said, "She left behind a small child, a husband and a sister, if I remember correctly."

"Right, and remember that I told you that Skye was a single mom?" Walt nodded again but looked even more confused.

"She's not a single mom, she's an aunt," Zak explained.

Dawning showed on Walt's face. "She's the aunt of the client. That's why you saw her with a small child and assumed it was hers."

"Yeah, well, you know what they say about assuming," Zak said.

Walt thought about it for a moment. "I don't see where it's really a problem. She technically isn't the client. So, unlike what I did, you don't have to worry about misinterpretation of the situation."

"The problem is that that is exactly where my mind went too. She's not the client, and she's not a single mom. Nothing to keep me from pursuing a relationship with her," Zak lamented. "Apparently, she doesn't agree."

"Why, what does she think?" Walt asked.

"Apparently, according to her friend Autumn, who has been texting me. Skye thinks that because I was reluctant to pursue a single mom, I would feel the same way about her because although she isn't the mother, she does spend a lot of her time helping with the kid. Sorry, that's another thing she was upset about. I kept calling her 'the kid,' and I didn't use her name. She thinks I will be upset because she has to spend a lot of time with Cassie."

Walt nodded; he was starting to see where this was going. "Ah. Okay, so Cassie is important to her, and she thinks that if you weren't ready to date a single mom, you wouldn't be able to date an aunt that is very consumed with her niece at this point."

"Yeah, and I apparently made the stupid mistake of being happy that we could pursue a relationship because she wasn't a single mom." Zak was really starting to understand what he had unwittingly done wrong. "And now she doesn't want to talk to me until she has time to think, but I need her statement for the case. I was wondering if you could possibly take care of that for me. She knows you a little, so it might be more comfortable for her than it would be with someone else."

Walt could see that his friend really was not happy with his own mistake. When he had been excited, he hadn't meant to discount Skye's feelings for her niece; it had simply felt like a relief to him to have that aspect of it taken out of the picture. "Sure, I'll have my admin call and set it up, or your admin can do it. I'll have my admin coordinate with yours," Walt offered. "And don't give up on having something with her. Misunderstandings happen all the time. Rayne and I had a huge one that almost ruined us for a while there. Rayne overheard me talking to my dad. You know how the partners can be. 'No fraternization, no, messing with the client, no possible scandal.' Rayne heard me telling him that she was staying at my house, but not as my girlfriend or lover or whatever. She thought that she was causing me issues at work, so she moved out. Went to some crappy motel and wouldn't tell me where she was. It was a mess for a few days, but we got it worked out. Just give her some space and time and maybe she will come around."

"I hope so," Zak said.

"By the way, it's nice to see that you have found someone you care about, other than just as a sexual partner," Walt encouraged him.

"I don't....hell, who am I trying to kid? Yes, I do, I realized I have feelings for her, and now I may have blown the whole thing because I didn't fully understand just what I had in front of me."

"I think you'll find a way to work it out," Walt said.

Chapter Nineteen

Skye was back at the same law offices on Friday morning. She had made it clear to the woman that had called that she didn't want to talk to Mr. Owens. The woman had assured her that she would be giving her statement to a Mr. Jensen. Maybe he would be the stodgy old attorney she had pictured before. As soon as she walked out of the elevator, she felt a tingle. She knew it was because she was so close to Zak, but she couldn't let herself think that way. She just had to remind herself that Cassie was the most important thing in her life right now. She and Zak would have to wait, or maybe they were just done for good. If he couldn't deal with her commitments now, he probably wouldn't just wait around for her to be finished with them either. It wasn't like this was only a few weeks' worth of a commitment. She could potentially be at least partially responsible for Cassie until she was grown and out on her own.

When she checked in at the main desk, she was directed down a different hallway than she had been when she gone to Zak's office. The administrative assistant buzzed into the office and told Mr. Jensen that Ms. Pierson was here to see him. She heard a voice say to send her in. She opened the door and there stood Walt, one of Zak's friends that she had met at the brunch. Had that only been last weekend? It seemed like it was a lifetime ago. Although that could be because she hadn't been sleeping much the last few nights, and when she did, she was back to having nightmares about Savannah, and she also had nightmares where she was with Zak and things felt so perfect and right, but then she would turn around and he was gone. She was searching down dark hallways and trying to open doors, but she couldn't find Zak.

She started to object, but Walt held up a hand to halt her objections. "I know that you and Zak have some things to figure out. But I promise you that I am only here to ask you questions that pertain to your brother-in-law's case. I won't try to convince you of anything about Zak. That is between the two of you," Walt assured her.

"Okay," Skye agreed. "What do you want to know?"

Walt explained that it wasn't so much a question and answer period as it was a statement from her as to what the loss of her sister had cost her, both emotionally and physically. Walt explained that he would imagine that part of that would have to do with her niece too. He knew that Skye had been left to help raise her sister's child.

Skye objected to that and told him that she didn't consider that a burden. Caring for Cassie would never be a burden to her. It was what any sister would do when the mom was taken out of the child's life.

Walt said, "I'm sure you don't. I'm sure your niece brings you joy and sadness both. Thinking of your sister every time you look at her. I don't mean that she is a burden, but this has caused you to have to change your lifestyle. According to the notes Zak gave me from his interview with David, you have moved into the apartment over his garage so that you can be there to help with Cassie. He also told Zak that you are responsible for her from 7:00 in the morning to around 6:00 in the evening. While I am sure that you don't consider that a burden, it very admittedly has changed how you live your life. That's the type of thing we need in your statement. The jury has to see that what happened to your sister has a further reaching effect than just David and Cassie. If I'm not mistaken, your sister was also your only remaining family, so that is a part of it too."

Skye was trying not to get choked up about all the things Walt was saying, but they were true. While she didn't consider it a burden, and she was happy to be able to step in, the loss of her sister had cost her so much, emotionally especially. She still had Autumn to rely on, but her sister had been there from the very first moment of Skye's life. She was the one constant for the last five years since their parents had died. She nodded and said that she understood. Walt asked if it was okay to record her statement so that they could be sure they didn't miss anything. He also told her that if she needed to pause at any point, that was perfectly understandable.

****

After Skye had given Walt all the information he had asked for, she stood to leave but turned around and asked him, "How is Zak doing?"

Walt looked at her with a sort of sad look on his face. "Well, he's been at work early the last couple of days, which isn't like him, but it's most likely because he isn't sleeping well. He looks like he hasn't slept a lot the last few nights." He continued, "Look, I promised you I wouldn't push to talk about anything having to do with Zak, but you asked, so, if I may, I would say that he realizes that he screwed up. Not in his feelings, but in how he expressed them. It wasn't that he doesn't want you to have a relationship with your niece. It was just that he has spent so much time dodging his parents wanting him to settle down that it's become almost a mantra to him to not want to have kids or be around kids really." Walt paused and then added, "I'm not saying I condone his words or actions; I'm just saying that I know where it came from. And it wasn't out of a distaste for you caring for your niece. It was a knee jerk reaction to him thinking that you were a single mom and all the commitments that come with that made him relieved to think that having a relationship with you didn't immediately make him someone's daddy."

"I understand," Skye said softly.

"On another note, if I may. When I told Rayne that I would be taking your statement today, I was told that I need to make sure you knew that Rayne and Sunni really enjoyed meeting you and that she hopes you can have a girls' day sometime soon. She wants you to know that whatever happened or happens with you and Zak, she would really like to spend time with you." Walt looked at her and added, "About a year ago, Rayne lost everything that was her life. Other than Sunni, she had no one and nothing to look forward to. She has found something to live for again, but I know she would really like to be your friend."

"I'll keep that in mind, thank you." And with that, Skye walked out the door. She thought that maybe she saw Zak walking around the corner away from her, but she wasn't sure. It could have been someone who just looked like him from the back. She made her way back to the elevator and left the building.

****

Zak had kind of been spying to see if he could get a glimpse of Skye. He had watched her from a conference room as she got off the elevator. She wouldn't have been able to see him—the glass was frosted for privacy—but he could see her. And then he had parked himself right at the corner where he would see when she left Walt's office. He really wasn't trying to stalk her; he just wanted to see for himself that she was okay. She looked about as tired as he felt. She looked beautiful as always, but there were circles under her eyes. He wasn't sure if that was because he had been an ass, or if it was because she was being reminded of her sister's death with the court proceedings coming up. Either way, he wished he could take it all away and make her feel happier. For a moment, a part of him had felt a bit of relief that she might be missing him as much as he was missing her, but he also didn't like the idea of him being the one to cause her to not sleep. He was beginning more and more to understand what she felt he had done wrong. And, admittedly, he saw where his words could have sounded the way she interpreted them. But if he never got to talk to her, he would never get the chance to try to backpedal and tell her what he had meant.

He decided to call Autumn and ask her to call him back. When she called later in the day, he said, "Look, I know that I don't have any right to ask this, but I really want to try to send Skye something that won't make her mad at me, but will let her know that I truly am sorry for the way I said things when she was here. I have realized that in that moment, yes, I did mean it the way it came out, but deep down, I didn't mean what it came across as. I was happy that she wasn't a single mom, because I am not sure that I am ready for that. In my mind, with her not being a single mom, we could get to know each other and just be a couple. I wasn't thinking about how much Cassie means to her and how much she needs to be involved in Cassie's life right now," he explained. "I don't know if that makes any sense at all. I just didn't mean it to come across the way Skye understood it. I really miss her."

Autumn thought about that for a minute. "Honestly, Zak, there's only one thing that I can think of that will change her mind right now and that's time and patience. Don't give up," she encouraged him. "Look, I know Skye has been trying to be all 'keep it light and easy,' but it might help if you know some things about her. Skye moved up here about four years ago from a little town in northern Indiana. Savannah had gone to Michigan State University and that's where she met David. When they graduated, they got married and Skye spent a lot of time up here. She's always been very close to her sister. That's when I met her. I won't go into that whole story, but we became almost instant besties. She really wanted to move up here a few years earlier than she did, but her parents weren't in great health, so she felt like she should stay and help them. I think she was pretty much a recluse down there at that point. She had lived in that town her whole life, but she really preferred it up here. All of her free time was up here with Savannah. When her parents died, it was an automatic decision to move up here. She didn't have a lot of friends down there. I don't know the whole story of that, but I know that she has always told me that I was the best friend she has ever had other than Savannah. When Savannah got pregnant, Skye doted on her. Skye took the training to learn how to do land and water yoga for pregnant women. She lost a lot the day Savannah died."

Zak tried to take all that in. He had parents, and even though they drove him nuts sometimes, he knew he could drop by anytime and they would welcome him with open arms. He had a brother and a sister. He had family. And he had his Sloth brothers. They were closer to him than blood most of the time. He had no doubt that losing any of his family would hurt like hell. He hurt for the fact that Skye had lost so much. He was quiet for a moment, processing all of that, and then he said, "Thanks for sharing all of that, it's definitely something I need to keep in mind."

Autumn told him that she was happy to help him understand. "Family is hard to come by for some of us," Autumn continued. "I have one question for you, though. Have you ever met Cassie?"

"No, I haven't," Zak admitted.

"You should. She's a pretty special little girl. She's a lot like her aunt that way," Autumn said. "Anyway, if I think of anything else, I'll let you know." And with that, she hung up.

Zak sat and stared out the window. He wasn't really looking at anything; he was trying to get his mind to focus on what he might be able to do to win Skye back. Maybe he could go meet the little girl that she was so in love with. If Autumn was right, and she was anything like Skye, she had to be pretty amazing.

Chapter Twenty

After a weekend spent mostly at the brewery trying to keep himself busy and his mind off of his situation, Zak found himself at the annual Labor Day party that the senior partners always held. It was always quite the event. There were kegs of several of the brews that Five Sloths made, along with kegs from some of the other local breweries. Of course, being the "end of summer," they had a barbecue. Not that any of the senior attorneys actually ran the grill; that was handled by the caterers, of course. It was usually a fairly fun event. He could hang out with his friends, and he always brought a woman along. Most of the time, he tried to bring one that was exactly the opposite of what his parents would want for him. He never brought the sweet 'possible future wife' material that his parents wished for—no, he tried to pick the one that had the biggest breasts, usually fake, and who was comfortable in a barely-there string bikini since the event was always held somewhere on water. This year, Zak attended it alone. He still hung out with Walt and Rayne and Pete, but it just wasn't where he wanted to be. He knew if he left early, his dad would give him shit about it though. So he stayed and tried to keep himself right on that ledge, drunk enough that very little mattered to him, yet sober enough his parents wouldn't think he was being overly obnoxious. It was a very fine line, but he was pretty sure he was doing a damn fine job of staying just to the 'right' side of it.

When the meal was over and people were mostly visiting and a few were playing the lawn games that had been set up, Zak's phone buzzed in his pocket. He looked at it but it was a number he didn't recognize. He almost let it go to voicemail, but, what the hell, maybe someone needed him to come bail them out of jail or something. He wasn't a criminal defense attorney, but you never knew when someone would remember you were an attorney and call hoping that you could get them out of jail. Then he could leave the party with a good excuse. He swiped across the screen and said, "Hello."

"Hello, is this Zak?" the voice on the other end asked.

"It is. Who is this?" If this was some telemarketer or something, he thought about maybe still telling everyone that it had been an important work related call and he needed to go and follow up on it.

"This is ADA Anderson," the man said. "You asked me to give you a call if we came up with anything on your trucker case."

That got Zak's attention, and he moved away from the crowd so he could hear better. "I did. You got something for me?"

"I do. Have you ever heard of an electronic on-board recorder?" he asked.

"No, can't say as I have," Zak admitted. He really hoped this guy had something worth hearing.

"Most people haven't. What this device does is record the time a vehicle is in motion, or when it's stopped. In December 2017, there was a ruling that mandated the use of this device in all semis with the exception of a few exemptions. The carrier in question in this case does not have an exemption," he explained.

"Okay, and what does that mean? This guy's truck didn't have one?" If that was the case, this would be easier to win.

"Actually, every truck owned by Allegiance Trucking has one of those devices. However, although they look perfectly normal to the naked eye, they aren't actually attached to anything. They have been rigged to always show a normal reading," Anderson explained.

"Okay, I'm still missing a piece here," Zak complained. "How does this help anything? What does it mean?"

"That device is placed in a semi to limit the number of hours a driver can be on the road before he has to stop and rest. The general rule is that they can drive eleven hours out of a fourteen-hour period, and in that fourteen-hour period, there should be a half-hour break. After eleven hours of movement, the truck is not supposed to move again until there has been a ten-hour break. It is supposed to keep drivers from driving tired. When working properly, it gives the driver a warning when they have approximately fifty miles to go before their drive time is up. That should give them enough warning to pull into a truck stop, or motel or whatever out on the road. If they ignore that warning, it gives them one more warning at approximately twenty-five miles to go. And if they ignore that warning, when working properly, the engine will disengage completely. Meaning they are sitting in a non-moving vehicle. So, obviously, drivers heed the warnings. Once the engine stops either by the driver shutting it down, or by it automatically disengaging on its own, the truck isn't supposed to be able to move again for ten hours."

Zak was beginning to understand now. "So this guy was most likely driving tired?"

"No most likely about it. I'll be honest, we aren't going after the driver in your case for much of anything. We are giving him a pretty decent deal on the criminal side of things because he is being very cooperative with helping us take down the bigger fish in this pond," the ADA said.

"He's informing on the company," Zak guessed.

"Yeah, not only informing, he's got logs to back up the fact that very often, their drivers are forced to drive twelve to fifteen hours a day, and their down time is often little more than four hours. The company basically tells them do it or find other employment. Most of these guys have families. They can't just walk away from a steady job."

"Most of these guys? You have others?" Zak asked.

"Several. Your guy was very helpful in helping us get several witnesses and we have enough to come down hard on the company. Within the next twenty-four to forty-eight hours, we will be filing charges against the company, the owners and the guy who figured out how to make the dummy device."

"So I'm better off waiting until you guys file criminal charges because then I have more to show a jury," Zak surmised.

"I would think so, and in my opinion, you can probably get a judgment against the driver, but you would get a much bigger settlement out of the trucking company," the ADA stated. "But it's your case as far as the civil aspect. You do whatever you feel is best for your client."

"Thanks for the information. Can you send me copies of anything that might be relevant to my side of things?" Zak asked.

"I'll send what I can. Some names and things may be blacked out, because the who won't matter to anything except the criminal side. But I can for sure send you the basic info on what they were doing and why the guy was so tired."

"That's what I need. Thanks again, Anderson," Zak said and then hung up the phone. That gave him a whole list of things to consider. Of course he had to give his client the final say in who they sued, and he knew it wasn't about money. David had said he wanted the driver to pay for what he had done. The money wasn't what cared about; he was looking for someone to be held responsible for his wife's death.

"Hey, you okay, man?" Walt asked, walking over to Zak.

"Yeah, just had a pretty interesting phone call," Zak replied.

"Oh, anything you want to talk about?" Walt queried.

"I do, but not here. You up for me and Pete coming to your place for a bit?" Zak asked.

"Let me run it by Rayne, since it's her house too, but I'm sure she won't mind being able to head out sooner rather than later. She aptly said this was the stuffiest barbecue she had ever attended. She wanted to know if the senior partners ever 'let their hair down.' I told her no," Walt stated.

After talking to Rayne and asking if Pete minded coming too, they said their goodbyes to their respective parents and explained that they had to leave because some potential information in one of their cases had just come up and they needed to get it sorted out. Of course, the one and only thing that a junior partner would be excused from one of the firm's events was if it was actual work. Billable hours were billable hours after all, even if they happened on a holiday.

Of course, when he said goodbye to his parents, Zak's mother made a point of telling him she was so happy to see that he hadn't brought one of his 'bimbos' this year. Those were her words, not his. He just kissed her on the cheek and walked away. It wasn't worth engaging her on that topic.

Even though the client would make the final decision, Zak felt better running the information past his friends since they worked at the same law firm. He just wanted to be sure that he was ready to present all the best options to the client before he actually met with him. Was there a way that he could make it sound like he needed Skye to be there too? Probably not, but he wished he could. He would really like to see her again.

****

When they got to Walt's house, he informed them of everything the DA had told him.

"That's some pretty heavy-duty illegal activity going on there," Pete said. "This could be opening a whole can of worms for the prosecutor. They have to look at any accidents where trucks from this company were involved. The more accidents they find, the heavier it will hit the trucking company. They may end up facing a long list of charges. It may even open up other lawsuits if the public finds out about this and realizes they were damaged by the drivers for that company."

Walt agreed. "I'm thinking that this may come down to a class action suit against the company if other injured parties come forward."

"I agree with all of that," Zak began. "And I have to talk to the client to see which way he wants to go on this. But I have a more important question." When they all looked at him, he continued, "Do you think it will have any effect on me being able to get Skye back?"

The guys both kind of just shrugged, but Rayne had obviously been hearing their conversation from her place at the kitchen counter. She turned to look at them and said, "I think there's hope. I don't know if this development will have anything to do with it, but from what Walt said about her visit the other day, she misses you as much as you miss her. You just have to figure out how to make her see that you came off as an ass, but you weren't really trying to be one."

"Gee, thanks for that, I think," Zak said.

Rayne just sort of shrugged off the fact that she might have offended him by calling him an ass. But if there was any chance of him figuring out how to get Skye back in his life, he would admit to just about anything.

Chapter Twenty-One

Zak called David first thing Tuesday morning to tell him that there had been a new development in the case, and he wanted to discuss it with David. When David answered, Zak thought he heard the baby gurgling in the background. "Did I catch you at a bad time?" he asked.

"No, not at all. I took a couple of days off to make a longer weekend to spend with my favorite girl," David stated. Zak could hear the smile in his voice. It was very obvious that his little girl made him happy.

"Well, there are a few things I need to discuss with you about your case. When would be a good time to get together?" Zak asked.

"I don't have anything big planned for today or tomorrow other than hanging out with Cassie," David volunteered.

"Actually, my morning is pretty clear. Would it be easier if I came to your place so you don't have to pack up your daughter and bring her here?" Zak asked.

"That would be great. Skye has already headed to work, so I wouldn't be able to ask her to take Cassie. It would save me some stress if you could come here," David agreed.

"Great. I'll head out now and be there shortly," Zak stated. When he got to David's house, he noticed the same SUV he had seen Skye with the first time he had noticed her on the street. Most likely when she had the little girl, she took David's car for car seat purposes. Skye's car was pretty small to be able to fit much baby stuff in it.

He walked up to the door and was just reaching to ring the doorbell when the door opened. David was standing there with the little girl Zak had seen Skye with a couple of times.

"Hi," David said enthusiastically. "Come on in, I'm just finishing up with Cassie's breakfast."

Zak followed him to the kitchen. David placed Cassie back in her little baby seat and grabbed a spoon and a dish of food. There were also a few pieces of crackers or something on the tray. Apparently, she was old enough she could eat finger foods but wasn't able to manage a spoon yet. Zak had no idea what stages babies went through and at what ages.

Zak began telling David why he was there. Every time he looked at the little girl, her smile about did him in. Her eyes were more hazel, most likely like her mother's, and her hair was more of a brown where Skye's was more amber, but that smile, that was one hundred percent Skye's smile.

"So here's what I know. I've been told by the ADA that there will be criminal charges filed most likely today or tomorrow," Zak began.

"Against the driver?" David asked.

"No, that's part of why I wanted to talk to you before it all went down on the news. The driver is going to get little more than a slap on the wrist," Zak began. When he saw the incredulous look on David's face, he continued on. "The reason for that is that he has proof that the trucking company was doing things that are illegal, that caused him and other drivers to be forced to drive tired or lose their jobs."

"So he's not being held responsible?" David asked.

"He has gotten some tickets and will have fines. He will most likely lose his ability to be a trucker anymore. But the DA says his information and cooperation is very necessary to their case. There is a device that is required on over the road semis that limits the number of hours the truck can be in motion without having a break so that the driver can rest. The company disabled those devices on all of their semis. That's highly illegal. Now, that doesn't mean that the civil case can't go forward against the driver. It does mean that we could also file a civil case against the company. Honestly, I know that you aren't in this for the money, but the company will have much deeper pockets than the driver. He would still very likely lose the case we will have against him, but his ability to pay will be limited. The other option is that we wait until the criminal charges are filed and then we go after both the company and the driver. That way, both are held responsible for the part they played in the accident," Zak encouraged him.

"Do you need my decision right now?" David asked.

"No, not at all. Honestly, if we are going to bring suit against the company, that part is better left until they have been formally charged with something. A jury is going to see that there is a legal case against them and be more likely to decide against them in a civil case. It's not always true, but if you are guilty of a crime, or sometimes even appear guilty, a jury awards damages in a civil case."

David was done feeding the little girl, so he grabbed some kind of wipes and cleaned off her face. She looked up at Zak and gave him another one of her beautiful smiles. "She's a charmer," Zak said.

"That she is," David agreed. "She's a pretty big flirt for such a little girl." He looked at his daughter and said in that kind of silly way that people seemed to talk to babies, "Aren't you? You're a big flirt." The baby smiled even more. No, CASSIE smiled even more. He needed to remember that she was a person and a person that was very important to Skye. She wasn't simply a baby or the baby, she was Cassie. Cassie looked at Zak again and gave him a big smile, reaching out both hands toward him. "I don't think he wants to take you, Cassie, he probably has to get back to work."

Cassie was practically falling out of her daddy's arms to reach toward Zak. "Actually, I have some time," he heard himself saying while holding out his hand to Cassie. She wrapped her little hand around his finger and pulled with all her might. If these people were important to Skye, it would serve him well to get to know them a little better.

"She's really taking to you; she usually smiles at strangers but never wants to go to them," David remarked.

Oh, what the hell, it wasn't like it would kill him if he held her, and she seemed very insistent that he do so. Although, she did just eat, so he might be risking vomit on his suit. Oh well, that's what dry cleaners were for, right? Maybe if he held Cassie, he would understand what Skye held so dear. He reached out both arms to her.

"Are you sure?" David asked.

"I'm sure, how hard can it be?" Zak asked. The little girl looked up at him when he took her in his arms and gave him the biggest smile he had ever seen on a small child. Not that he had seen a lot of them, but this one lit up her whole face. Her eyes had a sparkle in them that wasn't achievable by any adult. It was the pure happiness of a child. This little girl would grow up without a mother. He didn't always agree with his mother now that he was an adult, but she had been a really good mom. She was always there for him; she'd taken her turn at carpooling to sports or events. She always kissed his injuries when he was very little to 'make it all better.' This little girl wouldn't have that. But she would have her daddy, and she would always have her Aunt Skye. He got it now. He hadn't gotten it before. Skye wasn't a mother, but she was going to do her best to make sure this little girl never went without the things a mother would provide. Cassie laid her head down on Zak's shoulder and gave the deepest sigh. He felt her warm breath on his neck. He felt her little body relax like she hadn't a care in the world. She trusted that he would hold her; she didn't question whether or not he would let her fall. That was one thing that he did know about children this small: unless they had been given reason not to, they were usually pretty trusting. If they had always been surrounded by loving and supportive people, they just assumed that everyone was kind and would love them and support them too. Oh, being an attorney, he had seen the worst of the worst; he had seen kids that trusted and were taken advantage of. He hoped this little girl would never know any type of betrayal of her trust. The more she relaxed and relied completely on him, the more he understood. He leaned down to whisper in her ear, "I get it now."

"Did you say something?" David asked. He had been cleaning up from Cassie's breakfast, putting things in the sink and garbage.

"No, nothing important," Zak said.

David peeked around to see Cassie's face. "Wow, she must really feel comfortable with you. She fell asleep," David said smiling.

Zak panicked at that a little. He didn't want to wake her up. Should he move, or was he stuck in this position for however long Cassie slept?

David said, "I can take her if you want."

Zak asked, "Would it be easier if I laid her down? I don't want to wake her up."

"That would be fine," David said. "Follow me." He showed Zak to the nursery. It was decorated in story book characters. Some of them he remembered from the times his mother would take him to the library. Peter Rabbit, Goodnight Moon, Curious George, Charlotte's Web—this was a room that a loving mother had decorated believing that someday, she would read all of those books to her daughter.

Zak tried to lay her down as gently as he could. He thought maybe she was going to wake up when she shifted and took another deep breath, but she remained asleep. He and David walked back to the front room. And Zak said, "Well, you have time to think about it, and decide what you want to do. Just let me know how you want to proceed."

David thanked him for stopping by and told him he would get back to him after he had time to think.

Zak called his admin and asked if there would be anything keeping him from taking the afternoon off. She said the calendar was clear, and she promised to run interference if any of the seniors came snooping around. He told her she was awesome and then he hung up the phone. Zak wasn't exactly sure where he was going to go; he just knew he had some thinking to do. He found himself pulling into the entrance to a park. There were mothers with their children on the swings and slides. He put his car in park and watched the children having fun and playing. Before long, the images from his dreams came to him and he could see him and Skye sitting on a bench watching a little brown-haired boy. When he closed his eyes to try to let the image clear in his mind, he saw something he hadn't ever noticed in the dream before. Beside the little brown-haired boy was a child that looked to be a couple of years older. She was a little brown-haired hazel-eyed girl that had a smile exactly like Skye's. There was something about her that made him absolutely certain that it was Cassie. That sure gave him a lot to think about.

Chapter Twenty-Two

Skye had a voicemail when she got done with her classes on Tuesday. It was from Rayne.

"Hello, Skye, this is Rayne Davis. We met last weekend. Anyway, I was hoping maybe we could get together for a girls' night sometime soon. I don't have very many girlfriends. I only have Sunni. But I'd really like to get a chance to get to know you better. I promise we don't have to talk about Zak. Walt told me you two aren't together right now. I promise I'm not going to try to plead his case. I really just want to hang out and have fun. Okay, well, if you are interested give me a call." She then recited her number before ending the message.

Did Skye want to go out with Rayne? Kind of. She really didn't have all that many girlfriends either. She had known Autumn forever basically, and after moving to Michigan to be closer to her sister, she hadn't had much chance to meet anyone new. She knew some of the other instructors at the gym, but most of them were college students or just not at the same place in life as Skye was, so they didn't have a lot in common.

And Rayne said she wasn't trying to plead Zak's case. It wasn't like she hated Zak; she just realized that they were in different places in their lives right now. She couldn't imagine not being a huge part of Cassie's life and Zak wasn't ready to be around kids. It wasn't anyone's fault; it's just how it was. She called Rayne back, and they decided to meet on Wednesday.

******

When she met Rayne at the coffee shop they had agreed on, Rayne gave her a brief hug and thanked her for coming.

They talked about the upcoming wedding. "I really hope you will come," Rayne pleaded. "I hope that you will feel welcome even though Zak will be there. I don't know exactly what happened with you two, and

I don't need to if you don't want to talk about it."

"It's really not a huge thing. I just realized that we are in very different places in our lives right now. My sister died several weeks ago, and she left behind a little girl. I am trying to help my brother-in-law as much as I can with her, but Zak made it very clear that he doesn't have a place for any children in his life right now. And that's fine, I respect that, but I can't just put Cassie on hold for a guy. Cassie has to be my focus."

"Wow, I'm so sorry to hear about your sister. I totally understand what you are saying. Your niece needs you a lot right now. And I know that Zak has pretty much been a typical playboy from what I have heard about him. So it makes sense that you feel that way," Rayne consoled her. "Although I don't know if this means anything or not, but Walt was totally surprised that he didn't have a woman with him at the Labor Day picnic. Walt says he always brings some 'bimbo' to the party just to piss off his parents. This year he came alone, so maybe he's starting to think about things differently. Oh, who knows, I promised we wouldn't have to talk about Zak, and here I am, talking about Zak." Rayne laughed. "So tell me about you, your sister, your niece, whatever you want to talk about. I totally understand if some of those topics are too painful to talk about right now, though."

Skye began telling Rayne about Cassie and about Savannah. It was nice to be able to just share some of her memories. She got choked up at times, but Rayne just waited and put her hand gently on Skye's in a show of support and understanding. After she was done talking, she asked Rayne to tell her about how she had met Walt and anything else she wanted to share.

Rayne told Skye about how she had been a ballerina headed to the New York City Ballet, when she had been hurt in an accident. She told her about the rehabilitation facility and how Walt had come in as her attorney but had ended up being her knight in shining armor. He had pulled her out of a place of hopelessness and had given her a reason to not only live again but to dance as well. She talked about her dance school and how happy she was to be able to pass the experience on to other people. She offered for Skye or even Cassie when she was old enough to come and take classes.

"I'll definitely think about that," Skye said.

"We have daycare on site too, if that influences you at all," Rayne said with a wink.

"Even better." Skye smiled. "I would definitely love to see it sometime."

Rayne told her what days and hours they were open, but also offered a private tour anytime. Rayne also told her how romantic Walt had been when he proposed to her at the grand opening of the school.

They chatted a little while longer, and then got ready to part ways, but promised to stay in touch and Skye promised she would come to the wedding. She wouldn't let what was going on between her and Zak get in the way of enjoying a beautiful wedding.

"Actually, this may seem totally off the wall, but I really don't know many people. I was so engrossed in my dancing that I didn't really have time to hang out with friends. Would you consider being a bridesmaid? Walt has this whole list of men he wants to stand up with him and I've got very little resources to try to pair people up. I know that I am going to have to tell him that he just can't have all of them as groomsmen, but I hate to limit him to just one. The only person I have standing up with me so far is Sunni," Rayne explained. "If you think it's too weird, I totally understand."

"No, I actually understand quite well. I moved to Michigan to be closer to my sister. During the times that I had visited Savannah over the years, I met my best friend Autumn. But I don't know very many people either. I would be glad to help," Skye agreed.

"You are awesome," Rayne said, giving Skye a hug before they walked out of the café. "I'll let you know when the seamstress can see you for a fitting. I actually picked a color and am open to style. So you can pick any dress she has within my color scheme."

"Great. I look forward to hearing from you then," Skye said as they parted ways to go to their separate cars.

On Friday afternoon, Skye was with Cassie when she heard a car pull into the driveway. She glanced at the clock. It was a little early for David, but not so much that she was concerned until she heard the doorbell. When she opened the door, Zak was standing there looking oh so yummy in his suit with a briefcase in hand.

"Oh, Skye, sorry. I wasn't thinking. I am supposed to meet David to look over some paperwork. I'm probably early, but I can just wait in my car," Zak rambled.

"Don't be silly. You're welcome to come in. David should be here in fifteen minutes or so," Skye offered.

"Thanks," Zak said as he walked by her. "Well, hello, darlin'. Don't you look pretty today," Zak said as Skye closed the door.

Skye thought that was kind of an odd way for Zak to greet her. She turned around, ready to say something about where the hell that had come from when she realized he was talking to Cassie. Cassie was crawling to Zak, and when they met, Cassie stopped and reached both arms up. Zak picked the little girl up. He was talking to her and she was completely enamored. She gave him her biggest smile and was totally focused on him.

"That's really odd," Skye said. "She's usually hesitant around strangers, especially since Savannah died."

"Oh, we aren't strangers, are we, beautiful?" Zak asked Cassie. She just giggled at him. "No, we go way back, at least a few days," Zak said.

"You've been here before?" Skye asked.

This time, Zak turned to look at Skye. "Yeah, I stopped by to talk to David about the case on Tuesday."

Cassie just kept babbling at Zak, and he turned back to take in everything she was saying. "That's right, I agree totally." Silly little nonsense things about her babbling, but the little girl was obviously taken with Zak and the attention he was lavishing on her. Skye knew exactly how that felt.

Skye couldn't help but stare. Cassie was teething and was kind of drooly, but Zak didn't seem to notice, or if he did, he didn't mind. He just kept talking to her like he totally understood every single babble, and totally agreed. Who was this man? She was probably standing there with her mouth hanging open. Thank goodness Zak was too busy looking at Cassie to notice.

A few minutes later, David walked in. "Oh, hi Zak, I wondered if that was your car out there." Of course, as soon as she saw her daddy, Cassie immediately reached for him. He greeted the little girl as he always did when he got home from work. Zak didn't seem to be in any hurry. He waited patiently while David gave all his attention to his little girl. Skye excused herself and left. This was kind of feeling like the Twilight Zone to her.

Zak watched Skye walk across the driveway and go up the stairs on the side of the garage. David noticed him looking and said, "Yeah, Skye just moved into the apartment above the garage. I don't know what I would have done without her all these weeks. She's always here for Cassie, and she's been so strong for both of us. I know this settlement is supposed to be about Cassie and about me, but we wouldn't be functional if it hadn't been for Skye. I plan to do something for her, whether I win the case or not."

"Oh, you'll win, the company is already starting to backpedal. The criminal charges are hitting them hard. Now is the perfect time to hit them with the civil suit. They look guilty of some horrible things. Whether the courts find them guilty of it all or not won't be known for a while. So, we strike now, while they are all over the news, and try to get a court date set soon. In a civil case, it's not a matter of guilty or innocent, it's the percentage of responsibility for the accident that the jury has to decide. And they also have to decide on a dollar amount that they feel lines up with that responsibility," Zak explained.

David nodded. "I know nothing about this. I never thought I would sue anyone, but I understand that this is the way things go."

"I also wanted to stop by because I received an odd request," Zak continued. "The truck driver would like to have a chance to meet with you and apologize. First, you absolutely do not have to agree to his request. Secondly, if you do agree to his request, it would happen at my office, and there would be a record of the meeting. If he says anything that is out of line, the meeting ends. And, lastly, if you do meet with him, it in no way changes your ability to name him in the lawsuit." Zak stopped to let David take all that in.

David was quiet for a long while, pondering Zak's statement. "What would you do?" he finally asked.

Zak immediately started to object. "I can't tell you what to do. It's totally got to be your decision."

"I get that, but I'm asking, what would you do?" David asked again. "I don't have to do whatever you say you would do, but I'm curious."

"Okay, well, honestly, I personally would want to meet the guy. He's the one that is giving the prosecution all of their info in the criminal case. From what they have told me, he was very much under duress driving that day. He should have been somewhere sleeping, but the company told him to drive or find other employment. So I'd be curious what he had to say. It may be total BS and if it is, you walk out, and you have an impression of this guy and maybe have more of an idea if you want to name him in the law suit. If he is sincere, then you decide if you want to accept his apology or not. Just because you hear it doesn't mean you have to take it," Zak explained. "And you don't have to decide tonight."

David thought about that for a few minutes and then said that he would think about it and let Zak know. Zak handed him the paperwork that needed his signatures and took Cassie so that David could write. He really did think this little girl was adorable. He was sure that she wasn't always so happy and pleasant, and he probably wouldn't want to be around when she wasn't. But for now, she was adorable.

Chapter Twenty-Three

Saturday morning, Skye met Rayne at the bridal shop to look at bridesmaid dresses. Rayne had picked out a beautiful aquamarine color for them to wear. Sunni had chosen her style already, so all Skye had to do was pick something that would complement both the bride and the other bridesmaid. She chose a simple style with an empire waist and a medium length. It hit about halfway between her knee and her ankle. That should make it easy for walking and if there were any dancing at the reception it would flow nicely. Of course there would be dancing at the reception; it was a huge part of what had brought Rayne and Walt together. This would be a great dress for that. Although she didn't know if she would actually be doing any dancing. She assumed there would be one dance for the wedding party to participate in, but otherwise, she wasn't sure she would be dancing much.

When the seamstress put in a few pins to show them how it would look once it was tailored for Skye, it almost took her breath away. She had never owned such a beautiful dress in her life. In the small town she had grown up in, no one really dressed up for much of anything. She had been in her sister's wedding, but that had been a fairly small event and she had gotten a nice dress from the local boutique, but it hadn't been tailored to fit her and it had not been this beautiful. This dress had simple embellishments of iridescent pearls and small diamond-like stones along the empire waist and along the neckline. When she came out of the dressing room with it on, Rayne totally agreed that was the dress for her.

"It's beautiful on you. I never thought about it, but that color really brings out your eyes," Rayne enthused.

"It is, oh, my." Skye was in awe. This dress, with the right shoes and accessories, would be amazing. The dress was amazing in and of itself, but if she could find the right jewelry it would be even more stunning. She would feel like a princess in this dress, or a fairy if she had wings. It just flowed so beautifully. The seamstress had given her a puffy slip to wear under it so that the dress didn't hang flat.

When they were finished with Skye's dress, the seamstress had Rayne try her dress on again to make sure the things she had done were right. Skye loved the dress Rayne had picked out. Hers too was made for dancing, which made sense because dance had been a huge part of Rayne's life and also a key factor in what brought Rayne and Walt together as a couple.

After they were done at the dress shop, they went to a local deli for lunch. After they were seated, Rayne looked at Skye and said, "I have to tell you something and I don't think you are going to like it."

"Okay," Skye said hesitantly.

"So when my only bridesmaid was Sunni, I told Walt that he could only have one groomsman. No problem, Jason is basically his best friend. But when I added you, I told him he could pick one more. I figured there was about a 66 percent chance he would pick the right way. But he didn't. He went with the 33 percent odds." Rayne was kind of cringing.

"What do you mean 66 percent and 33 percent?" Skye looked puzzled and then dawning showed on her face. "Oh, there were three other sloths, there was a 66 percent chance he would pick Jeremy or Pete, but he went with the one other choice and picked Zak."

"Bingo," Rayne said. She really did look like she was afraid that Skye was going to be upset with her. "I was hoping that you would find a dress you loved so much that it wouldn't be so bad to find out that you would be walking down the aisle with Zak."

"Listen, it's fine." Skye assured her. "It's not like Zak and I hate each other. We just don't work. I've already seen him because he is David's lawyer and if that goes to court, I will be seeing him a lot more. Just because we don't work as a couple doesn't mean we can't function together like adults in your wedding."

"Are you sure?" Rayne asked. "I could tell Walt that it's not okay and he has to switch groomsmen. The other two are going to be ushers, so it's not like anyone is being left out. Zak can be an usher and Pete or Jeremy can take the groomsman spot."

"No, seriously, it's fine. This is the only time Walt will get married, he deserves to have the people he wants stand up with him." Skye paused and then added, "Zak is a conundrum to me anyway."

"What do you mean?" Rayne questioned.

"Well, yesterday, he stopped by David's house with some paperwork while I was still there. David hadn't gotten home yet. He walked in and immediately Cassie crawled right to him and asked him to pick her up. She usually isn't like that with new people. Especially since her mom's gone, she's been a little more clingy, which we totally get."

Rayne nodded her understanding of that.

Skye continued, "He picked her right up. She was all drooly because she's teething but he didn't seem to mind. And then, I about fainted when he started responding to her baby babble. Apparently, he was there earlier in the week when David was home and she took to him immediately. She even fell asleep on his shoulder and he went and laid her down in her crib."

"Seriously, that's not anything I've ever imagined with Zak. I haven't known him long, but I've always seen most of the guys as typical playboys," Rayne stated.

"I don't know. The way he came off before, I would have thought that kids were like the plague or something, and then I see him with Cassie, and he looks totally smitten. Although Cassie can have that effect on people," Skye admitted with a smile.

"Maybe it's Cassie, and maybe it's you," Rayne suggested. "Maybe he realized that he was being an ass about it all. I know he says he's not ready for kids, and I get that. I'm not really there either, but Cassie isn't with you 24/7, so maybe he's finally starting to see that it may be worth it to know her if it gives him time with you?"

Skye just shrugged; she really had no idea. She wished she could read Zak's mind and figure out what he was really thinking. But for now, she had to keep Cassie as her main focus.

She asked Rayne all about the details of the wedding. It was pretty easy to get the bride to talk about all of her plans and forget all about trying to match make Zak and Skye.

Rayne asked Skye if she wanted to invite her friend Autumn to the wedding so she would have a friend to hang out with. Rayne would be pretty busy with the guests, so she wanted Skye to feel like she had someone she knew to talk with. Skye agreed that it would be great to have her bestie there, so Rayne gave her an invitation to pass on to Autumn.

Chapter Twenty-Four

Zak got a phone call from David the following Tuesday saying that he would agree to meet with the truck driver, but he would also like Skye to be present. If the man wanted to apologize, he owed it to both of them and to Cassie, but she was too young to understand. David also made it clear that they wanted to have the right to respond if they felt the need to say something. David promised that they would keep it civil, but he did want the man to know that they might have questions or comments. Zak assured him that he would make that a stipulation to meeting with the man when he contacted the driver's attorney.

The meeting was set for Friday morning.

When Skye walked into his office, Zak wanted nothing more than to go and wrap his arms around her and tell her how much he had missed her. But he had lost the right to do that. The biggest problem was that he had lost the right to touch her over something that he had said totally wrong from how he meant it. He hadn't meant it to sound like he expected her to give up her time with her niece. He had just been relieved to find out that she wasn't actually a single mom, because he just wasn't sure he was ready to have that responsibility all the time. He totally got that she had to help with Cassie, and after having met the sweet little girl, he saw the attraction of wanting to be a part of her life. He just didn't know how to backpedal without it sounding like he was just trying to get her back. He totally was trying to get her back, but he didn't want it to sound like he was only saying things so that she would think he had changed and take him back. He wanted her to know that he was completely sincere in what he felt now, not what he had seemed to be saying then.

He dreamed of her pretty much every night. Sometimes he saw her with Cassie, sometimes he saw that little brown-haired boy, sometimes he just saw her. The worst ones were the ones where he watched her walk away and no matter how hard he tried or how loudly he yelled, she never turned around and came back to him. Those were the ones that made him wake up in a cold sweat. He would not let himself believe that he would never get her back. He just had to figure out how.

"David, Skye, thanks for coming today," Zak said. "Please take a seat." They were in one of the small conference rooms at the law firm. The truck driver and his attorney wouldn't be allowed back until Zak informed his admin that it was okay. He wanted to talk to David and Skye first.

"I wanted to go over a couple of things before we get started. First, as you know, this is a civil case, not a criminal case. If it were a criminal case, I have no doubt that the attorney for the driver would not have requested this meeting. In a criminal case, if the driver said the wrong thing, he could be found guilty of a crime. In a civil case, if we sue him, it isn't a matter of innocence or guilt. It's a matter of how much or what damage was done and who is responsible for that damage. It also doesn't have to be a 100 percent thing. A person can be found at fault in a civil case if they are even 51 percent responsible for the reason of the case. Percentage of responsibility is also used in determining the amount of settlement at times. For example, if there was a loss of a million dollars the jury would most likely find that the person who was 51 percent responsible would have to pay 51 percent of the amount of damage, while the person who was 49 percent responsible would have to absorb 49 percent of the loss. This situation is a little different because you can't put a price on a life. Oh, sure, there are ways to figure some of it out, such as if there was a loss of income, that would most definitely be a part of the calculation of loss. What you have to decide is if you want to pursue a case against this man. If you do, the jury will have to determine what percentage of the loss was caused by the illegal actions of the company and what percentage was caused by the driver. It's never an easy thing to calculate, but that's basically a simplified explanation of what happens in these cases. If you decide not to sue the driver, the jury will still determine if he had a percentage of fault and the trucking company would have to pay their percentage, but the driver would not if he isn't named in the suit."

Zak looked from David to Skye. "I know that's a lot of legal mumbo jumbo, but do you understand the basic concept anyway?"

They both said that they did.

"Great, so I have talked to his attorney and it's been agreed that the driver has a statement that he would like to make. You will then be allowed to ask questions and make a statement if you choose to. It's also agreed upon that if either side becomes belligerent or violent, the meeting is over, and the case will proceed within the court system." Zak then asked if they were ready for the meeting or if they had any questions first.

Neither of them had any questions, so Zak called his admin to send them back. A minute later, a woman in a business suit preceded a man who looked to be in his late fifties into the room. They both went to the opposite side of the table. The attorneys greeted each other and shook hands. The driver seemed to be mostly looking down at the table.

When they were all seated, Zak began, "I have already explained this to my clients, but just to clarify that we are all still in agreement, Mr. Sanderson will make his prepared statement, after which my clients will have the opportunity to ask questions, or make a statement of their own if they so desire."

"As another point of business, I have told my clients and I want to make sure your client understands that agreeing to this meeting in no way obligates them to not pursue a lawsuit against Mr. Sanderson if they so desire," Zak stated, then looked at the other attorney and the man across the table. "Is that agreed upon?"

The attorney and the driver both stated that they understood.

The man's attorney looked at him and nodded for him to begin. It was at that point that he finally looked up and made eye contact with both David and Skye in turn.

Skye realized that while the man might appear to be in his fifties as far as hair and stature, his face had the haggard appearance of a man much older.

As he began speaking, his voice faltered often from the emotion of what he wanted to say. "First, I know that there is absolutely nothing I can say that will make up for the horrible pain that you have experienced. And no apology is going to make you feel any better. So, while I will say that I am so very very sorry for what I did, I thought if I could at least explain what happened from my point of view, you would at least have a better understanding of the situation." He paused and took a deep breath, and then continued. "I had been driving for basically fifteen hours straight. Other than fuel and bathroom breaks, I had been on the road. Regulations say that I am only supposed to drive about eleven hours of that before taking a mandatory sleep break. I should not have been behind the wheel of that truck that day. I knew I shouldn't be behind the wheel, but my company had other feelings. If I didn't make the delivery before the receiver closed for the day, my job was in jeopardy. Looking back, I should have quit that company a long time ago. As soon as I realized that the company had jimmy-rigged the EOBR on their trucks, I should have left the company altogether."

Skye and David both had puzzled looks on their faces, so Zak said, "If I may, could you explain to my clients what the EOBR is and what it does?"

"Sorry, an EOBR is an electronic on-board recorder," he said. "It is a device that is supposed to limit the number of hours a truck can roll down the road. It records and reports to agencies like the Department of Transportation how many hours that truck has been in motion. It is supposed to make it so that the truck's engine can keep going, for heat purposes and all of that, but the actual drive train won't engage for a set number of hours to insure that drivers take a break and sleep. The trucking company had found a way to disable that. If we were stopped by the DOT our numbers always appeared to be legitimate, but they weren't. We were often put in positions where we drove twice the amount of time we are supposed to by law. Like I said, I should have left the company as soon as I knew that. But I guess we all have a certain amount of feeling invincible in us. I convinced myself that I needed that job, so I would do what it took." Mr. Sanderson shook his head at his own foolishness.

"Anyway, I know I had no business being behind the wheel that day. And very honestly, I did not know that I had caused an accident until the police came to my company looking for records of who had been driving that route that day. Eyewitnesses had reported the name of the trucking company from the accident. When I was told that someone had died because of my carelessness, I submitted my resignation. The company wants me to stay quiet, of course, so instead of having me resign, they gave me early retirement. They paid me out on my 401k and retirement benefits." He looked directly into David's eyes and stated, "It feels too much like blood money to me, if you know what I mean. I don't want that money under these circumstances. I want you to know, I am not doing this to try to convince you not to sue me. I believe you have every right to do that. This is separate from that; I have talked to my attorney and she tells me that it is completely legal for me to take my retirement pay out and put it into a college fund for your little girl. I don't want that money for myself, but if it can do something good in this godawful situation, then that is what I want to do." He paused and looked down at his own folded hands for a moment and the tears started quietly rolling down his face. He looked back up and said, "I will never forgive myself for taking that little girl's mother from her or for your loss of a wife and sister, and I know that this doesn't make up for that loss, but I am hoping that you will let me do this so that college is one thing you won't have to worry about for her future."

David and Skye both had tears in their eyes, and they were holding hands on the table. Skye looked at David and squeezed his hand to let him know that she was 100 percent behind whatever decision he made. David took a while before he answered and then said, "I understand what you mean about this feeling like blood money. I would not take it if I felt like you were trying to persuade me not to sue, nor would I take it if I felt that you were trying to absolve yourself of any guilt in this accident. But I don't feel that you are. I think you honestly just want to try to make that money at least help in some way." He looked the man in the eyes and said, "I still have not decided what I am going to do about the lawsuit, but I will accept a college fund for my daughter as long as there is no stipulation that she ever have to know where that money came from. She doesn't need to experience that. Right now she is too little to understand what is going on, and she won't be reminded of it later in life when this money becomes available to her. You have no right to know my daughter or speak to my daughter or have any contact at all with my daughter. If this is set up totally anonymously, it would be unfair of me to decline something that could help her have a brighter future."

With that, Mr. Sanderson nodded and said a very quiet "Thank you." His attorney took a file out of her case and handed it to Zak. "As you can see, the fund has already been set aside. All you need to do is read this and if you agree, have your client sign it and fill in the name and information of who the account belongs to for the future."

Zak took the paperwork and sat it on the table, then he stood and escorted the two visitors out to the hallway that would lead them to the elevators. When he returned, he stood outside the door because Skye and David were talking, and he didn't want to interrupt.

"Do you think I did the right thing?" David asked.

"I think so. I didn't get the sense that he had any ill intent in doing this. I think he really does feel bad about what he did, and he definitely doesn't want to profit from it. The money will help Cassie, regardless of how much it is. It's a start on her college fund," Skye consoled him.

When it seemed like they were done talking, Zak reentered the room. He picked up the file and opened it. "This looks to be in order. I can fill it out, or you can. It's basic information, like Cassie's full name, current address, parent or guardian name, things like that. It's been set up at one of the local banks, pending this information being returned so that the account can be placed in Cassie's name." He handed the paperwork to David for him to look over.

David wasn't really sure what half of this meant, so he asked if Zak could help him fill it out. They sat together and filled in Cassie and David's information. David signed it where Zak told him to and then Zak picked up the file and said, "I can drop this off at the local branch. When it's all filed with the bank, you should get a statement for Cassie's $100,000 college fund."

David and Skye both looked at each other with stunned expressions. "When he said it was his retirement, I was thinking maybe ten to twenty thousand tops," David said. "I had no idea it would be that much."

"Yes, Cassie will be able to go to pretty much any school she chooses when she is old enough, and this will also gain interest, so it will be more than that when the day comes," Zak informed them.

David had a decent income, but with normal expenses, a mortgage, car payments and things, he would have never had a college account of that size for Cassie. It still kind of felt like blood money, not so much on Sanderson's part, but definitely on the part of the trucking company. They were obviously trying to get Sanderson to have some sort of loyalty to them but, from what Zak had told him, Sanderson was the biggest informant on what the trucking company had done wrong.

Zak knew he couldn't get into a discussion of what had gone wrong between him and Skye right here at the firm and not with David standing there, but he did say to Skye, "I miss you Skye, and if you can give me a chance to explain, I would appreciate it."

Skye just looked at him and nodded. She was beginning to thaw a bit when it came to him. She was seeing that she might have misunderstood his intentions, but she just wasn't at the place that she could talk about it yet. Maybe after the case was done and he wasn't David's attorney, after things had been settled and they were more comfortable with the new normal they were trying to build since Savannah's death. She walked out of the office before she could break down. She had to be strong in front of David. She didn't want him to think that he and Cassie were a burden or that they were standing between her and Zak. It had nothing to do with her commitments to her family and everything to do with Zak not wanting children in his life.

Chapter Twenty-Five

When David and Skye got back home, they thanked Autumn for watching Cassie while they were gone, and Autumn left after Skye promised her they would have another girls' day soon. David asked Skye if she could stay for a while so they could talk. He felt he needed her opinion on some things.

"I really want your opinion on what to do with the lawsuit," David began. "The company, that's hands down. Obviously, I am going to do what I can to make them pay. You know that it's not at all about the money, but they were doing things illegally that caused this accident to happen. I hope they get the book thrown at them for the legal aspects, and I hope they have to go completely out of business. I don't care if I only get one dollar from them because they are out of business and broke; it is the principle of them being held responsible. But, honestly, I don't know what to do about the driver."

"I agree, it's a tough one to decide," Skye began. "I guess what I see is that he really is remorseful. And not just because he started the college fund for Cassie. It was on his face, and he even admitted that as soon as he found out that he had caused an accident, he resigned. The company just kept up their horrible business practices until the police stepped in and stopped them. They gave the guy his retirement money hoping to keep him quiet. I wouldn't be surprised if they padded that some too. They wanted it to be a payoff for him to stay quiet."

"Right, that's what I was thinking," David agreed. "And I've never done anything illegal, but I think everyone who has a job has at times been faced with a situation or a boss that wants you to cut corners. Some of those corners don't really hurt anyone, but some of them do. Big companies are in trouble all the time for releasing a drug before it's fully ready or for using a lower grade of lumber to make a project cheaper."

"Yeah, it's not generally the workers that want to cut corners. They are usually told by the higher-ups to do it or leave." Skye said. "I know that even at the fitness center, rules get lax at times. I guess what you need to decide is if you feel that he is being honest when he says the company made it obvious to their employees that they needed to do this or find other jobs."

"It says a lot to me that he was the one to give the information to the police. The company most likely believed that he would remain loyal, especially after the pay-out, but he went to the police anyway," David stated. "I guess I feel like the guy has already made restitution for his mistakes, but if you don't agree, I need to know it. I know that I am the one bringing the lawsuit, but you have a stake in this too."

"No, I do agree. I don't think suing him would prove much of anything at this point. Like you said, it's not about the money, it's about responsibility and he obviously feels responsible and is trying to make up for it," Skye agreed.

"Okay, then that decision is made. Now, on a personal note," David continued, "did I sense something going on between you and Zak? He was looking at you like a man who is really into you, but you won't give him the time of day."

"We had a little fling before I knew he was your attorney. It was just a couple of weekends of fun. We both agreed before anything started that neither of us was in the right place to consider something more than just 'no strings attached fun.' Then when I did meet him as your attorney, some things kind of clicked into place for both of us and I realized it just wasn't going to work," Skye said. David thought she looked like she really wasn't happy with the fact that it hadn't worked out.

"You do know that he's my attorney, so there is nothing saying you can't have a relationship with him, no strings attached or any other kind, right?" David asked.

"I know, and it had nothing to do with him being your attorney. We just realized that we are in different places. He's not ready to get serious and have kids or even consider kids, and while I'm not ready to have my own kids, I am a big part of Cassie's life and I intend to stay that way. I don't think he can accept that right now," Skye stated.

"You don't think he can, or he told you he can't?" David asked pointedly.

"I just don't see it working, right now anyway, that's all," Skye said with finality.

"Okay, well, you know your situation better than I do, but knowing that does make some other things make more sense to me now," David admitted.

"Like what?"

"Oh, just some things that he said the first time he came over and met Cassie. It's not important. I'm not even sure that he said what I thought I heard," David admitted. "I just don't want me or Cassie to stand in the way of your happiness. If you need to back off a little to focus more on you, you have every right to do so. I appreciate what you do for Cassie and me. But we do have to figure out our lives without Savannah, and that doesn't mean that you have to give up yours."

"I know," Skye assured him. "I'm not doing anything that I don't want to do one hundred percent."

"Okay, but if you need me to find other day care or babysitters for Cassie so you have more time for yourself, please let me know. I would feel horrible if you gave up something you really wanted to be able to take care of us."

"I will," Skye assured him.

Chapter Twenty-Six

David called Zak the following Monday to let him know what he had decided about the lawsuit. He told him that he had decided against going after the driver, because he felt the company was really the most responsible for the situation. He also asked Zak if there was any chance that they could meet for dinner or something; he had some other things he wanted to discuss. Zak agreed, assuming he was probably wanting to make sure that Cassie was provided for in case something happened to David, and maybe he even wanted to make sure that Skye would get custody of Cassie if anything happened to him. Whatever it was, Zak told him he would be glad to meet. He suggested that they meet at Five Sloths on Tuesday. Zak would be managing, but it really wasn't difficult to have a meeting while managing the place; he was usually just there in case. And he called Jason just to let him know that he was going to be talking to a client for a while in case Jason wanted to drop by too just to make sure they were covered.

When David got to the brewery, Zak seated him at the same table where he had sat with Skye and let him pick his brew. "So, what's up, David? Is there some other legal information you need, or are you just wanting to go over the case so you feel more at ease when we get to court?"

"Neither. I want your side of what happened between you and my sister-in-law," David said point blank.

"Oh, she told you about that?" Zak kind of hedged. He wasn't sure what Skye had said, most likely she had made him look like the bad guy, because, let's face it, he actually was.

"Not much," David conceded. "I admit that I noticed that you two seemed to know each other, but not be comfortable with each other the other day at your office. So I asked her. She said that basically you two are just at different places in your life and so it wasn't going to work. I have a feeling that it's because she is so involved with Cassie and that isn't something you feel okay with. I don't want to be what stands between Skye and someone that she may really have a connection with."

"That's not completely accurate. And I'm the one at fault for what made Skye walk away." Zak ran his hand through his hair and then continued. "A few weeks ago, I saw Skye getting out of your SUV at the fitness center. Basically, she was the most beautiful woman I had ever seen. And then she got into the back seat and pulled out Cassie. So immediately, my mind jumped to the logical conclusion that she's a single mom." Zak took a drink of his microbrew to try to keep his courage up. This guy was probably going to realize that Skye had dodged a huge bullet when they split up. "Anyway, not that this justifies it, but my parents and I have been going at it a lot lately. They want me to settle down and get serious, think about marriage, and maybe start planning for maybe having kids and a house. I have balked at that idea, mainly because of how much they shove it at me. So anyway, I was not in the market for a single mom, at least I was pretty sure I wasn't, but Skye was so beautiful, and I kept thinking about her. I decided to join the gym to meet her, and fairly quickly, I asked her out, with the stipulation that it be a no strings kind of thing. I never told her that I thought she had a kid and that was why I wanted to keep things simple between us. I admit that I am a horrible person, but I wanted the sex without being tied down to a kid." Zak paused to take another drink. "Anyway, fast forward a few great weekends of getting to know her and spend time with her and in she walks to give me her statement in your case. It was then that I realized that she was not Cassie's mom; she was her aunt. I handled it horribly because I was excited to know that she didn't have a kid. I know, totally an ass. But in my mind, that solved all the problems. With no kid, we could maybe have more of a relationship because I didn't have to think about a kid in the mix. I came across as wanting her to basically pick me over Cassie. I never said that, but I think it was kind of implied when I was so excited to know that she didn't have any 'real commitment' to Cassie." Zak used the actual air quotes with his fingers. "Skye basically told me how wrong I was if I thought that she didn't have a commitment to Cassie, and pretty much told me to stick it and walked out."

"Ouch, I get where that would definitely set her off. But I have to tell you, as valuable as she is to both Cassie and me, if you have real feelings for her, I don't want to stand in the way of that," David conceded.

"I appreciate that, but I don't really know for sure what Skye and I have. Probably nothing at this point," Zak admitted.

"I have one more question," David interjected. "When you held Cassie that first time, I thought I heard you say, 'I get it now.' Is that what I heard?"

"Yeah. I've never really held a baby. I've been around one that a friend of mine has. He's not a baby anymore, and I have seen him since he was born. But I hadn't really spent much time with him until he was basically walking and talking and past the baby stage. When I held Cassie, and she let out that deep sigh of contentment in my arms, I could see how small she is and how much anyone like Skye would want to help her have as normal of a life as possible without a mom. She's so sweet, and at this stage pretty much helpless. It made me remember how much my mom was always there for me when I was growing up. And despite how much we don't always see eye to eye on my life right now, I know that she has always wanted the best for me," Zak explained.

David let all that sink in, for both of them. Then he just nodded. "That makes sense, and thanks for explaining it to me. And I will say that Skye doesn't have family besides Cassie and me. If you decide you want to be a part of our family, I would welcome you, but if that's not something you are interested in, I will be Skye's big brother and protect her if you hurt her." He met Zak in the eyes and Zak could tell that he was serious on both accounts.

"I hear you; I don't think Skye wants anything more to do with me anyway," Zak said.

"I think you would be wrong on that," David objected. "I admit, she's going to be skeptical for a while, but I think she really does miss being with you." David stood to leave, but before he walked away, he pulled out a pen and wrote something on a napkin. He handed it to Zak and said, "If you do decide to listen to your mom, there's a really great house up for sale by this realty company. It just happens to be next door to mine, you know, if you want to have good neighbors or whatever." He smiled and then walked away.

Chapter Twenty-Seven

Walt's bachelor party was in full swing at Walt's house. Pete, Jeremy and Jason had threatened to hire strippers if they had it at the brewery on a night they were closed, so Walt had offered his home. He had a large home, and he had a housekeeper that knew how to cook and make great snacks for the party. Walt had promised Rayne that if any strippers showed up at the door, he would not let them in. Rayne was on her way out to her bachelorette party too. She was getting together with some girlfriends over at some spa that was staying open late so they could all have a night of pampering and champagne.

For the most part, the bachelor party was a lot more like a bunch of guys getting together to eat and talk sports than what most men had for bachelor parties. No wild parties for these guys, at least not now that one of them was seriously in love with his soon-to-be wife. Walt and Zak were out on the back deck catching a breath of fresh air. Rayne had said that the guys could drink and have cigars, but only in the media room. She didn't want to be trying to get that smell out of her living room furniture. Funny how she wasn't even married to him yet, but she was definitely the queen of her castle. And Walt was what a lot of single guys would call "whipped," but Zak was starting to see it in a different way. He would say that Walt was content, he was in love, and he was happy.

"So how did you end up here?" Zak joked.

"What, in love and getting married?" Walt asked.

"Yeah. I guess I just didn't see any of us getting to this point until at least mid-thirties," Zak admitted.

"Hell, I didn't either," Walt said. "But when the right woman comes along, you just can't help but want her in your life more and more and eventually you realize that you want her there forever."

"I hear that," Zak said quietly.

"Wait, are we talking about Skye here?" Walt asked. "I thought you were just having some fun with her and now it's over."

"Yeah, that's what I thought it was too. At first, when I found out she wasn't a single mom, she was an aunt, I blew the whole thing by my stupid comments. I still thought it was probably for the best. I mean even though she's not the mom, she is very much a huge part of Cassie's life and that won't be changing anytime soon. So I figured things had worked out the way they were supposed to."

"Something happen to change your mind on that?" Walt asked.

"I don't know that I have fully changed my mind, but I did have to go to David's house for some legal business one day. And Cassie was there. She held her arms out to me, so I figured what the heck, how hard can it be to hold a baby? And I needed David to look at some papers, so I took the baby."

"And, she won you over." It was more of a statement than a question from Walt.

"She snuggled her head down on my shoulder and gave this sigh that was so huge for such a little thing. I felt her warm breath hit my neck, and within seconds, she was asleep," Zak admitted. "It kind of made me think of my mom. As much as we disagree on things now, she was always there for me when I was growing up. You know that our dads were always busy building this big law firm, but our moms took up all that slack and were always there."

"Yeah, that's very true," Walt said. "I'm still not really close to my dad. But our moms were always great at filling that void."

"Right. So, I got it, I understood why Skye has to place so much importance on Cassie. She doesn't have a mom to do that, so it falls on Skye, at least for now," Zak explained.

Walt nodded his head in understanding, and then said, "And you fell in love."

"What? No, I'm not in love, but I do understand things differently now," Zak argued.

"Would you like to rethink that statement?" Walt asked. "I think you fell in love with Skye and you kind of fell in love with Cassie that day too."

Zak thought about that. Had he fallen in love? Did he even really know what love was? He didn't think so on either account.

"Okay, humor me here," Walt said. "How many nights a week do you have any type of dream about Skye?" Zak just looked at him like he was pretty sure Walt knew the answer. "Okay, then how many times a week do you have a dream that has Skye in it that isn't sexual in nature?"

"I don't know, maybe four or five," Zak admitted.

"And, last question, have you ever, while awake or sleeping, seen Skye in an event that you know is in the future?"

Zak just sort of growled and shook his head, not as a sign of a negative answer but as a 'how the hell did this happen' sort of thing.

"Well," Walt said, "I can honestly tell you that there are worse things a man can do than fall in love with a beautiful, smart woman."

"Let's just keep this to ourselves for now, okay?" Zak said.

"Deal," Walt agreed. "But for what it's worth, I'm betting that Jason isn't far behind you."

"You think he and Sunni—" Zak didn't finish the question; they both knew what he was asking.

Walt stood up to head back into the party and looked at Zak and said, "Pretty sure, yeah."

Zak nodded; he could see Walt's point. So far, Jason was keeping it simple because he wasn't sure how to handle things with Sunni once she knew about his son, and he wasn't sure how well his son would handle a woman in Jason's life. But he really did seem to be into Sunni way more than he had with any other woman. Even Ryan's mother.

The next day, Zak called the realtor; it wasn't like it would hurt to go look at the house. Maybe he could use it as an investment property. She was available to show it to him that afternoon and he took her up on that. Skye would be at the gym, so she wouldn't see him there and think he was being a stalker or something.

The neighborhood wasn't one of the most affluent in the area, like where his parents lived, but the house was a really great home. It had a lot of character. It was older, but not historic, and it had been refurbished with a lot of modern aspects. It was a four-bedroom, four bathroom home. The kitchen was ultra-modern. He didn't even know if Skye cooked, but that wouldn't matter; he could always hire someone like Walt did if needed. He asked the realtor if he could just walk through on his own after she had shown him around and pointed out all the features. He walked into the master bedroom, which wasn't huge but could definitely hold a king size bed with room for a comfortable chair and nightstands. The walk-in closet wasn't as big as Walt's, but it had plenty of room for two people to adequately store all their stuff. The master bath was great, a deep bathtub big enough for two with a separate shower if one wanted to soak while the other was hurrying off to work.

He walked down the hall. The first bedroom from the master was decent sized. Most couples would consider it for a nursery. He liked the house; it would be perfect for a family. Not that he had a family, but he might someday. As he turned the corner to go back downstairs to look at the finished basement again, for a brief second, his mind pictured a little brown-haired boy chasing a little brown-haired girl down the hallway. He shook off the image. He really was losing it.

The basement was finished for the most part. It was divided into two parts, not really halves. More like two thirds and one third. The smaller would made a great workout room/gym and the other would be a good place for a big TV and comfortable couches. Yes, he was still primarily looking at this as a bachelor pad. He had no reason to be sure that it would ever be anything else. But it was right next to David's house. Maybe Skye would at least consider spending time with him there. If not, he could always watch the real estate market and sell when it was optimal.

As he pulled away from the property, he saw a little girl riding a bicycle down the road. This one wasn't a dream, she was a real girl, but it was proof that this was a great neighborhood for kids.

Chapter Twenty-Eight

Two weeks after the meeting with Mr. Sanderson, Skye was walking down her stairs to go to David's when she noticed a moving van at the house next door. It had been empty for a few months, so apparently they were going to have new neighbors. She tried to see over the fence what they were moving in to try to get an idea of what type of family it might be; ages of kids and that type of thing was often pretty easy to figure out by what was being moved in. She didn't really notice anything that was a dead giveaway on who it might be, so she went in to David's house to gather Cassie up; she was taking her to the park. It was getting to be chilly most days and today would likely be one of the last with warmer temperatures and sun. Next weekend was the wedding and then it would be Halloween and not long after that the snow would fly in Michigan and they would all mostly hibernate for several months.

"I see we are getting new neighbors," she said to David as she walked into the kitchen.

"Yeah, seems like a pretty good guy. I met him," David said.

"Do you know how many kids they have?"

"None, it's a single guy," David said. He was feeding Cassie, so he didn't look up at Skye.

"Hmm, that's kind of odd, this is kind of a family neighborhood. Not many single guys would want to live there unless they are creepers or something." Skye laughed.

"No, he doesn't seem like that to me," David said. "Seemed like a pretty professional guy. Maybe he's starting a family soon and wants to have a place."

"Maybe. Still seems odd though," Skye said. She was still trying to see if she could see anything over the fence. "Is Cassie almost ready to go? I figure this might be one of the last days that the park is an option, so I was going to walk her down there if you don't mind."

"That's fine with me. Just a few more bites." He continued to feed his little girl. When he finished feeding her and started to wipe her up, he asked her if she was excited to go to the park. She babbled in her typical baby way and giggled.

She was such a happy little girl. Fortunately, she was really too young to understand anything that had happened these last few months. Skye put Cassie in the stroller and began down the street toward the park on the corner of the next block. She still couldn't imagine why a single guy would want to move into this neighborhood. Of course, maybe he was newly single and had kids that he had full or partial custody of. That would be a definite possibility and so would what David had said: maybe the guy was single now, but was getting married soon and hoping to start a family right away. If he was a professional like David seemed to think, he might be ready to settle down. He'd gotten his career on track and now it was time to start a family and move to the next stage of life.

Of course, when she thought of weddings and getting married, she thought about Rayne and Walt. Their wedding was only a week away. She was so excited for Rayne, but she really was not looking forward to seeing Zak. She knew she had to get over it and deal with it. It wasn't like she had to spend all day with him. Walk down the aisle, stand through the ceremony, walk back up the aisle and one dance at the reception. She could handle that. She would handle that, for Rayne and Walt. They really were nice people. She had really enjoyed herself at the bachelorette party. She had taken Autumn too. Rayne had said the more the merrier, so she had asked Autumn to go with her. Autumn was going to the wedding too; she was Skye's plus one. She didn't have any guys she would want to invite, so her bestie got to be her plus one. And that would help with the whole Zak thing too. She would have Autumn there to help shield her from Zak if he approached. She could always claim her friend was ill and they needed to leave. She would meet her obligations, but there was nothing saying that she had to stay for the whole party if it was too uncomfortable to be there.

While Skye was pushing the swing for Cassie, she thought she saw Zak's car drive by. She was sure it was his; not too many people drove little bright yellow sports cars in town, especially not in this neighborhood. Maybe he had some paperwork for David, or maybe he had another client in this area. She didn't know, but she felt his eyes on her as he drove slowly down the street.

When she was done at the park, she lingered a little longer because she was hoping that she would see Zak's car pull back past, signaling that he was leaving the neighborhood, but she hadn't seen him, and it was very possible that he had gone another direction. She was hoping to not run into him at David's, but she couldn't keep her niece out here forever; the day was starting to get more cloudy and the air more chilled. So, Zak or no Zak, she needed to head home. She didn't see Zak's car anywhere along the way and thankfully he wasn't in David's driveway either.

"Was Zak here at all today?" she asked when she saw David.

"No, why?" David asked.

"I just thought that I saw his car when we were at the park, so I thought maybe he had to stop by here about the case," she explained. She thought that David was kind of acting weird, but maybe it was just her own mind. Maybe she hadn't even seen Zak's car. She was seeing him in her dreams often, so maybe now he was an apparition in her waking hours too.

Skye made sure David didn't need anything else from her and she headed up to her apartment. She needed a drink and maybe a long bath, or maybe a bath and a few drinks so she could sleep. She was pretty sure after having seen what she thought was Zak's car, she wouldn't get through the night without dreams of him.

****

Zak had seen Skye at the park with Cassie, and a huge part of him wanted to stop. He thought about making it about Cassie, that he had noticed her and wanted to say hi. But he was pretty sure that Skye would have seen right through that. He needed to stick to the original plan. He only had a week to wait before he would see her at the wedding, and he would hopefully get a chance to talk to her and try to convince her that he had finally seen the light.

It had taken Walt to convince him that it was love. He wouldn't have used that word personally, but when he thought about it, Walt was completely right: he was falling in love with Skye. He didn't know what the future held for them, if that little brown-haired boy was a real glimpse into his future or not. But he knew that he would never know what could or would be if he couldn't get her to at least sit down and let him apologize for his idiocy when he had found out she was Cassie's aunt and not her mother, and hopefully ask her to give him a chance to see if they could build something real. He would explain that what he had said on the spur of the moment had come out wrong and it wasn't completely how he felt. He had realized that he had no problem with her helping with Cassie, and he wasn't opposed to being around the little girl himself. He had just meant that he wasn't ready for kids full time and it had come out all wrong. He hoped that would sound plausible to Skye.

Chapter Twenty-Nine

It was finally the day of Walt and Rayne's wedding. Skye was looking forward to it and dreading it at the same time. She knew that she was going to have to be close to Zak, and that was going to be difficult to do without wanting to go back to what they had before. She was resolved to be the best bridesmaid she could be and focus on making sure that Rayne's special day went off flawlessly, even if that meant that she had to ignore her feelings for Zak and act like they hadn't had a relationship in the past, one that she really wished was still happening in the present. But the point was that there really was no future in that, so wishing wasn't going to change how Zak felt about kids, and hoping wasn't going to change the fact that she was needed to help with Cassie for the foreseeable future. She would never hope that she didn't feel the commitment to Cassie and David, but she could hope that someday that wouldn't matter to Zak.

When she got to the small church where the wedding was being held, she saw Zak's car in the parking lot. She most likely wouldn't see him until the ceremony was starting because the groomsmen were kept away from the bridesmaids so that the groom didn't see the bride in her dress before she was walking down the aisle.

Skye had tried on her dress with the seamstress a few times, and had tried it with her shoes, but she had never had the full ensemble put together until today. Rayne had bought her a necklace that was beautiful, and she had small pins in her hair that had the same gems that were in the necklace, small aquamarines that matched her dress but also matched her eyes. She felt like a fairytale princess in the outfit. She had gone earlier that morning to have her hair put into an up-do. The pins were scattered all around her hair so that whichever way she turned her head, there were sparkles in the mirror.

"Oh, my God," Sunni exclaimed. "You look amazing. My dress is beautiful, but the color doesn't match my eyes like it does yours. It's like the whole thing was made just for your coloring."

Skye thanked her and told her she was beautiful too; Rayne had picked out the most amazing colors and accents for the whole wedding.

It was a small church, one that apparently Rayne had gone to as a small child. The ceremony was limited to mainly close friends and family because of the size of the church. It was a beautiful historic building. The setting was perfect for a fairytale wedding. The decorations were almost mystical. The groomsmen were on one side of the church, the bridesmaids on the other in small rooms waiting for the ceremony to start. Apparently, Walt would be waiting at the front, but Jason and Zak would be walking their partners down the aisle. Skye and Zak were to go first so that they could step apart and take their place on the appropriate sides of the church. They hadn't had a rehearsal because it was only the six of them and it was going to be a really simple ceremony. It was easy to just explain; they didn't really need to practice. Skye had been relieved to hear that because it meant one less time she had to see Zak and try to remain unaffected by his presence.

****

As he walked up the steps to get into his position for the processional of the wedding, Zak stumbled a little when he saw Skye directly across the lobby from him. She looked more beautiful than any woman he had ever seen in his life. Her hair was partially pulled up but was left down and free in small curls around her face and chin. It looked like she had little blue diamonds in her hair, diamonds the same color as her eyes and her dress. He didn't know anything about styles or fashion for women, but the dress looked like it had been designed specifically for Skye. It fit her perfectly, and it was just the right combination of elegant and sexy. At least he thought she was sexy. Maybe that wasn't what someone else would call the dress, but it was incredibly sexy to him. Not that it showed of a lot of skin, or cleavage, it just fit her so perfectly and while not showing off too much skin, it did give just a hint of the beautiful curves that he knew were beneath that dress.

When he stumbled, Walt had bumped into him and at first had said, "What the..." but he trailed off when he saw what Zak was looking at and just changed it to, "You're in trouble, man. She is gorgeous, every guy at the reception is going to be all over her."

"Not if I have anything to say about it," Zak grumbled. "I don't plan to leave her side." At least that was Zak's plan. He wasn't sure that Skye would agree, but he sure as hell was going to try. He had some plans for the day.

Skye looked up and across the small room and her eyes met Zak's. She saw the heat in his eyes and the appreciation he had for her appearance. She thought she saw some pain there too, but she wasn't sure. She realized that even though she hadn't meant to, she had really fallen hard for Zak. It was going to take a long while before she was over him. That was okay, though. She wouldn't have to worry about how long it took to get over him; she wasn't planning on even dating until Cassie was a little older.

They continued to the top of the stairs into the small vestibule. He put out his elbow and Skye dutifully placed her hand in the crook of his arm. He felt a zing of electricity go through him; did she feel it too? He looked at her and she had a stunned look on her face and started to pull her hand away as if she had been burned. He just placed his hand over hers to keep it in place and said, "I feel it too, Skye. We have things we need to talk about later. But I have to say you are amazingly beautiful today."

"Thank you," Skye said quietly. She had felt that electric zap when they first touched. And she had to admit that Zak looked amazing in anything, but Zak in a tuxedo was beyond human comprehension. His shirt matched her dress perfectly. Of course, that was the way Rayne had planned it because they were paired up for the wedding, even if they weren't a couple anymore.

She wasn't sure that they had anything to talk about, but she would do him the courtesy of listening to what he wanted to say, and then she would tell him that she thought it best if they considered what happened to be forgiven but also keep it in the past. She didn't need reminders of the amazing times they had had together, and she needed to make her head and her heart realize that it was time to refocus. Zak was a great lover, and he had given her some mind-blowing experiences, but she needed to keep entanglements like that out of her life for at least a few years. Maybe once Cassie was in school, or maybe at some point if David found another woman he fell in love with. Skye knew David wasn't moving on anytime soon; after a death, there needed to be time to mourn, but at some point, she hoped that David would love again. She knew her sister would have wanted that for him. As long as the woman loved David and Cassie, Skye would be happy for them if that time came. Until then, Skye was committed to them. She wasn't necessarily putting her life on hold forever. If a man came along that could understand her commitment to Cassie, then she wasn't opposed to building a relationship with that person over the course of time. On the other hand, she knew that she wasn't going to be in any hurry because she was sure it would take a long time to get over Zak.

The wedding was as beautiful as Skye had imagined any wedding could be. She walked back down the aisle with Zak, and then the guests left. The wedding party stayed for a few more photographs, but Rayne had made it clear that, while she wanted a nice number of photos to remember the day by, she also didn't want her guests waiting hours for the wedding party to arrive. The reception was being held at her dance studio where they were able to invite more people than had been able to attend the actual wedding. Rayne didn't want them all sitting around forever.

When they arrived at the studio, the party was kicked into gear. A full buffet dinner was set up downstairs while the second floor had a large open dance floor with all of the decorations and lighting for a real party. Once Skye was cleared of her photograph duties, she began looking for Autumn. They were all going to eat and then at 2:00 the actual wedding dances would begin upstairs. There was already music playing so that anyone who finished eating could make their way upstairs.

Skye looked around for Autumn. She hadn't been at the wedding, but she was supposed to be here for the reception. Skye spotted Autumn coming her way from one of the tables off to the side. Zak just happened to be standing right next to Skye, so she kind of felt obligated to introduce Zak to Autumn; after all, she had heard so much about him. The problem was what exactly did she refer to Zak as? She couldn't really say, "Hey, Autumn, this is the guy I was banging until I found out that he can't deal with me being a part of Cassie's life." That wouldn't go over well, so in the end, she just referred to them each as her friend. "Zak, I'd like you to meet my best friend, Autumn; Autumn, this is my friend Zak." There, that was easy enough, right? Unfortunately, Autumn shook his hand and said, "I've heard so much about you." Zak couldn't say the same thing. He had no real idea that Skye had a best friend other than a few random texts right after they had broken up. They had never talked about their lives in that type of capacity. So Zak just replied with, "It's nice to meet you."

As she was starting to walk away with Autumn, Zak gently took her elbow and pulled her closer to him. "I meant what I said, Skye. We have some things that we need to talk about. If you will hear me out later, after the party, I promise I won't bug you ever again."

"Okay," Skye said softly and then continued to follow Autumn to the table she had picked out. As much as Skye didn't want to have to have a talk with Zak, because it would break her heart to do so, she did realize that closure was probably a really good thing. So she would sit down and have this talk and wish him well. She had absolutely no ill feelings toward Zak. At first she had been hurt that he had seemed so heartless when it came to Cassie. But over time, she had realized that he hadn't really meant that the way it had come out. He had just said it wrong. He didn't have any negative feelings about Cassie as much as he just wasn't ready to have a child be an interruption in his relationship. She could understand that aspect of it too. When it was new and fresh, a couple generally focused on each other to let things develop and see where it would go. If the focus had to be divided, some people wouldn't want to move forward.

Zak really badly wanted to just drag Skye out of here now. He wanted to get this over with one way or another. Either she would forgive him and they could try to build something real or she wouldn't, and he would do his best to avoid her and maybe, someday, he would actually be able to move on. He wouldn't drag her out now; Rayne would probably have his hide or, more accurately, she would get Walt to take off his hide.

The reception was pretty informal, really more just like a huge party than a wedding reception. Autumn had been introduced to all of the five sloths, and of course, she knew the story. She seemed to kind of like Pete a little; at least she kept looking at him and flirting a little.

Zak kept his eyes on Skye as much as he could without seeming like a total stalker and without being rude to people who approached him to talk to him. Of course Walt had been obligated to invite all of the senior partners, although only the ones who were related to the sloths had actually made an appearance. Zak thought about introducing his parents to Skye, but that seemed kind of pointless if Skye never forgave him. His mother would ask about her continuously if she didn't see her with Zak again.

When the formal dances began, Rayne and Walt danced their first dance as husband and wife while the same song that he had apparently proposed to her by played. It was then time for the wedding party to dance. Walt and Rayne were in the middle of the large open dance floor area with Zak and Skye and Jason and Sunni joining them. Eventually,

Jeremy and Pete joined them too. Jeremy was dancing with some woman that Skye had never seen, but she was surprised to see Autumn dancing with Pete when he came on the dance floor. The five couples danced to one song, and then the dance floor was opened up to anyone that wanted to join them. Skye tried to move apart from Zak after the one song, but he just wrapped his arms a little tighter. "Just one more song," Zak protested. "I haven't held you in so long. Just give me this."

Skye thought he sounded a little dominant and commanding, but what he sounded mostly was content to be holding her and a little hopeful that maybe she liked it too. The problem was, she really really did. When the song was completed, the music changed to something more upbeat, and Zak did give her the opportunity to move away if she wanted to. Skye moved to go to sit with Autumn, but she realized her friend wasn't at their table. She scanned the dance floor and found her still dancing with Pete.

As the party progressed, Skye noticed that if a song was upbeat and not really a "hold your partner close" type of song, Zak was totally content to sit at the table with his friends and watch. Whether or not Skye had been asked to dance by anyone, Zak sat out all of the faster songs. But a pattern began to emerge. Skye got asked to dance by a handful of guys, but if she was out on the floor when the song slowed to a couple's type of song, Zak came and tapped the shoulder of her dance partner and took their place. "Why are you doing this, Zak?"

"I just am not ready to see any other guy hold you close, Skye," Zak admitted. "If we talk later and get things settled one way or another, I will do my best to respect whatever you want me to do. But, for now, it's too soon to watch other guys hold your body next to theirs. I have missed being close to you. Just give me this at least."

"I've missed it too, but I'm not sure that missing this is what we need to fix things," Skye debated.

"I know. Look, I know we need to talk, and I am more than willing to leave right now and do that. But I'm not sure how happy that would make Rayne and Walt, and I know you are here with your friend. I am more than willing to wait as long as you want. If you want to stay until the party is completely over, that's fine too. All I am asking is that you hear me out. In the meantime, don't expect me to watch other men hold you close. If you would like me to stop stepping in, I would be fine with it if you just didn't dance slow dances with anyone else. If you want to sit out the slow songs, I won't bother you again until you are ready to leave."

Skye could register that it was said out of jealousy. What she couldn't be sure of was the reason for the jealousy. If it was just about the physical aspects, she could understand that to a point. She wouldn't want to see another woman draped across Zak either. But being physically connected wasn't the means for a relationship. She knew that he wasn't ready for anything more than that, especially not with her, so the jealousy had to have been about the physical and not about anything else. They didn't have a commitment or any kind of emotional ties. Well, Zak didn't; she couldn't say the same for herself. As much as she had tried to convince herself that separating from him was the best idea, that didn't mean that her heart didn't hurt because of it.

She danced with Jeremy, who apparently was one of the sloths. He had gone to law school with the other guys, but he wasn't a practicing attorney. His father was a local senator, so Jeremy worked in his office. According to Jeremy, his father was trying to groom him to take over the Senate seat when he retired. Skye couldn't be sure, but he didn't seem like maybe that was the plan he wished for his own life. But maybe he just wasn't ready for that yet.

Walt asked Skye to dance. It was one of the slower songs, but apparently, Zak was okay with that. It was pretty obvious to everyone in the room that Walt only had eyes for one woman.

Walt had noticed that Zak had pretty much monopolized all of Skye's slow dances. He had also noticed that Skye seemed to look for Zak when she and Walt started dancing, almost as if she were expecting Zak to step in again. Walt was pretty sure that wouldn't happen; his friend would know he wasn't there for any other reason than to talk to Skye. He was also pretty sure that a part of Skye was hoping that Zak would tap in. Not that she wasn't okay with talking to Walt, but he was pretty sure that she would have rather been talking to Zak.

"So I just wanted to thank you for standing up with Rayne today. I know that your new friendship means a lot to her," Walt said.

"Oh, it's really not a problem," Skye assured him. "Rayne and Sunni have both made me feel like we have known each other forever. They have accepted both me and my friend Autumn into their circle."

"Well, I'm glad you have connected," Walt reiterated. "I must say that my wife must have had you in mind when she picked the wedding colors. The dress and jewels are the same shade as your eyes." Walt smiled.

"I've received so many compliments today," Skye said. "It makes me feel beautiful."

"You are beautiful, Skye." Walt paused and just danced with Skye for a bit before he continued. "Look, at my office that day, I promised that I wouldn't plead Zak's case. And, for the most part, I still won't. But I think that if you give him a chance to explain, he really does feel bad about the way things came out that day in his office."

Skye remained quiet but gave a small lopsided smile at what Walt had said. Walt continued, "We men can put our feet right into our mouths sometimes. All I ask is that you keep an open mind where Zak is concerned. Sometimes we are a little thick headed." Walt smiled, and when the song was done, he again thanked Skye for being there and for being so supportive of Rayne.

When the older people had mostly left, the younger crowd turned the music up and it really became a party. Rayne and Walt made their way around the room and said good night to their remaining guests. They were flying out on a late-night flight to New York to spend a few days, and then they were going to fly to Moscow. Rayne had always dreamed of seeing the Bolshoi Ballet in person, and Walt was going to make that dream come true. Along with lots of other historical sites.

When Rayne got to Skye to tell her good-bye and thank her for being a bridesmaid, she too told Skye that she believed that Zak could change and that if Skye would give him time and patience, he might come around someday.

When the couple had exited to cheers and the throwing of birdseed, Skye walked back into the dance studio to find Autumn and make sure that she was okay to drive. She had been drinking a little more than Skye had. Not that her friend was super drunk, but she did want to make sure she was okay to drive. When she got to Autumn, she was still with Pete. Pete promised Skye that he would make sure Autumn got home safely.

So it looked like her bestie was going to have a fun evening. Skye was totally okay with that; Autumn was a kindergarten teacher and she came from a very strictly religious family. They were very traditional in how they felt their daughter should behave. Getting out to have a few hours of fun wasn't something she accomplished often without getting grief for it. Skye didn't really know Pete, but she knew he was one of the attorneys at the same firm as Zak and Walt. She knew he was also part owner in the brewery and if he was a friend to the guys, Skye felt she was safe.

Chapter Thirty

Skye felt Zak approach before she actually saw him. There was definitely still electricity there. Apparently, her head and her heart needed to sit down and have a long talk with her libido. When he was at her side and asked her if she was ready to go, she agreed that she was.

When they walked out to the parking lot, Zak turned to look at Skye. His eyes told her that anything he would say right now would be totally honest. "Thank you for giving me a chance to talk to you, Skye. It really means a lot to me. I was kind of hoping that I could take you somewhere; I have something to show you. Would you please go for a ride with me?" Zak looked so contrite and pleading that she really couldn't say no, but just for good measure, Zak added, "Please, just give me a half hour and then if you still can't forgive me, I'll do my best to stay out of your life other than what I have to do for the court case."

That didn't really sound all that wonderful to Skye. It wasn't that she didn't want to be with Zak; she just felt that right now she had to have different priorities. Cassie wouldn't always need Skye as much as she did right now, but it had only been a handful of weeks since Savannah had died. To be honest, Skye probably needed the connection to Cassie as much if not more than Cassie needed her. But if this was what it took for them to both be able to move on, then this was what she had to do. She agreed to go for a ride with him.

Zak picked up what looked to be a satin sleep mask and asked Skye if she would be willing to wear it until they got to their destination. She almost denied that request, but there was something about Zak that made her feel like this was important, and not just to him. She was thankful, however, that he hadn't chosen to use his tie as the blindfold. She put it on and sat back for the ride.

As Zak began to drive, he also began to talk. Skye wondered if the talk was really the biggest reason for the blindfold. Sometimes it was easier to say things to someone if you didn't have to look them in the eye.

"First of all, I want to apologize for being such a humongous ass that day at my office," Zak began. "I know that I totally came off as the super villain in all of this, but please, hear me out and let me explain. From the moment I had seen you going into the gym that day, my mind was such a mess. You were and still are the most beautiful woman I have ever seen. But I was also absolutely certain that I was not ready to have kids. I had gone over it and over it in my mind, how much I wanted you, but how much I wasn't ready for kids. And then we went on our dates, and you spent the night at my place, and I knew that I was getting in way deeper than I had planned." He paused and ran his thumb lightly over her wrist, almost like he wanted to be sure that they still had some sort of connection. Skye felt the heat immediately. It wasn't that they didn't have a physical connection; they had that in spades. It was the rest of the relationship that seemed to be a problem.

"Anyway," Zak continued, "I kept telling myself that I could have you as a sex partner and not have to worry about the other parts of life. You could be a mother, but that didn't have to change the physical relationship that we had. The thing is, I was starting to think about you more and more. And I was starting to think about wanting you for more than just a sex partner, but something in my head kept objecting because you're a mother. I can't handle kids. I kept telling myself that so much that when I realized that you weren't a mom, that you were Cassie's aunt, I thought it solved all the problems. I could have my cake and eat it too, as they say.

"I know that what I said that day, and the way I said it, just came from this part of me that was so relieved that my life could go on as planned. I could have more of a relationship with you without having to spend any time with a kid. My mouth was pretty much attached to my dick at that point, by the way. Had my head or my heart spoken first, I might not have blown it so badly."

The car turned into what felt like a driveway and then the engine shut off. "Stay there and I'll come around and help you out. We're almost to my surprise," Zak said.

Skye waited until he came around and opened her door and then took her hand. He walked her several feet and then told her that she had three steps to go up and to rely on him if she felt unstable at any point. He helped her up the steps and then she heard a door open. He led her into wherever they were and then stopped. She had no idea where they could possibly be.

"Okay, let's take your blindfold off now," Zak said.

As her eyes began to focus, Skye could tell that she was in a house, albeit a pretty empty house. She looked around but didn't see much of any sign that someone lived here. "Okay, what is this?" she asked. "Where are we?"

"Well, this is the house I just bought. As you can see, it's pretty empty, but I am hoping that maybe you will help me pick out things that will help make it our place," Zak said with a bit of a cringe, like maybe he was afraid she was going to tell him he had utterly lost it. And, most likely, he had. She probably thought that he believed that he could apologize for being an ass, and then she would forget all of the reasons that this would not work in her life right now.

"Zak, I can't move here. I just moved into the apartment over David's garage so that I can help with Cassie. There are days that I need to be there before 7:00 a.m. Adding a drive time to that is just too much. That's why I moved out of my old apartment."

"Okay, I understand, but can I just show you the house, and maybe we can figure out some way to work with that? It's a great house. It has so much potential. I just want you to think about it. If you can't move here right now, maybe you can spend weekends here with me, or whatever works for you. And maybe in the future, when you fall in love with all of the great features of this house, you'll want to spend more time here. All I'm asking is please forgive me for being an ass and look at the house objectively."

"Okay, give me the tour," Skye said rather flippantly. She could not believe that he was trying so hard, but he just wasn't getting how important this was to her. She could forgive him for the way he had handled things in his office that day. She could see where it had been a shock to him, so he hadn't thought before he spoke. But that didn't mean that they could have a live-in relationship right now.

Zak showed her the great basement, which already had his workout equipment and the TV and furniture from his apartment. It made it into a really great man cave or TV room or whatever. It would be a good place for him to have his friends over to watch sports on the weekends.

He showed her the four bedrooms and the four bathrooms, most of which were basically bare and waiting for someone to come in and fill them with some sort of life.

"It's a really nice place, Zak. And I will be glad to help with pointers or tips on decorating or whatever, but I don't think you should plan this house around me. Right now, I'm just in a different place in my life than you are."

"Okay, wait. I have one last feature to show you and if you still feel that way, I won't say anymore tonight," Zak conceded. "I won't promise to stop trying to wear you down over time, though." Zak took her hand and walked her onto the back porch.

"It's a nice backyard, Zak," Skye admitted. "It's got a lot of room. You could make it a great place to grill and have friends over."

"It is a great back yard," Zak agreed. He turned her to face him and put his hands on her shoulders. "But the back yard isn't the best feature of this place."

From behind her, Skye heard a small child say, "Kye, KYE." She turned around because she knew that voice. Toddling toward her from the gate in the fence that ran along the property was none other than her niece. She looked up to the gate and there stood David. "I don't understand," she said as she went down the steps to pick up the little girl.

"Yeah," Zak said, running his hands through his hair and following her down the steps. "The best feature of this place is that we have a pretty cute neighbor."

"Why, thank you," David said with a bow. "The little girl that lives here is pretty awesome too," he added with a grin.

Zak just looked at David and shook his head and chuckled. "Whatever. I think maybe you need to be like that neighbor on the TV show that was always behind the fence."

Skye turned to look over the fence and sure enough, that was the second floor and the roof of David's house. She almost stumbled, but she caught herself and leaned down to pick Cassie up. Zak came to stand beside her, and Cassie immediately lit up and said, "AK."

"Yeah, we need to work on that Z at the beginning there, angel. It's Zak," he said, enunciating very clearly.

Cassie just giggled and gave him her best smile. "AK."

Zak shook his head like this was going to be impossible. But Cassie reached a hand out to Zak's cheek to try to pull him closer and when he leaned in, she put her forehead to his forehead and said, "Love AK."

Zak just smiled as his heart melted even more and said, "I'll take it. We'll have time to work on the Z. I live next door, after all."

Skye had tears in her eyes. She knew what that meant. Cassie would accept hugs, and even kisses if you gave them, but her way of showing her love was to press together forehead to forehead. Zak had won her niece over hook, line and sinker. She couldn't blame the girl; he was pretty awesome.

She looked at David, totally bewildered. "You don't have a gate in your fence."

"Apparently, my new neighbor had one installed this afternoon. It locks from either side, for privacy or safety concerns," David informed her.

"But it can also remain open when it's helpful," Zak added.

"So how did all this happen?" she asked, looking back and forth between the men.

"Well, the first day I came here, Cassie reached right for me. I figured it couldn't be that bad to hold her, and I had papers David needed to sign. While I was holding her, she let out the biggest sigh you could imagine for a girl this small. I felt her warm breath on my neck, and she cuddled her head down on my shoulder and in a few minutes, she fell asleep. I got it. I realized just how special both you and Cassie are, and I knew that I would be a better person if I could have both of you in my life," Zak explained.

"I just told him that I knew of a great house for sale in the neighborhood." David shrugged.

Skye threw herself into Zak's body with Cassie sort of mushed between them and put her arm around his neck. "I love that you did this."

"Well, I realized that I love you, so I had to try to do what I could to fix this for both of us," Zak explained.

"I love you too," Skye said through her tears.

"Does that mean you'll move in with me and help me decorate this place? It's in desperate need of more furniture and more people," Zak said.

"Yes, I will move in with you," Skye said. She was overwhelmed with thoughts. Apparently, David had liked Zak and approved of them being together since he had been the one to get Zak to consider the house. Cassie was obviously totally smitten, and it was very obviously a two-way street. Zak seemed just as smitten with the little girl. Her family approved and supported her in having a relationship with Zak. It was pretty easy to see why David had been in Zak's corner; the man had bought a house just to make sure that Cassie and Skye would still be able to be close. Who could ask for a better man? They kissed and apparently, Cassie was tired of being squished.

She started to wiggle and then she said very loudly. "KYE-AAK!"

All of the adults started to laugh. David took her and said, "We definitely need to work on those beginning consonant sounds, baby girl."

"Hey, we have our own couple name, like Brangelina." Skye giggled.

"After what happened with that couple, I'm not sure couple names are something to consider a good thing," David said and excused himself to head home. He walked away with Cassie after she had given her appropriate good-bye kisses and several waves and "good-byes" and closed the gate behind him.

Zak took Skye's hand and said, "I am so glad my bed got moved already." He turned to kiss her and then looked into her eyes. "Would you come upstairs with me, Skye? I've missed you so much."

Skye didn't answer; she just pulled Zak's hand and headed back into the house and up the stairs.

Before they turned up the stairway, Zak grabbed the blindfold that she had worn to come here. It might come in handy; one never knew. Skye noticed him grabbing it and shook her head no.

"Okay," Zak said as he tossed it back over his shoulder. "No more blindfolds then, I take it?"

"Oh, you can blindfold me anytime," Skye replied. "But I prefer your tie. It adds to the sensation when I have your smell so close to my nose."

"I can do that," Zak agreed. He started unzipping her beautiful bridesmaid dress. This wouldn't get tossed to the floor; he hoped she would wear it again when they went to a nice dinner party, maybe with his parents. As he unzipped her, he asked, "To keep my promise of being understanding about your commitments, do you have any responsibilities for Cassie or anyone else tomorrow?"

"Nope, tomorrow is Sunday." Skye smiled. "I'm free of commitments all day."

"Good, that was what I was hoping, because I have really missed you and we have a lot to catch up on. We may end up sleeping quite late by the time I am too tired to keep going," Zak said.

"Oh, well, I will take you up on that. I have a lot of catching up to do myself," Skye said, turning to begin unbuttoning his shirt. He had lost the jacket and tie when they had walked in the door.

"Skye, I need to tell you, I am probably going to go off really fast because of how much I have missed you, but I don't think I can wait long enough for a lot of foreplay either. I promise there will be a second time, and I will take care of you, but I'm just too hot for you right now," Zak stated honestly.

"Trust me, I'm almost there myself just from being close to you and kissing you," Skye agreed. And she was. No man had ever gotten her this aroused this easily just from kisses and undressing each other, but her body knew exactly what Zak could do to her and it was.

Round one was exactly what Zak had predicted: hot, fast, and hard. Round two took more time as they both reacquainted themselves with the other's body. The third round came after they had taken a short break to eat the pizza Zak had ordered and then decided on a shower.

Round four—now, round four was something very different. After their shower they began to work on filling in some of the blanks that they hadn't talked about when they were trying to keep it light and somewhat anonymous. They lay with Skye's head on Zak's chest and talked about the things that most people talk about in the early stages of dating. Zak told her about his parents and his siblings. Skye told him more about her family, even though they were all deceased. It was time for them to get to know each other.

After they had talked for hours, Skye pulled her head away to look at Zak. In some ways, it felt new, now that they had connected on a less sexual but more personal level. She leaned down to kiss Zak. It wasn't their usual hot, steamy, passionate kiss. This was slow and easy and lasted until they were both a little breathless.

Zak leaned up and took over the kiss, just kissing her, and the new level of connection he felt with her made him want to do something he had never done before. Zak wanted to make love to her. This time, he touched her and kissed her and aroused her in a slower, sweeter fashion than he had ever done. Before tonight, it had always been about the satisfaction that sex could bring. Tonight, he realized that there was so much more to be had than just physical satisfaction.

This time, when he reached his orgasm, he looked directly into Skye's beautiful blue eyes and said, "I love you, Skye."

She responded with, "I love you too, Zak." They settled back into their position of lying with Skye's head on Zak's chest and his arm around her holding her tight to him. Skye started to drift off a little, totally content to just lie there and be held by the man she loved.

Zak's mind was full of so many thoughts. That had been the most satisfying encounter of Zak's entire life. Maybe it was the love that he was feeling, or maybe it was the fact that he was realizing that he never wanted to lose this amazing woman, but Zak found himself opening up more than he ever thought he would. "So you may think this is crazy, and it probably is, but while we were broken up, I kept having these dreams and flashes of you and me with a little brown-haired boy. I saw us watching him at the park and I even got a quick flash of him running down the hall the first time I looked at this house. I can't predict what our future holds, but I do think we will be together for a long time, at least I hope we will." At first, Zak wasn't even sure Skye had heard him. Her breath was slow and soft like she might be asleep, but then he was pretty sure that he felt her cheeks move like she might have smiled.

They both drifted off to sleep, content to just hold each other and absorb love and support from the other. When they woke up it was late morning. Zak wasn't sure why, but he asked Skye if she would like to meet his parents. She agreed that she would love to, so Zak got on the phone to call his mother. When his mother picked up, he said, "Hey, Mom, I was wondering if this evening would be a good time to stop by?"

"Of course, dear." His mother sounded a little indignant. "You don't have to make an appointment to come see us. We don't see you often enough, you always have an open invitation."

"Well, I wanted to check before I just came over because I would like to bring a guest." Zak looked up and Skye was smiling at him from across the kitchen counter. She was making them a brunch to help reboot their bodies after their amazing night together.

"A guest?" his mother questioned. "Oh, Zak, I hope it's not one of those floozies you normally hang out with."

"Look, Mom, if you don't want me to bring her, I'll just stay home," Zak retorted.

"Oh, no, please, do come over," his mother pleaded. "We never get to see you anymore. We would love to have you to dinner."

"Great, we'll be there at six," Zak said and then hung up. He wasn't sure that taking Skye to see his parents was going to be a good idea, but she was going to be a regular part of his life, permanently if he had his way, so they needed to know who she was.

****

At five minutes to six, Zak pulled up to his parents' grand estate. Zak never really understood why his parents had felt the need for such a huge home. Even when the kids were little, they had way more space than they could possibly need. Now that his parents lived here alone, it was even more of a waste. But Zak supposed that one of the senior partners at a prestigious law firm needed to impress people with his wealth. And his mother wouldn't be caught dead inviting someone from the country club to a home that wasn't one of the biggest and most expensive in the area.

"Lifestyles of the Rich and Famous," Skye said with a teasing smile.

"Yep, something like that," Zak lamented. He had to admit, Skye had done her best to impress his parents. She was dressed beautifully and with class. He knew she didn't have the budget to dress in the designer clothing his mother always wore, but she was just as classy and elegant as his mother had ever been. Damn, he loved this woman. "My mother wouldn't be caught dead at the country club without a house like this to invite people to."

"It's a lovely home, from what I can see," Skye consoled him.

"That's the thing," Zak began. "This is way more of a house than it ever was a home. My mom was great and did her best to fill in for my father, who was always at work trying to build a name for the law firm. But this was never really a home." Zak took Skye's hand and turned to look her in the eye. "Promise me if I ever become a work obsessed or money hungry like my dad you will call me out and that you will not let us live in just a house."

Skye saw the sincerity in Zak's eyes. Just because someone had money, it didn't mean they had love and happiness. She kissed the back of Zak's hand and said, "I promise."

Zak got out of the car and came around to open Skye's door just as his mother opened the door to welcome them, and no doubt to check out the 'floozie' Zak had brought with him. She was in for a huge surprise, now wasn't she?

As he reached his mother, he leaned in for a partial hug and a brief kiss on her cheek before he said, "Mother, I'd like you to meet my girlfriend, Skye."

Skye reached out her hand and said, "It's a pleasure to meet you, Mrs. Owens."

Zak could tell that his mother was a little confused as to how to respond to that, so she just reached out and shook Skye's hand. One thing no one could ever accuse his mother of was not knowing how to cover in a social situation. "It's wonderful to meet you too, dear," she said.

They shared a nice dinner conversation. When Skye told them about her family, Zak's father looked at Zak with a bit of recognition in his eyes. He was putting together exactly who Skye was. He knew the case Zak was in the process of representing. He hoped his father wasn't going to try to tell him that he shouldn't be dating someone so close to his client. But if he did, he would be told to butt out.

Zak's mother asked if her family lived in the area. "They live right next door to us," Skye stated.

"Oh, isn't that lovely?" his mother said.

"Yeah, Zak was super amazing and bought the house right next to my brother-in-law so I would still be able to help with Cassie," Skye said.

Zak could tell by the looks on his parents' faces that they were both surprised and happy that this might mean he was settling down. The evening went as well as it could. His mother was always going to be nosy and pushy, but that was okay. Probably most mothers were.

Just before they left, his father pulled Zak aside and said, "The case you're working on just got a whole lot bigger. We've had five more people come forward to sue the trucking company. There isn't one specific driver involved, so their best bet is a class action against the company as a whole. Find out if your client wants to continue with his suit or if he wants to join the class action. If he joins, I want you sitting first chair since you have been in on this from the beginning. I was thinking that we should put Walt as second chair because you two work so well together and then the two of you can add more from the younger pool of the staff if you feel you need them."

Zak told his father that he would check with David in the next twenty-four hours and have an answer. His father told him that he was hoping they could start taking statements and doing research by no later than Wednesday.

"I think you should approach Walt then; he can get started on it because if my client doesn't want to join then Walt can take first chair. Either way, you know he and I won't care who has first chair and who has second if we end up working together on this," Zak stated.

They promised to have his parents over when they had their house all furnished to show it to them and then left.

On the way home, Zak said, "Speaking of getting the house furnished, what does your schedule look like this week? As much as I love spending time with you in bed, we might eventually want to get a couch or something."

"I don't have to work tomorrow, but I have Cassie from eight in the morning until about six in the evening," Skye said.

"Do you think Cassie would be up for a little shopping, or is that something she doesn't do well with?" Zak asked.

"She doesn't mind it; we go to the mall sometimes. As long as she can nap in the car a little here and there," Skye stated.

"Great. Let's plan on at least going to a few places. We can play it by ear and if it seems Cassie is getting tired of it all we can always finish another day," Zak suggested.

Skye agreed and then asked, "What was your father talking to you about just before we left?"

"Oh, it was just some work stuff," Zak explained. He really didn't want to talk about David's case any more than he had to. He knew every time he did it just brought painful memories for Skye.

"He wasn't upset that we're together because you are representing my brother-in-law?" Skye asked.

Zak squeezed her hand and assured her that it wasn't about that at all. "It's just that since the news about the trucking company came out, five other people have contacted our firm wanting to bring a class action suit against them. If David wants to keep his case separate, he can do that, but if he wants to join the others, then my father wants me to be first chair in the class action," Zak explained.

Chapter Thirty-One

The following day, they went over to Skye's apartment next door and Skye showed Zak the few pieces of furniture she would want to bring with her. They were nothing fancy, but they were special, things that she had brought with her from her parents' home. Once they knew what they had to start with, they headed out to find more things for their home.

Skye was impressed with how well Zak did with Cassie. For being a guy who had only recently been willing to accept a small child as any part of his life, he had really taken to being totally committed to Cassie's every need. He insisted on carrying her around every store they went to. He of course passed the diaper duty off to Skye, since he had never changed a diaper in his life. He promised to learn, but that might be best done at home. The only time he wasn't carrying her was when Skye insisted that it was getting close to her nap time and she needed to be in the stroller so that she could properly rest. Skye had taken many pictures of the two of them, some posed and some totally candid photos that they probably didn't even know she had snapped. Zak might not realize it, but that little girl was totally connected to her Uncle Zak. He might not be her uncle by marriage, but that didn't matter to Cassie. She loved him unconditionally.

When they stopped for lunch, it was Zak's turn to take pictures of Skye with her niece. He really did find Skye so beautiful, and the more time he spent with her, the more he realized that he was in love with her inner beauty even more than he was in love with her outer beauty. He snapped a series of photos while Cassie was pressing her head to Skye's forehead in her sign of love. He was pretty sure one of those needed to be printed in a very large size to hang on a wall somewhere in their home. And he did realize that it was a home. It wasn't a house to him anymore. Sure, it might still be pretty much bare of furniture and adornments, but having Skye there with him made it a home. Having

Cassie come over would make it seem even more so. That gave him an idea. "What would you think of making one of the bedrooms into a place that Cassie could stay if David ever needed to be away for some reason?" he asked.

Skye pondered that for a moment and said, "It has some merit, because there have been times that David has gone out of town on a business trip or something, but I think we should check with David before we put any effort or money into it. He may prefer that she stay in her own bed at his house."

Zak could see that point and he conceded for now, but he insisted that they start getting some toys to have at their house for when she came over.

By the time the day was done, they had the basic furniture all picked out. They decided the accessories such as pictures, lamps and things like that would be best to wait until the furniture was in place and they could get a better idea of layout and what was needed to fill the space.

Over the course of the next few weeks, they settled into their new home and into a routine that became comfortable. The days Skye didn't work, Cassie was at their house. The days she did, she took her to the fitness center. David had decided to join the class action lawsuit, so Zak and Walt were busy preparing for the upcoming trial. Zak always made it home for dinner, though. He made a point of being out of the office no later than five and was home roughly twenty minutes later. The only nights he wasn't home was when he had duties at the brewery. Skye often went with him when he was managing the bar. She sat with Sunni at a table or at the bar if Sunni was there. Jason wasn't there every night of the week. Usually the earlier days of the week weren't all that busy, but the later days in the week, the pub could be pretty crazy with customers, so Jason tried to be there to help out. It seemed to Skye that Jason took his job as manager of the brewery very seriously. His relationship with Sunni, not so much. He was always flirting with her, and definitely seemed to be hot for her, but Skye didn't really see anything that felt like a commitment on the horizon. Oh well, it wasn't her business what type of relationship they had; that was their business. She really did like Sunni, though, and would hate to see her get hurt if Jason wasn't as into her as she seemed to be into him.

It was such a comfort to Skye how easily they just fell into a routine and were so comfortable with each other. Sometimes moving in with a person took a lot of adjustment, but to her it seemed like she and Zak were just in sync with each other. They sat down each morning to a breakfast. Depending on what their schedules looked like, they took turns with the cooking or sometimes they worked on it together. Every evening they sat at dinner either at home or out at some restaurant and discussed their day. Zak couldn't always tell her much about the actual lawsuit because of attorney-client privilege, but he still told her about how his day had gone. David had agreed that it might be a good idea for them to have a place for Cassie to sleep if she ever needed to spend the night or a place to nap if she was spending the day at their house, so they had gone out and bought a crib for her and some bedding and muslin blankets. Skye didn't say it to Zak, but the things she picked out would transfer easily into the way she would want a nursery if she and Zak ever did get to the point of having children of their own.

****

It seemed like the weeks had flown by because Thanksgiving was just around the corner. Apparently, the Five Sloths guys had made it a tradition to have a huge Thanksgiving dinner catered for their employees. Not all of them attended if they had other family commitments, but Zak had told her that the guys and many of the employees planned other commitments around the employee dinner. They always had it catered, and they always gave each employee a bonus based on how long they had been working at the brewery. Apparently in the past it had been held at the pub, but this year, they decided that Rayne's dance studio was a better option. That way they could set up bigger table options than the pub had allowed for. Zak had said it always seemed sort of disconnected to have everyone in booths or tables. This year they were going to be able to have everyone closer together, so it felt more like one big family instead of a bunch of small ones.

When the day of the dinner arrived, the guys and their ladies all met at the dance studio early to make sure everything was set up to their liking. They rearranged a few of the tables for easier traffic flow and made sure the buffet tables were all set up ready for the food to arrive. About an hour before the guests were scheduled to be there, the caterers arrived. They began hauling in more food than Skye had seen in one place in her lifetime. It was obvious that the guys did not skimp when it came to thank their employees for their loyal service.

Zak had invited David to bring Cassie. Although the four of them had a small dinner the evening before and they were all going to Zak's parents' for a dinner on the weekend, he wanted David to feel like he was a part of the Five Sloths family. As soon as David walked in the door, Zak made a beeline to him and asked if he could introduce Cassie to all of his friends. David walked over to Skye and watched as Zak took the little girl around the room to meet all of the new people.

"He's telling everyone to meet his niece, Cassie," David observed. Yes, Skye had noticed that too. She just wasn't sure to make of it. She felt like she and Zak were definitely committed to each other, and to her it felt long term and even potentially permanent, but she didn't want to assume that Zak felt the same way. "This is quite the event," David said.

"Yeah, apparently they do it every year. They used to hold it at the brewery, but now that Rayne owns this place, it's a perfect location. This is where they had their wedding reception too," Skye stated.

"It's nice of them to do all of this for their employees. Most bosses don't show much thanks to their staff," David said.

"Yeah, and this isn't the half of it. They also give each employee a bonus of one thousand dollars per year they have worked at Five Sloths. Zak said they give it to them today rather than waiting to make it a Christmas bonus so they can use it to make a better Christmas for their families," Skye explained.

"Wow, maybe I'm in the wrong line of work," David joked.

Zak had told her that the guys had always tried to move around the pub and make sure each employee was thanked individually, but this year, they were going to sit at different tables so that each group had an owner at their table. Skye sat with Zak at a table that included a woman named Holly. From what Skye knew, Holly had only been at the pub for a few months. She was the second cook. There was a head cook and Holly had trained under him to learn the way things were cooked and served at the brewery. Skye had eaten there several times and she honestly had never been able to tell if there was a different cook in the kitchen. Holly had apparently been a quick study and learned the menu well. She also had a young son. He sat next to her at their table. Holly seemed like a quiet, more reserved person. Skye had to wonder if she had a bad situation in her past, or maybe even her present. She would have to ask Zak if he knew anything about her. Skye felt a connection to her; there was just something about the woman that drew Skye to her.

By the end of the meal, the owners had all stepped aside and gotten the envelopes with thank you cards in them for the people who were sitting at their table. When Holly opened hers, tears began to fall down her face. It was obvious that the bonus inside had meant something to her. Skye was a little curious, though, because she knew that Holly hadn't been there a full year. She didn't know what the guys gave the ones that had been there less than a year, but apparently whatever they had done had meant something to her. Skye leaned over and asked Zak, "So with employees like Holly who have been there less than a year, do you give them a prorated amount or something?"

Zak whispered to her, "Normally, anyone that has been there less than a year gets a five hundred dollar bonus. Holly was a special case. About a week ago, we were approached by some of the employees asking if they could give part of their bonus to Holly. Several of them asked us to give her five hundred dollars of their bonus. Everyone knows that she is in a tough place right now. None of us knows the details, but we know that she asks for as many hours as she can have and for a mom, that's not the normal way things go. We suspect that her child's father either isn't in the picture or doesn't contribute much, so we all look out for her." Apparently, there was yet another reason to love how amazing her boyfriend was.

****

The dinner with Zak's parents went really well, considering that it was a group of people who didn't really know each other. Skye met Zak's brother and sister. His brother, Luke, apparently was the rule breaker in the family. He was going to Yale; it was explained to Skye that this had always traditionally been a Harvard family. Whatever school he went to, Skye liked him a lot. He was funny and friendly. He even made a few flirtatious comments to Skye about 'Yale men doing it better,' which always got Zak to glare daggers at him, but it was all done in fun. His sister, Monica, on the other hand, seemed like the traditional 'rich bitch' in Skye's opinion. She was all about the designer bag and the Louboutin shoes. Skye had thought that Zak's mother was a little 'stuffed shirt' the first time she had met her, but the minute Cassie arrived, Mrs. Owens melted into a baby babbling grandma type. It was pretty obvious that she would love to have grandchildren of her own someday. David seemed to be comfortable with Zak's family. They had all expressed their sympathy over the recent loss of his wife. But after that brief melancholy moment, the rest of the day had been filled with laughter and lively conversation—well, with the exception of Monica, who seemed to be more invested in texting on her phone than actually talking to real people.

By the time the dinner was done, Skye felt like she could really connect with this family, and she was happy that it seemed like David and Cassie fit in too. It wouldn't necessarily be often that they all got together, most likely just holidays, but it would be nice if those weren't awkward.

Zak pulled into their driveway and they all got out of the SUV. He stopped David for a minute to ask him a favor. "I was thinking, it's winter in Michigan, and I worry about Skye having to go to your garage to get her car every day. How would you feel about me moving my sports car into your garage and moving Skye's car over here? I don't really drive the Boxter much in the winter anyway. So it would be like me putting it in storage. Then Skye doesn't have to walk across the yard if the snow gets deep."

David replied, "Yeah, that's fine with me. Make the switch whenever you want to." He then headed across the yard to put his very exhausted daughter to bed.

Zak and Skye walked to the front porch, Zak made sure she got inside okay, and then he went to make the vehicle switch. The weather hadn't been too bad lately, but it was late November in Michigan, and you never knew when you would wake up to a foot of snow.

Chapter Thirty-Two

The next couple of weeks were good, but they also taught Zak exactly how different their upbringings had been. Skye insisted on going out to the local nursery and cutting down a fresh real tree to decorate for their home the day after Thanksgiving. Zak had grown up with artificial; under no circumstances would his mother allow pine needles to infest her home. Zak would have assumed they would go to Macy's or something like that and buy a large box of color coordinated decorations for the tree. Skye insisted on going to Frankenmuth and picking out individual ornaments that would have some significance in their lives. She picked out a lawyer one for him and an aerobics one for her. She picked out an 'our first Christmas" one and had it engraved. She also got one that represented their new home. Each ornament was picked out with great care. She bought a sloth and a beer mug. She bought ornaments with each of their names on it, including David and Cassie. She picked out multi-color garland and lights. His parents had always had white lights and silver and gold garland with gold, silver and white balls.

When he and Skye finished decorating the tree, he had to admit he liked Skye's much better. He could see the ability to add ornaments for special occasions—maybe someday a 'baby's first Christmas' ornament might adorn their tree. Who knew, maybe someday there would be a few of those on the tree? They turned on all the Christmas lights and turned off every other light in the house. It was a magical feeling. Zak embraced Skye next to the Christmas tree and right then and there, he made a decision. There would be one very small box underneath the Christmas tree this year. He just hoped that Skye would accept it. "This is the most amazing tree," Zak told her. "My parents always had a white, silver and gold tree. It was very distinguished but not any fun at all. We weren't allowed to touch it. This tree feels like something it's okay to touch."

Skye smiled. "A few of the ornaments are breakable, but they can all be replaced, and we made sure that all of the ones on the lower branches were safe for Cassie, so we should be good."

"I know," Zak said, "but I meant that it feels more relaxed yet amazingly beautiful. What would you think of asking the guys over for a party on Christmas Eve? We usually just hang out at the brewery or something, but I think it would be great to have them all here to show off this amazing tree."

"It's the kind of tree I grew up with. Of course, ours always had handmade ornaments that Savannah and I had made at school and new ornaments got added yearly. The sentimental ones stayed on no matter how old they got to be, but some just got old or broken so we would find a new one to take their place. We often picked up something that reminded us of a trip or a special time." Skye was quiet for a while, and Zak completely understood why. Really, Skye had no family to speak of. Cassie was her only living blood relative.

Thinking about that gave him an idea. "Hey, what do you think about me calling David and if Cassie is still up, they can come over and see the tree. I'll bet Cassie will love it."

That seemed to brighten her right up. "Oh, that's a great idea," Skye agreed. "Call him and if they are coming, I can make some hot chocolate and get out some of the Christmas cookies we bought today. That's what we always did growing up. When we finished the tree, we had cocoa and Christmas cookies. They were always baked by my mom, but I haven't had time to bake any yet, so store bought will have to do."

Zak called David and he said they would be over as soon as he could get Cassie bundled up. That set Skye in motion, she was off to the kitchen to prepare a snack for them all to enjoy. He was glad that he could give her some of the traditions that she had grown up with and for her to be able to share them with Cassie. They had saved one ornament for the tree. Skye had wanted for Cassie to be able to put her own name on the tree, or at the very least try to, and they would make sure it got placed in the exact spot she picked for herself. Zak turned the regular lights back on and the Christmas tree lights back off so that Cassie could get the full effect once she and David were in the house and unbundled from their winter gear. Skye came out from the kitchen with a tray of cookies and three mugs and a sippy cup.

Cassie already seemed fascinated with the tree, even though it wasn't lit. The ornaments alone were captivating to her. Skye couldn't wait to see her reaction when the tree was lit with all the house lights off. Skye pointed out some of the special ornaments to Cassie and told her what they meant. The little girl didn't really understand, but she listened and looked at each ornament in turn as Skye pointed them out to her. Skye took one of the ornaments off of the tree and showed Cassie how she put it back on and then she handed Cassie her special ornament and tried to help her put it on the tree. Of course, Cassie didn't understand the hook and how to put it on, but she tried. Skye helped her get it in the basic location she was trying for.

Zak went and plugged in the tree lights and Cassie's eyes got as big as saucers. When he turned off the house lights, she squealed with delight and clapped her hands. The tree was obviously a hit with the toddler. They all sat on the floor around the base of the tree and enjoyed their hot chocolate and cookies by the glow of the Christmas lights.

When David headed home to tuck Cassie in for the night, Skye leaned over to Zak and asked, "Do you want to know a fantasy of mine?"

"Of course. I want to know everything you dream of so I can try to make them come true," Zak said.

"I've always wanted to make love on the floor under the edge of the Christmas tree with all the pretty lights shining around us. My mom told me once that she and my dad did that when they were young and didn't have kids to worry about," Skye said softly.

"I can definitely do that," Zak agreed. "I'll be right back," he said before jogging up the stairs.

Skye wondered where he was going until she saw him coming back down with the big fluffy comforter from their bed. No one could blame Zak of not thinking ahead. The hardwood floor wouldn't feel all that great under her, so he had gotten her a bit of a cushion. He spread out the blanket right at the edge of the Christmas tree and sat down on it. He leaned over and started kissing Skye on the neck and behind her ear. He began unbuttoning her shirt as she began unbuttoning his. Soon they were both naked and stretched out on the big, soft comforter. Zak positioned her so that her head was right under the lights of the tree and began kissing her all over her torso, paying extra attention to her breasts. He loved her breasts and she seemed to love having the attention too. When she was sufficiently squirming under his attentions, he moved down her body and spread her lips open so that his tongue could feast on her plump wet pussy. She soon began writhing with her orgasm and Zak made a place for himself between her legs. When they had finished, Zak grabbed the throw that was kept on the back of the couch. He lay down, wrapped Skye in his arms, and tucked the throw around them. He kissed her forehead and said, "We need to make that a tradition."

"A yearly one," Skye agreed.

"I was thinking more like nightly," Zak stated.

Skye just smiled; that didn't sound like a bad suggestion at all. She drifted off to sleep with Christmas lights twinkling overhead.

Chapter Thirty-Three

As December slowly rolled in, Zak and Skye continued to become more and more comfortable with their day-to-day routine. Cassie was often a part of outings. Zak became more and more convinced that his plan for Christmas Eve was the right way to go and less and less worried about what the visions of the little brown-haired boy had meant. He talked to Pete about the jeweler that was pretty much on his mother's speed dial. She was most likely one of the man's biggest clients. Pete connected him with the man, and he set his plan in to motion. Skye had a birthday coming up and he wanted to buy her a real version of the necklace and earrings she had worn at Walt's wedding. The ones she had were beautiful and matched the dress amazingly well, but he wanted her to have the real thing that would last forever. He requested the pieces to be made with the large aquamarine stone in the middle and a frame of diamonds around the center stone. The ring, however, was just the opposite. The large diamond in the center was surrounded by small aquamarines. The ring wouldn't be part of her birthday present, though.

When Skye's birthday arrived, Zak had a huge party for her at the brewery. It was Monday so the brewery was closed for the evening. He had invited all the guys and their girls and of course David and Cassie. He was surprised, but even his parents came. It was very obvious that they were trying to keep an open mind about where Zak's relationship with Skye was going to go.

At one point in the evening, his mother pulled him aside and told him, "If you have any sense at all, you won't let that girl get away."

"I don't plan on it, Mom. I know she's the best thing that ever happened to me," Zak admitted. She seemed happy with his statement and went back to her table to sit down.

Skye had noticed Zak's mother talking to him, so she went over to find out if everything was okay. "Anything going on? It looked like she was a little intense," Skye stated.

Zak pulled her closer to him and said, "Yeah, sweetheart, it's fine. She was just telling me that if I was smart I wouldn't let you get away. I've never been accused of being a highly intelligent being, but I do know a keeper when I see one." He winked at her and leaned down to kiss her. "I want to give you your present. Go sit on that stool over there and you can open your gifts where everyone can see." Zak nodded toward one of the barstools that had been pulled into the center of the tables that had been pulled together for the party.

Skye sat on the stool and one by one, Zak handed her the gifts their friends had brought. Walt and Rayne had gotten her a beautiful painting that would match their living room perfectly. It was signed by a local artist that Rayne said she had always loved. Her best friend Autumn had gotten her a subscription to a cheesecake of the month club. There was definitely something to be said about best friends who knew you well. Zak's parents had gotten her a beautiful silver picture frame and had gotten a picture of Cassie put in it somehow. They had most likely gotten it from Zak, or maybe from David himself. The others got her the typical variety of things you would expect from people who don't know you well enough to get something personal. Mostly gift cards for spa services or nice restaurants. Zak saved his gift for last. When Skye opened the package, she couldn't believe her eyes. The necklace and earrings looked so much like the ones she had worn at the wedding and yet they definitely sparkled more and were very obviously real.

Rayne took the opportunity to joke with Zak and say, "Hey, I already got her one of those!"

Zak laughed and said, "I know and they looked so beautiful on her I wanted her to have the real thing."

Skye pulled Zak to her and gave him a totally appropriate for public consumption kiss and thanked him for his beautiful gift.

When they got home, the continued their nightly tradition and made love under the lights of the Christmas tree. When they were both sated, Zak carried Skye upstairs and tucked them both into bed.

****

On Christmas Eve, all of their friends came to their new home to enjoy a catered dinner. Zak had been trying to talk Skye into considering hiring a housekeeper or even just a cook, but she said she enjoyed doing all of the domestic stuff, although she had agreed that catering was the better way to go when they were having so many friends over. But she had baked several kinds of cookies and other Christmas goodies to have after the meal was done. Walt and Rayne were there, as were Jason and Sunni. Pete and Autumn were both there, but they weren't together anymore, apparently. They still flirted with each other and talked about how they had to get together again after the holidays settled down. Apparently, Pete had been involved in a major legal battle and had been busy and therefore neglecting his time with Autumn. Autumn said she understood, but it was obvious that she had taken a step back to wait and see if he followed through on his comments. Jeremy was there with a young woman who seemed far too stuffy for him, but apparently, as a senator's son, he was cautious who he went out with. Couldn't have Daddy getting bad press on his account. David and Cassie had come over for the dinner but said they wouldn't stay long. Cassie needed to get to bed before Santa Claus came.

Skye had realized a week ago that Zak was pretty much going to give that girl every reason to believe in Santa Claus if he continued to buy her as many presents as he had and labeled them from the North Pole.

The dinner was amazing. Zak had ordered only the best from the caterer. They had prime rib and lobster with all of the sides a person could dream of. Everyone passed on the dessert saying they would have some in a while once the food had settled.

It was time to open presents, and David got up to excuse himself. He wanted to get Cassie home, and he would be exchanging gifts with Zak and Skye the next morning when they came over to see the haul that Cassie had gotten from her grandparents and her Uncle Zak and Aunt Skye. Before he could leave, though, Zak asked him if he would mind staying a minute. He had something he wanted David to be present for. That confused Skye, but David agreed to stay.

When they were all seated around the living room and with the Christmas tree all lit, Zak took Skye's hand and walked over to the tree. He started to bend down, and she thought he was probably picking up a gift from under the tree, but instead, he got down on one knee and pulled a small box out of his pocket. Before he opened it, he said, "Skye, I was such a fool when we first met. I almost let seeing you with Cassie stop me from meeting you altogether. But you were so beautiful that I couldn't get you out of my mind, so I decided to try the whole friends with benefits and no commitment route. I thought that was the perfect solution since I thought you had a child. Turns out, I was an idiot to think that I wouldn't fall in love with both you and Cassie. And even though she is your niece and not your daughter, I am so happy to have her in my life. She brings joy to everyone she meets. Seeing how beautiful she was made me fall in love with her. Walt told me at his bachelor party that he thought I had already fallen for both of you, and he was right. It just took me longer to realize it. I am so thankful that you gave me that chance to talk to you at their wedding and gave me a chance to fix things between us. I love you so much, Skye. I want to spend a hundred Christmases with you. I want to wake up every morning for the rest of my life with you by my side. I want to have little brown-haired boys with you some day, or maybe little brown-haired girls. I don't really care which as long as it all happens with you." Zak opened the box and then continued, "Skye Pierson, will you marry me and make my life complete?"

Skye had had tears running down her face within seconds of the time his knee had hit the floor. Men didn't get into that position unless they intended to propose. When he finished his speech, she was pretty sure she looked like a mess with her make-up all running down her face, but that didn't matter. She reached her hand down for Zak to put the ring on her finger and said, "Yes, I want a hundred Christmases with you too. I love you so much, Zak."

Zak put the ring on her finger and then stood up to give her a kiss. The woman that had been hired to serve the dinner came out at that moment with the tray of champagne glasses that Zak had asked her to prepare. It occurred to him that it would have been pretty embarrassing if Skye had said no and he had this woman all ready to bring out champagne to celebrate. Thankfully, she had said yes, and his celebration was going to proceed as he had hoped. Everyone took a glass of champagne and several toasts were made to the couple. Lots of hugs and pats on the back went around the room too.

When David came over, he shook Zak's hand and said, "Welcome to the family." He turned to Skye and gave her a hug and said, "I am so happy for you two. I kind of take credit for part of it, though, since I was the one who told him about the house." He gave her a big smile, then he said to both of them, "I need to get the munchkin home, she's about ready to drop, but thanks for asking me to stay for a bit, Zak. I would have been bummed if I had missed this. See you in the morning."

He brought an almost asleep Cassie over to wish them both goodnight, and after kisses and hugs, she very sleepily said, "Night, night, Kye, night. Night, Ak." With that, she and David walked out the door.

The rest of the night was filled with exchanging gifts and congratulations. Zak had gotten Skye another present and she told him that he didn't have to, since he had already given her a beautiful ring. But he insisted that this gift was as much for him as it was for her. When she opened it, she could see why he had said that. It was a very thick pillow-type thing, something like what might be on a futon. She knew that he had bought it so that she could sleep comfortably underneath the tree and they could make love then on a softer surface than just a blanket.

When Zak opened his present from Skye, he found that she had framed several of the pictures they had taken over the last few months. Pictures of them with Cassie, pictures of them together and candid shots that they had taken of each other. Some were enlarged and some were only about five by seven, but he could imagine how they would look all arranged on a wall together. The story of the beginning of their forever together.

Epilogue

The guys had always tried to have a weekend getaway shortly after the first of the year. The firm had a cabin—well, they called it a cabin, but it was more like a personal ski lodge. It was close to some of the best skiing in the state, but it also had a large hot tub, TV rooms that were great for things like the Super Bowl or other sporting events, and all the luxuries of the best hotels. The firm also paid a caretaker and his wife to keep the place up year around. She was the cook and the maid, and he did all the upkeep and things like shoveling. In the summer, it was on a small lake that was great for fishing. So the guys always put their names on the calendar for having it Super Bowl weekend. They knew that they could get bumped from that schedule if a more senior partner wanted to, but in the last several years, no one had bumped them. It was in the northern part of the Lower Peninsula of Michigan, and none of the older guys wanted to be that far up in the snow during this cold weather. Which begged the question as to why they had bought it in the first place, although several of them did avail themselves of it in the summer. And it was a great tax write-off if they could claim fishing trips with client or ski weekends as "staff team building exercises." So the five of them found themselves on their usual guys' weekend, but it wasn't a guys' weekend anymore. Walt had brought Rayne, Zak had brought Skye, Jason had brought Sunni, and Skye had also invited her friend, Autumn. It seemed like Pete maybe had a thing for Autumn, although no one had ever seen them date or anything other than dancing and flirting at Walt's wedding. Maybe he just thought she was good looking or something because he looked at her a lot, even though he never talked to her other than just the cordial conversation when they were all at the table or watching a show.

The 'cabin' was made to house at least twenty people easily. Four of the rooms had their own private bath, and the rest of the rooms were set up more like a suite with a bathroom between two bedrooms. The couples each took a private room and by general agreement, Autumn got the other private room. Pete and Jeremy took one of the sets with a bathroom in the middle. It had every luxury anyone could imagine from the best hotels. The bathrooms had laundry chutes that went directly to the laundry area downstairs. If they wanted to throw in personal laundry, they could, but generally, they only sent down things like washcloths and towels. They took their personal things home. If there was ever a spill or something, they had no doubt that Mrs. Gilbert would wash it and return it to them, but they didn't want to require that of her for the most part. Although they had no doubt that some of the senior partners had her wash everything for them.

They had come up on Friday, and weren't going home until sometime Tuesday. So it would be a nice, long, relaxing weekend.

On Monday afternoon, the women had all decided to venture out to Traverse City for a wine tour on the Old Mission Peninsula. The guys were all sitting around watching TV and enjoying a beer when Mrs. Gilbert came and stood in the doorway, politely waiting for them to acknowledge her.

"Hey, Mrs. Gilbert, did you need something?" Walt asked.

"Uh, well, I was just getting ready to put the towels and such into the laundry when this dropped out onto the floor. With the way the chutes run, it could have come out of any of the master suites," she said, holding up a small white stick.

Jason got up and walked over to her and took it out of her hands. He had seen one of these before. And, he definitely knew what the word "yes" in the little window meant too. "Thanks, Mrs. Gilbert, we'll handle it from here." As she walked back out of the room, Jason turned to his buddies and said, "Guys, one of the women here is pregnant."

"What?" Walt exclaimed.

"Well, I guess that leaves me and Pete out," Jeremy said. "We don't have women here." He seemed pretty smug about that.

"Wrong," Pete said.

The guys all turned to him with raised eyebrows.

"Look, at Walt's wedding, Autumn and I did a lot of flirting, and quite a bit of drinking. We decided to go to a hotel for the night, and well, I'm sure you can fill in the blank. After that night, we realized that we had really put the cart before the horse as my grandpa used to say, so we decided to just go on a few actual dates. We went out a few times, then it seemed like she was always busy, or always had an excuse, so I figured she just wasn't into me and I stopped trying to call. We used protection that night, but I know nothing is 100 percent sure, so, yeah, I'm a possibility too."

"Wow, I do not envy you guys right now. Not so much about the baby part, but about the whole finding out who part," Jeremy said. "Obviously, whichever one it is, she wasn't exactly anxious to tell you the news."

The four possible daddies decided to just sit the women down and ask them point blank who it belonged to. It wasn't like any of them would be pissed off that it had happened. It takes two to tango, and whichever woman it belonged to would have the full support of the man involved and the rest would be supportive of whatever the couple decided.

When the women got home, the guys all had them sit in the big open living area. Walt stood up and started pacing. "Uh, ladies, I'm not really sure how to go about saying this, but we all want you to know that we will be supportive and happy for whoever this belongs to. Mrs. Gilbert found this in the laundry this morning." He held up the white stick.

All of the women looked at each other and looked at the men. It took a few minutes of everyone looking around. It seemed no one wanted to say it was theirs, but on the other hand, none of them wanted to out one of their friends by denying it either. Finally, after several tense minutes, Autumn stood up and walked over to Walt. She held out her hand and said, "That's mine, thank you." He handed it back to her and she went up the stairs to her room. Sunni started to get up and follow her friend, but Pete stopped her and said, "Let me." Sunni nodded and Pete went up the stairs. He knocked on Autumn's door and asked if he could come in.

Autumn met him at the door and said, "It's not yours; you don't have to worry about it." She seemed very nonchalant for a woman who'd just found out she was pregnant. Maybe she had a boyfriend that she was happy to be having a baby with.

"Autumn, we were together a couple of months ago. Are you sure?" Pete asked. "I am totally willing to step up if it's my baby. I will support you in whatever you want to do."

"Well, it's not your baby. A week or so after we spent the night together, I got my period, so I know that it's not yours, okay?" Autumn seemed pretty defensive, but he couldn't make her let him help if she didn't want him around.

"Okay, I just wanted to be sure. You don't have to be upset with me. I had a right to know if it was mine," Pete defended.

"Yes, I know, but it's not, so don't worry about it." And with that, Autumn closed the door. She was quiet and pretty much stayed to herself for the rest of the trip.

Pete could understand her being quiet. It had probably been a shock, even if she was with a regular guy. He hoped that whoever the father was, he would step up and do the right thing. He would hate to see someone as great as Autumn left alone to make those decisions and to possibly raise a child.

The End

Excerpt from Fallen Rayne
(Five Sloths Brewing book 1)

Walt cleared his throat to get the attention of the young woman who was sitting staring out the window. Apparently, she hadn't heard his knock on the door, so he had pushed it open slightly to see if anyone was inside. She appeared to be lost in thought. When she heard him, she turned toward him, and he realized he was looking at the single most beautiful woman he had ever seen. Her skin was pale olive, her hair was a long wavy auburn mass that flowed most of the way down her back, her cheekbones were high and perfect, but her eyes, although a beautiful rich amber, were haunted, almost like there was no life in them. It took him aback for a moment to see someone so beautiful yet so lifeless inside.

He cleared his throat again to try to regain some control of the voices inside his head, the voices telling him that this woman needed him, and as more than just an attorney. He suddenly wanted to help her find life again. He just wasn't sure how to do that. He stepped into the room, reaching out his hand to her as he drew closer. "Hello, Ms. Davis. I'm Walter Jensen, your attorney." She took his hand, but again, he almost felt like there was no life in the woman sitting in front of him. Yes, obviously, she was alive, she was breathing, and she spoke softly when she said, "Hello." But there was no life there, not really, no vibrancy that he would expect from a woman so young and so beautiful. "I'm here to ask you a few questions so that we can get started on your case, if that's all right with you."

"That's fine," she said. "The sooner we get this taken care of, the sooner those bastards pay for what they did to me."

Ah, there was the life, at least a small spark of it, although not in the way he wanted to see her eyes light with emotion. This was pure loathing, utter hatred for the persons involved in the lawsuit he was hopefully going to win for her. Maybe that would give her some happiness. He very likely could make her a very rich woman with this case. After all, the defendant was obviously negligent. For some reason, though, he got the sense that money wasn't really going to do anything to change her demeanor. He also got the sense that those eyes would be almost like a slow burning flame if she were truly passionate about something. If she were truly passionate about someone. He briefly pictured those eyes staring into his with a different type of passion.

Whoa!! Walt, what the hell, dude? Totally not appropriate to be drooling over the client. Even if she was the most beautiful woman he had ever seen. He had seen his share of women and had probably dated more than his share. Being an attorney, a part owner of a microbrewery and a former frat boy at a prestigious law school, he had always seen beautiful women and truth be told, he had taken several of them to bed. But there was something about this woman. Maybe it was her sadness, maybe it was her physical beauty, and maybe it was the fact that she was a victim of a horrible injustice, but whatever it was, he was reacting to her like he had never reacted to someone before.

Get your head back in the game, Walt, he silently scolded himself. Yeah, it would seem totally professional to be drooling like a school kid for the initial interview with a new client. The thing was, though, that even though his body had definite thoughts about her, there was something else too. It wasn't a sexual draw, not that he would say there was nothing sexual to this, but there was something about this woman that made him want to put a smile back on her face, to see her lively and vibrant again. He had no doubt that at one point she had been vivacious and happy. Her case file said she had been a dancer all her life, so she had obviously had a deep passion for something—well, something other than revenge, that is.

He hesitated, not quite sure how to move forward. He had seen plaintiffs before that were bitter, he had seen ones that were in pain, he had seen ones that were angry, but he honestly didn't remember ever seeing one that seemed like the incident had literally taken the life from her. Finally, he shook his head to get his mind back on the matter at hand.

"Yes, well, of course," he said, trying to figure out how to move forward with the questions he needed to ask her. "First of all, thank you for taking the time to talk to me today. I think we have a great chance of winning this case. I believe it's pretty cut and dried that the construction company was negligent. I am very optimistic that we will get a very generous settlement."

"How much can they possibly pay? There is no amount that will get my life back. Life is over for me; no amount of money can fix that. But yes, I do want to make them pay, I want to make them pay to the point that they have to go out of business, I want to ruin their lives as much as they have ruined mine." The words came out almost like venom; there was pure hatred behind them. He had been wrong, it wasn't that there wasn't any life there; it was just that the life that was there was so bitter and hateful that she couldn't focus on anything but making someone pay for the situation she found herself in.

"Yes, well." Again, he found himself not knowing exactly how to respond. This petite beautiful woman was so hateful, so spiteful, so....so.... and that was when he saw what she really was. She was so hurt, so horribly, completely broken that she did not know how to even function in a normal manner. Maybe his best bet would be to try to find out from others what they felt had happened to her. Not the details of the accident, he could read those in the reports, but what had really happened to her, to the lively young woman that he could tell had been in there at some point.

"Actually, maybe it would be best if I get you to sign some release forms for me so that I can talk to your doctors and the other medical staff involved in your case, I might be able to get a better idea of what we are dealing with from them, before you and I sit and talk strategy for the case."

"That's fine. Whatever you need from me. I just want to get this over with," she said softly.

He gave her the usual forms, the retainer naming him as her attorney in the case of Rayne Davis vs Charmichael Construction, releases of her medical files, permission to talk with doctors, therapists, police, and anyone else who might have any insight into her case.

She signed paper after paper, pretty much before he had a chance to explain to her what she was signing.

"Are you sure you don't want to read over any of these before you sign them?" he asked.

She looked up at him and again, he was touched deeply by the lifelessness of her eyes. "I'm sure that there is nothing in here that can harm me any more that what this incident has already done. If you are worried that I may be signing away things that I shouldn't, trust me, Mr. Jensen, I don't believe I have anything more to lose than my life and the future I dreamed of."

Walt walked out of the room at the rehabilitation facility almost in a fog. He felt something so deeply for that young woman. It wasn't pity, not really. Although he did feel extreme sorrow, it wasn't pity, it was a deep and utter sickening at the pain and loss that he had seen in that young woman's face. He vowed that he would do whatever it took to bring life back to those eyes. He knew it wasn't about money for her, so he had to figure out what it was about. And then he needed to fix whatever it was. He wouldn't stop, he wouldn't rest until he saw some spark of life in her eyes again. He just wasn't sure how he was going to do that.

Rayne sadly shook her head as the attorney left her room. That was one handsome man. She had never really had much experience with men. She had always been so involved in her dancing, from lessons to exercise to choreography planning, that she had never really had time for boys when she was younger and definitely not for men once she got old enough to start working toward becoming a member of the New York City Ballet. She had always thought there would be time for that later. Most prima ballerinas didn't work much past the age of thirty or thirty-five. She was only twenty-three. She'd thought she had plenty of time for dating and marriage and children, later, after her career had peaked. Now, though, she would never know that life. Who would want to marry a woman who was so sad, so utterly broken that she didn't see the way to ever be happy again? Life was just throwing her all kinds of hard hits lately. She'd lost her dream to dance and then she lost her dream to have a family someday.

No, she knew that she would always be alone. No one would find her attractive, no one would want to be involved with someone like her. A woman that was possibly never going to get out of a wheelchair or at best would have a horrible limp. But still, she couldn't help but think about how gorgeous that man had been, with his deep black hair and those emerald green eyes. Well, at least she would have a good-looking man around long enough for her lawsuit to finish. Even if there was no hope of having someone like him in her life forever.

Excerpt from Encouraging Autumn
(Five Sloths Brewing book 3)

When everyone was done eating, they worked together to clear the table. Then Pete took his place next to Autumn turning his chair so that he could look more directly at her. "I know that you don't want to talk to me about this. But I believe I have some ideas that may help you if you will be honest in your answers and keep an open mind to my suggestions. I promise you that whatever you decide nothing that I already know, nor anything that you tell me today will go any further than this room unless you decide that it does. And, I will assure you that none of what I am asking will result in any kind of judgment or condemnation."

Autumn could see why Pete was considered a good attorney. He was very professional, and he seemed very ready to argue whatever case it was that he was going to try to make. "I understand." Autumn agreed.

"First, how far along are you?"

"About a month." Autumn said quietly.

"Good, that's great." Pete encouraged. Autumn did not see what was so great about it all. "Correct me if I am wrong, but this is the way that I see it. With your family, if you had eloped and gotten pregnant on your honeymoon, while being disappointed that they didn't get to throw you a huge wedding, they would at least be happy that you were not an unwed mother?"

"I suppose, yes, that's true, but it's also irrelevant." Autumn protested.

"Not necessarily." Pete stated. "Here is what I propose, no pun intended. I think we should head to Las Vegas for the weekend and get married." He saw the protest already rising in Autumn's mind, so he held up a finger to keep her from saying anything just yet. "A marriage in name only, I'm not expecting you to sleep with me. Although, I do think we need to live together to keep up appearances. For now, we can live in my apartment, or yours. We would start looking for a house together. If your family still wants to have a wedding, I am not opposed to it as long as they understand that we ran off to Vegas because I just couldn't wait the time it would take to put a whole wedding together."

Was this man crazy? "I can't marry you; we aren't in love." Autumn protested.

"We know that, they don't. You got pregnant on our trip to Vegas. I know it's close to a month off timing wise, but we will work on that as we go along. First babies are often late anyway, so if this one holds off a week or two, it just helps support our story. If it doesn't, babies are also known to come early sometimes, which would also help support our story. I will be the father of this child in every way as far as anyone outside of this room knows. And, when the time comes, if you will allow it, I would very privately and discreetly adopt the child and regardless of what happens with our relationship, this child would always have my support as a father." Pete continued, "As far as not being in love, no, I suppose we aren't the picture of romantic love, but people marry for all sorts of reasons, social status, money, companionship, why not for this reason. All I want to do is support you and help you in this situation."

Autumn looked around the room, Skye looked pretty much as gobsmacked as Autumn felt, but for some reason, Zak didn't seem to be surprised about this crazy idea. Most likely, Pete had talked to him about it before. "So, even though we aren't in love, and you know nothing about the real situation, you just want to step in and be my husband and the father of my child, why?" Autumn asked.

"First, yes, I know we aren't in love, but we got along well when we were dating. We can be friends and keep this completely platonic other than having to appear as a real couple when we are out in public." Pete encouraged. "As far as the other aspect, as a man and as an attorney, I will admit that I want the man who did this to be appropriately punished, but that will remain completely up to you whether or not you want to tell me. I will guarantee you that if you tell me, I will do everything in my power to protect you from any backlash of what he did to you."

Autumn just nodded her understanding so Pete continued, "I know that this is not a situation you would have ever wanted to find yourself in, and I know that this isn't the proposal of your dreams, but I am trying to be practical and help you in any way that I can. If it doesn't work, when you feel it's appropriate and safe to do so, you simply tell your family that we have decided to divorce and go our separate ways. I don't know your family, you do. I'm committed to this for the rest of my life if that is what you want, if not, then I will make sure that any separating is done on your terms."

"Why, why would you do this?" Autumn pleaded, "It's crazy to even think about."

"I can't go into them right now, but I do have reasons, and some day, I promise I will tell you. Right now, what I would like to do if it's okay with everyone is go home and let you discuss this with Skye and

Zak. I think everyone will eventually agree that this is the best plan of action. I have a flight scheduled for ten in the morning to take the four of us to Vegas. I will be at the airport. You have three choices of how to handle this. You can just not show up at all, and I will know that you do not want my help. You can show up with Zak and Skye, but ask me to not get on the plane and I will know that you want to have a fun weekend with your friends but you don't want my help. Or, you can come and get on the airplane with me and we will all work together to make the best of this weekend and I will help you with all of it." Pete promised. "Since I am leaving, I give Zak permission to answer general questions about me. You know a lot about me from dating, but if you have questions, you can ask Zak." He looked to his friend and they shared some sort of eye movement, head nod, non-verbal conversation and then Pete headed for the door and was gone.

Triskelion
A spin-off from Five Sloths Brewing
Coming Fall 2020

Brett...big brother...first to become a Green Beret… first to serve his country, first to protect his siblings…. first to step up and make a place for his brothers to come home to.

Trevor… middle kid…. wasn't the oldest, wasn't the youngest, so he became determined to be the smartest. When he joined the Green Berets, it was because the Marines would rather he was hacking for them than into them.

Riley… little brother...baby of the family. When your only family is already Green Beret, what else are you going to be? Sometimes he wishes he had died with his squad….sometimes he's glad he didn't, but all the time, he wishes he could really walk away… not from life, not from reality, not from the only blood he's got left… but from the pain and the memories… yeah, those he wishes he could walk away from.

Triskelion is a series about Brett, Trevor and Riley Lawson. Three brothers, all former Green Beret.

Triskelion Motorcycles, their bike shop is their 'every day' job. It's also the location for the offices of their bodyguard and private investigating services for people that need their skills.

Triskelion turns the heat up a few notches from my Five Sloths Brewing series.

About Robin Andrews

Robin Andrews still lives in the same small town that she grew up in. She began college headed for a legal career. While she still went into the legal arena, she set aside the idea of becoming an attorney for the much more rewarding life of a mother and grandmother. She has been married for thirty-five years. She lives with her husband and her miniature Labradoodle, Hope.

She is the mother to three adult children (two boys, one girl) and grandmother to three grandchildren (two girls, one boy). She loves taking her family to the local fitness center for family swim days.

Her greatest joys in life are writing, reading and spending time cuddling with her grandkids.

Website: www.robin-andrews.com

I would love to have you join my readers group on Facebook: Robin's Readers Nest.
https://www.facebook.com/groups/898899640504649/?ref=share

Other Books by Robin Andrews

Fallen Rayne Five Sloths Brewing Book 1
Encouraging Autumn Five Sloths Brewing Book 3
Coming June 2020
Resistant Summer Five Sloths Brewing Book 4
Embracing Sunni Five Sloths Brewing Book 5